Walking With Irma

ANN O'CONNELL RUST

Author of the Award Winning Series
"The Floridians"

**Amaro
Books**
Fiction

Published by
Amaro Books
9765-C Southwest 92nd Court
Ocala, Florida 34481
E-Mail: amarobooks@aol.com

First printing 1999
ISBN NO. 1-883203-05-8

Library of Congress Catalog Card No. 99-94675

Printed in the U.S.A.

Cover photograph: Irma Lichtendahl
Cover Artists: Joyce Popendorf / M.A. O'Connell
Graphic Artist: Karen Fulford

Books by Ann O'Connell Rust:
The Floridians - a five-volume series
Vol. I: Punta Rassa
Vol. II: Palatka
Vol. III: Kissimmee
Vol. IV: Monticello
Vol. V: Pahokee
Dessa
Nonie of the Everglades
Walking With Irma

About the Author...

Ann O'Connell Rust is a native Floridian and is a well known and respected Florida historical novelist. She is a popular speaker/lecturer and shares her love of the state as she travels to schools, libraries and bookstores.

She and Allen spend their time between their home in Ocala, Florida, and their ranch in Wyoming, and when time permits, babysit their nine grandchildren. Three of their five children live in Florida.

ACKNOWLEDGMENTS

The author wishes to thank A. Fennell Rust, Editor/ Copy Editor, Eileen Dockham, artist, Jim McNealey, sculptor, Hazel Halling, valuable information, Lucile and Earle Barnes, historical information, and the people in the Hoback Ranches and Hoback Basin, neighbors and friends. A special thank you to Joyce Popendorf and Karen Fulford for the award-winning cover.

Dedicated to Irma and Charles Lichtendahl,
wonderful neighbors and beautiful friends.

ONE

Jo traced the raised pastel floral design on the cover of the journal with her forefinger. Slowly, methodically she retraced the same flower. Sighing deeply, she gave in to her sadness and turned over on the pale flowered coverlet. The four-poster bed she and Ben shared since they moved into the big house usually gave her comfort, but not today. "I don't dare tell Ruthann that I've written only four pages in the journal." Running her small hand through her thick, ash-blond hair, she murmured aloud, "She's a thoughtful daughter and truly believes that it will help me forget."

"If you write everything down that happened, Mama, then it'll help. I'm sure of it. There was an article on depression in last month's issue of *Family Circle,* and I've seen several shows on TV about depression, and they all said to just write it down, then read it aloud." When Jo began to protest, Ruthann threw her hands up just like she had seen her mama do a thousand times and said, "You've gotta try! You've just gotta try, Mama."

The tears quickly came, and Jo went to her. "Don't, Baby. Please don't. I'll try. I know that Dad is worried since he's never seen me like this. You know what a happy person I usually am. This is just not like me." They patted gently each other's cheeks, like they'd done since Ruthann was a wee one, and smiled. Turning to page one Jo read aloud as Ruthann had suggested.

I'll never forget the date, and I'm terrible at remembering dates; I was, even in school. But the year 1989 is a year that I'll never forget. Neither will Ben or the other people in the Hoback Ranches.

You see, Ben, my husband of almost thirty years, and I built our summer place up in the Hoback Ranches in Wyoming in '86, three years before that fateful date. They aren't actually ranches. I mean that some of the people had pleasure horses but no cattle or sheep or anything like that. But I'm getting ahead of myself. I believe when you write in your journal that it's customary to introduce yourself. Seems

1

that I read that somewhere.

I'm Jo, actually Joan Catherine, but I've been called Jo since I was little. I was born a Pierce but married Ben Daulton the June after our graduation from Jacksonville University in Jacksonville, Florida.

But to get back to why '89 was such a memorable year I'll naturally have to return to '85, the year we went to Las Vegas to Ben's convention and subsequently to Yellowstone, Jackson Hole and...

She put down the journal and thought, it seems much longer than four years in some ways, but when I think about that bizarre, unbelievable time, the years in between almost evaporate and the fears return, fresh, just like it all happened yesterday. The sounds, the smells of the evergreens and that clear crisp mountain air we all bragged about, until that summer, that is. She remembered how the acrid smoke from Yellowstone had crept down to the Hoback Basin and then to the Ranches. We weren't prepared. We just weren't prepared. Heavens, I can even hear Maggie barking, and she's been gone since then. None of us in the Hoback Ranches will ever be the same. How could we? And to think that we all started out with such hope and excitement—a new beginning. Not just for Ben and me, but especially for Liz.

"Here, Ben, sit on this!" Jo called into their dressing room. The *this* was the large blue brocade suitcase that she had insisted on taking on their trip.

"Good grief, Jo! We'll be gone only two weeks. We'll be overweight!" When he saw her bite her lower lip he did as she had asked and sat on it. Ben was an easygoing man and enjoyed pleasing his mate and knew what her lip biting meant.

"There, that'll do just fine," she mumbled as she managed to zip it closed. When she looked up at him she was again smiling. Hugging him, she squeezed his slight shoulders, then pecked his cheek and resumed their conversation.

"There will be the two banquets, and I know everyone will want to go to some of the shows. Mimi said you dress, and I mean DRESS, in Vegas. So I'll need the dressy things, then the casual clothes for our trip to Yellowstone. It might be cold in June," she said.

"Just when did Mimi Carter get so knowledgeable? Didn't think that she and Chet had even been north of Georgia or west of Florida."

"You stop that, Ben Daulton! You know full well that they were in Wyoming a few years back and won that trip to Hawaii only last year. Besides, Chet brought scads of brochures home showing pictures of Vegas and the park. That's more than I can say about someone else I know."

"I knew Mimi would beat me to it and I didn't want to spoil all her fun."

"Sure you didn't. You got so busy at the plant that you didn't even think about brochures or our first real vacation in years..."

"What do you call our trip to Maine last year, a campout? Cost over $4,000.00! What was that, Mrs. Daulton? Chopped liver?"

Jo grinned. "That was lovely, dear, but this is true excitement. I mean seeing all the shows and celebrities and getting to dress up, plus Yellowstone. Do you think we'll see any grizzlies? Why are you frowning like that? One of the brochures Mimi had showed a picture of one and..."

"Was it wearing a cap that said Smokey on it?"

"Really, Ben..."

"Oh, I'm kidding. I doubt that we'll see any bears. They're supposed to be very shy, and you're not allowed to feed them. Everyone is warned to keep food locked up, etc. Besides, we'll be staying at the Inn for only a few days before going east to Cody, then down to Jackson. You'll need western wear, you know, cowgirl boots, fringed leather jackets, jeans. You know, maybe we'd better get out another suitcase so my fashionable wife won't feel out of place."

"Well, mister, you can tease me all you want. I don't care. I like to look nice for you..."

"Come here, woman. You always look nice and you know it." He chuckled as he stroked her arm and then headed for the den. Calling over his shoulder, he asked, "You want a drink before dinner, hon?"

"I surely do. Why don't you have Andrea fix a batch of margaritas? She's doing chiles rellenos and refried beans, and I think they'll go better with Mexican than...

"Ben," she called, then waited. "Ben, did you hear what I said?"

"Of course I heard what you said!" he yelled. "You said you wanted me to fix some daiquiris."

She walked to their bedroom door and called to Andrea, who was in the kitchen off the great room. "Andrea, would you please inform Mr. Daulton that I said margaritas, not daiquiris. And would you please be so kind as to ask him to put in his hearing aid?"

Andrea returned her smile and said, "Yes, Missy. I'll try." She shrugged her shoulders and walked toward the den.

Jo thought, he'll not put it in even for Andrea. Why are men so obstinate? She continued looking for her black embroidered moo-moo in the large dressing room. They had taken part of Ruthann's bedroom and added it to their already large closet, using the remainder of the room for Ben's computer equipment. The other wing of the house had been son Robbie's room and great room, but with the kids married and on their own they really didn't need Ruthann's room too.

She and Ben had bought the oversized lot in the fashionable area of Ortega, south and west of downtown Jacksonville. They waited 'til they could afford their dream house before building and didn't regret having lived in the smaller house on the west side. The children had had plenty of playmates and she had made lifelong friends there: Mimi and Chet Carter were two of them.

Ben was fortunate to be hired by the Maxwell House Coffee plant even before he was graduated from JU. He had risen rapidly in the company, loved his work and was very respected. They had a good life. The children had never given them any trouble, and Jo was happy that she had decided to be a stay-at-home mom. She put her home-ec degree to work in decorating their small starter home, making most of her and Ruthann's clothes, cutting corners on their grocery bills and smart shopping that challenged her creative mind. The entire family enjoyed her desperation casseroles, as she called them.

Vacations consisted of camping out in state parks in the Southeast, mostly in Florida and Georgia in those days. She missed it, but when Ben suggested that they stay at the Old Faithful Inn in Yellowstone for over $100 a night she didn't argue. Besides, it wouldn't be much fun camping without the children and grandchildren.

She found the moo-moo that Mimi had brought her from Hawaii and slipped into the black thong sandals. "Grief! I forgot to polish my toenails. I'll do them on the patio while we have our drinks." She selected a neutral shade of polish from the large, filigreed, mirrored tray and pushed her dark blond hair back from her forehead. Looking closely into the mirrored wall over the long dressing table, she studied her new hair style.

"Think Patsy put too much yellow in the hair rinse. I'll have to speak to her about it. Don't want to go brassy on our trip, but I'm glad we decided on the perm. It does look natural and should hold up with just a shampoo and blow dry." She smiled at her image. Why am I so excited about this trip? She heard Ben call her. "Coming, hon." she responded.

"What a gorgeous day!" she said, taking her frosted margarita from Ben. She looked around her. "I love tropical flowers. Wish we didn't have to cover the bougainvillaea during the winter months though. Would you just smell that gardenia? Are we in paradise, Mr. Daulton? Look at the flowers reflected in the pool. Why would we ever consider leaving here? I mean it!

"We are indeed in paradise. Have just enough winter to kill the insect larvae and a gorgeous fall and spring. Well, I'll admit that the summers can be beastly, but with AC…"

"And the bills that go with the AC."

"I haven't noticed that you've stayed off the golf course even in July, sir."

"But, I'll be honest, I've noticed the heat more in the past few years. Maybe we should build a cabin in the mountains like the Lavertys did. They seem to love North Carolina."

"Not like they did before their house was broken into last year. Stole everything of any value and left the place in a shambles. Joyce isn't as keen on it as she once was. We'll think on it though."

"Ruthann and Karl would like it, since we'd be close by, and we'd get to see Kris and Kimberly more—get to know our grands better. "

"I know they've suggested it several times, but, hon, well, I'd like to look around some more. I love it here, right here. At least we've come to know Rachel and Casey. Did you see those two Sunday? I'm glad Robbie approved of my caring for them two days a week. Don't know when Julie and Robbie would get them to the club for swimming lessons, and that Casey is as aggressive as a boy. Wish Julie would consider having another child. Robbie wants a boy in the worst way. Did you see Casey dive?"

"Of course I saw Casey. I'm deaf, not blind, young lady. Robbie puffed up like a peacock. Now aren't you glad that I talked you into hiring Andrea and Carlos? You'd never have found the time to care for the kids if we hadn't signed up for them. Reverend Long said at Rotary last week that the church is sponsoring ten more Filipino families as soon as they can get jobs for them. You know, I think several of the men there will consider hiring them, and they're not even Lutheran."

"I think that's wonderful, hon, really I do. It's hard for me to remember what my life was like before they came to work for us." She screwed the cap back on the nail polish bottle and put her feet up on the diving board to hasten the drying.

"You'd better have Carlos clean the pool just before we return. Casey informed me that she wanted to learn to dive backwards. Do you think I should let her? After all, she's only four and a half..."

"As long as you're right there, what could it hurt? Do you want another margarita?"

"Don't think so. I'm feeling this one..."

"You're supposed to feel it. Why else would you drink it?"

"Because it tastes so good, mister smarty pants. That's why!"

TWO

As Ben had predicted, their bags were overweight. Jo had rearranged her packing several times but could not seem to discard anything without replacing it with another garment. Mimi and Chet were already at the Delta check-in counter when Robbie came stumbling in with some of his parents' luggage. The porter carried the remainder.

"I bet we've called the house three times. Where were you? Andrea said you left an hour ago!" Mimi chastised a frustrated Jo as they sought an empty bench.

"I was ready for a solid hour before Robbie came for us. Guess who was still packing when he got there? Ben always thinks he can do everything in fifteen minutes. I even had his dress clothes laid out, but you should see the old things he's bringing to wear in Yellowstone," Jo lamented.

"Why didn't you exchange them? I always pack for Chet. He never takes the right clothes, and besides he likes for me to."

"Well, that's Chet. But you know Mr. Independent Ben." She sighed. "I bet my blood pressure is sky high. I'm not going to let him upset me until we're home again."

"Is that new?" Jo commented, referring to Mimi's mid-calf khaki skirt and Madras jacket."

"Found it on sale at Ivey's—one of those red-dot sales. I think I could actually live in Liz fashions."

"Never thought they'd be mixing burgundy with khaki," Jo said. "That was one of the NEVERS I learned in clothing and construction, but I like it. Glad the designers are breaking all those old rules we grew up with. I wear blues with greens without blinking an eye anymore. Remember when that was a no no?"

Ben and Chet were animated as they came toward them. "Gate three, my dears," Chet called. Ben winked at him. "Overweight, Miss Jo, as I predicted."

She shrugged, smiled and said, "I don't care one whit, Mr. Ben." She grabbed his arm, and the foursome walked happily toward gate three.

They changed planes in Atlanta, and, as Ben commented when they landed at the Las Vegas airport, "Those stewardesses kept food and drinks coming so often that I couldn't finish *The Times* crossword puzzle..."

"Do you ever finish one, Ben?" Chet questioned, eyebrows raised in amazement.

"Actually, I sometimes do..."

Jo interrupted. "What he's too modest to admit, Chet, is that he always does."

The airport was crowded, the atmosphere festive. John Aschenbeck hailed them. He was the convention chairman and was meeting the dignitaries. "The hotel courtesy car awaits the contingency from Jacksonville."

"What! No limo? You're slipping, John," Ben responded jovially while shaking John's large, square hand. He looked more like a television wrestler than a bigwig with the company.

John laughed. "Hey, would you mind waiting for the four forty-five from Tucson? Grey Butler and Inez are on that."

"Of course not. Could use an afternoon libation, couldn't we, Ben?" Chet laughingly said, turning back toward Jo and Mimi. "Join us, girls?"

They did.

The hotel was as ostentatious as Jo had hoped, and just as noisy. The decor was red and black. Checker colors, Jo thought, trying to keep her mouth from hanging open—gawking. She was so excited she was almost giddy. The slot machines in the huge room off the lobby rang loudly, punctuated by the players' shouts of joy and moans of disappointment.

"What're you grinning about?" Ben questioned.

"Just being here, I guess, and the anticipation of a fun-filled four days, but mostly the change of pace. As much as I love Jax, it is laid back..."

"You can say that again," Mimi interjected, "but you're going to love Jackson even more than Vegas, Jo. Now that's a fun town. Chet and I were supposed to be there with the tour for only two days. That's when we left the tour, stayed for three more days and would've stayed even longer if he hadn't been called back to the plant. You remember, in '82 when the strike was called. Still haven't forgiven him for calling Jax to check on things."

"What did you find to do in Jackson? You don't even ski."

"A lot of other women didn't either, I found out. We sat around the Jackson Lake Lodge and drank lots of hot buttered rum, played bridge and discussed our husbands' shortcomings and children and grands. Plus did a lot of shopping in the quaint shops in town. It was beautiful. Nothing prettier than the Tetons in winter. Wish we were flying in instead of driving. You'd see what I mean, even though there won't be a lot of snow at this time of year. And I did learn to drive a snowmobile. How glorious it was at night!"

"But, Mimi, we can see a lot more on the way to Wyoming if we drive. Besides, who's in a hurry?"

The four days flew by. While Ben and Chet convened with the other Maxwell House execs, the wives and girlfriends were kept busy with tours. The most memorable was the Hoover Dam—unbelievable, Jo told Ben later. The men's meetings ended after lunch, and they were in their rooms to rest or in the casino to hit the gaming tables by two o'clock each day. The evenings were filled with cocktail parties hosted by the company, two awards banquets, then their free time for dinner and into-the-morning floor shows.

Monday morning arrived, and a bedraggled foursome was met by the rental-car driver with their minivan. "I'm glad he came to the hotel," Mimi exclaimed. "I don't think I could walk even three blocks. I never sleep worth a darn when I'm not in my own bed."

"That's two of you," Ben said. "Jo drags out like a zombie, mumbles that she'd sure like a cup of coffee, and I remind her that she'll have to wait for room service or get dressed and go down to the coffee shop. Then she really moans."

Ben had insisted on renting a 4-wheel drive for the rugged country and hoped they'd have the opportunity to use it. Jo and

Mimi slid into the back seat, and Ben took the wheel. The back was filled to the top with luggage.

"Pilot to co-pilot. Pilot to co-pilot," Ben said loudly to Chet. "Check with the navigators for directions."

Mimi and Jo both had maps, guide books, brochures and various other materials. "We want to go into Yellowstone at the west entrance through Montana. So our two nights at the park will be at the Old Faithful Inn. Right? I've heard that it's spectacular. Margie Branch said that it's the largest log hotel ever built. She and Julian stayed there an entire week."

They all agreed on entering the park via the west entrance. "OK, then let's take it easy and stop at Salt Lake City and go on into the park Tuesday. That's when our reservations are, isn't it?"

"That's right," Jo answered. "And check-in time is noon. I'd like to get to Salt Lake early enough to see the Mormon Tabernacle and whatever else there is of interest. What do you say?"

Mimi was quick to say that they'd already seen the tabernacle, and frankly she intended to take a long, hot tub bath, fix a couple of martinis and do her nails—she was exhausted.

"Well, Ben and I'll do the sightseeing. I've heard that it's a beautiful city."

The trip to Yellowstone was uneventful. They spent two and a half days at the park doing all the tourist things. The Inn was as fascinating as Margie had told Jo, and she wished that they had more time to enjoy it. She did take the forty-five-minute tour, and as they were finishing, everyone rushed to the side portico to see Old Faithful go off only a few seconds late. They saw scads of bison, deer and elk and sat through a lecture about bears. It was so dry even Ben complained, and he was not a complainer. Jo's main concern was that her hair didn't respond to that dry air, that she needed some of that good old Florida humidity to make it curl. They'd just have to smear on more moisturizers.

The park rangers cautioned everyone about the potential danger of fires and warned them to use the receptacles to put out their cigarettes and cigars. Everyone laughed when he said that Smokey was getting up in age, and he didn't want him to have to work overtime. Someone in the audience asked about the drought and was told that snowfall and rain had been way down for over five years, and no change was expected for at least three to four more years. "Most are calling this the eight-year drought," he said.

"Before we go to Cody in the morning I want to have breakfast in the dining room one more time," Jo said. "Please, honey. Can't you just feel the presence of all those tourists in the early 1900's dressed to kill and being treated royally? We need to dine out more, and I don't mean at the club. What are you laughing at, Ben Daulton? You tell me! I'm going to tickle you if you don't tell me. I mean it!" Ben managed to roll over on the bed just as the phone rang.

"Darn it all! That'll be Mimi." It was. "Now you'll have to behave yourself in the dining room, young lady, or the ambiance will be ruined. I'm sure that those ladies would find your forward behavior offensive. Tickling your husband just wasn't done in those bygone days, Miss Jo."

"Of course it was. They didn't talk about it, that's all."

After dining on fresh salmon with caper sauce and a vegetable quiche they again packed the van and were off to Cody to visit the Buffalo Bill Museum and stay overnight, then head to Jackson. Mimi had been right. It was a delightful tourist town. They checked in at the Snow King Resort, and after an abundant and delicious dinner at a quaint Mexican restaurant headed for their rooms and a much needed rest.

The following morning arrived too soon. After breakfast at the hotel Ben and Jo drove Mimi and Chet to the airport for their return trip to Jacksonville. Chet had an important conference to attend, so they had to cut their vacation short. But, as Mimi said, they'd been there before, and she was anxious to get home. They had a cruise planned for the fall, and it would take her that long to get rested up for it. The usual laughs ensued.

On the way back to Jackson Jo said, "I want to call Liz when we get back to the hotel, hon. Oh, how she'd love it here! Everywhere you look there's a scene to be painted. I wish that she and Avery had decided to come with us. Now, don't say it!"

"No, I am going to say it. Jo, you've got to allow her to work out her own problems. I know that she's like a sister to you, but really, hon, you're not helping her."

"All I do is listen. I've stopped giving advice. She won't take it anyway. I truly get upset with her. Why does she put up with him?"

"Maybe because she loves him."

"There is such a thing as self respect, Ben. I'm afraid she's lost hers and stays with him because she's so down all the time. You remember what a delightfully witty girl she was, and she has more talent than should be allowed one person. Her work is respected and admired, and she could be one of the most famous artists in the Southeast. Everyone says so."

"It takes more than talent…"

"Yes! It takes confidence, and he's destroyed hers, messing around with those bimbos. Maybe not bimbos, but they might as well be. In the old days they were called gold diggers. That's what they are, honey. They'll do anything for a free ride, even ruin a marriage, and one of them was even the church secretary. Imagine! I wish she hadn't found out. She'd be better off not knowing."

He patted her hand and said, "I think you're right on that one. Call her when we get back, hon. She might need cheering up. And, it'll cheer you, too. Hey, this is our great get-away, remember? Don't get down on me, young lady."

"Why can't Avery have some of your compassion? Why is he so darned self centered?" She sighed deeply.

"Gonna put a nail in your coffin, Miss Jo. Isn't that what your Aunt Ruth used to say when you sighed?"

She smiled. "She surely did. I'd forgotten that." She squeezed his hand, but when he looked at her he knew that she was thinking of her best friend Liz.

"When we get back to the hotel, why don't you drop Robbie a note and send him those brochures you got of the Inn? Think he'll get a kick out of the Inn's architect beginning his career at age thirteen with no formal education to speak of, just working in an architectural firm. You know, that blows my mind, as the kids say. It's hard to conceive, isn't it?"

"I thought the same thing when our guide said that. When I

think of how hard it was for Robbie, especially the math. I want him to have the chance to come out to see the Inn for himself. We could keep the kids. He does beautiful work, and we're proud of him, but I truly believe some people have a special gift. Certainly Robert Reamer did." Ben knew that she was thinking of Liz and not of the Inn's architect.

THREE

The original plan was to spend two days in Jackson, then head down to Flaming Gorge National Park, the Dinosaur Park, then back to Salt Lake City, where they'd turn in their rental vehicle and catch the plane for their return trip home. But, as Jo had said many times since, the best laid plans...

"I'm glad to be by ourselves," Ben said. "You know I love Mimi and Chet, but it certainly is nice to be alone and not have to listen to her chatter. I don't know how he puts up with it!" Ben was lying on his back on the king sized bed, arms underneath his head, watching Jo blow dry her hair.

"He tunes her out, that's how. Haven't you noticed that when she asks him a question he always has her repeat it? Well, he does. She thinks he's getting deaf, but I know full well that he's just not listening."

"Do you want to eat here at the hotel?"

"No indeed! Let's just wander around the square and soak up some western culture. We might see a restaurant that's appealing. Doesn't that sound like fun? Might even have a drink at the Wort's Silver Dollar Bar. You know, play tourist."

"Sounds fine to me. I just don't want to make a single decision. Is this western shirt all right, hon?" Ben called to Jo, who had gone into the bathroom where the light was better to put on her makeup.

"Wear the dark grey one. Looks a little dressier, not that anyone dresses here. Oh, the black western-cut slacks and your casual shoes and bolo tie. How is that for playing tourist? Now, aren't you glad I bought them in Vegas?"

"Yeah, and paid much too much for them, I'm sure."

"You simply couldn't wear those rags you brought from home, Ben Daulton, and you know it."

With their arms around each other they walked the wooden sidewalks, dodged other tourists and didn't stop smiling the entire time. "Doesn't the air smell delicious? Pure mountain air…"

"Pure my eye. You're inhaling exhaust fumes just like back home…"

"But it's more fun here. There's the Wort Hotel. Is that English Tudor design or alpine?"

"Jo, you know better than to ask me that, but Robbie would certainly know."

"Are you game, sir? I mean pardner? It's only four thirty."

"Sure, why not, my little filly. Let's do it up right." They entered the Wort, and that's where it all began, the turning point in their lives.

"Isn't this beautiful? No, handsome is a better word. Ben, wait up, I want to look at the paintings. Wouldn't Liz love these? And the fireplace. Magnificent! Even though it's July the fire doesn't look out of place, and it does get nippy when the sun goes down. Wonder what kind of stone that is."

"Here, Jo, take this brochure and you can find out all about it while we have that drink."

Jo took it but continued looking at the large paintings of mountain scenes on every wall except the stone wall of the fireplace. Ben grabbed her arm and said, "You can look 'til your heart's content when we come out. That bar is already noisy. You want to sit at the bar if there's room?"

"No, but I do want to find out from the bartender how many silver dollars are imbedded in it."

"We can do that while we order. Here, hon." He pulled the chair out from the small table for Jo, and a waiter approached.

"That's what I call quick service. A glass of white wine for my missus, and I'll take Jack Daniels straight up, please. Oh, before you leave, my wife wants to know how many silver dollars are on the bar."

"Two-thousand thirty-two 1921 silver dollars. I'll bring back a brochure that describes the Wort when I return with your drinks. What kind of wine would you like, miss?"

"Something not too sweet, please. A white Grenache or

Chardonnay would be fine." When the waiter left Jo asked, "Why didn't you tell him that we already have a brochure?"

"This one might be different." The bar was already half full. Lots of laughter, foot-stomping western music, but sedate. After all, it was the Wort. Ben suddenly reached over the table and took her hand.

"Are you aware, Mrs. Daulton, that I've loved you for thirty-three years?"

"I should certainly hope so, Mr. Daulton."

Neither noticed the gentleman at the table opposite them next to the wall that was covered with large western paintings. He was smiling slightly as he observed the twosome. Had he not overheard the conversation, he would have guessed that theirs was a second-time-around marriage.

The waiter approached him with a familiar expression. "Mr. Wilson, are you ready for another?" It was obvious that he was a regular patron.

"Hit me again, Greg, but make it light. Mardie is upstairs getting all gussied up for the big blow out at Hallings'.

Jo had looked over at his table when she heard the waiter. She was smiling. The elderly man returned her smile and rose.

"Want to welcome you to the Wort. I'm Kraemer Wilson, but most folks around here call me Will. You passing through?"

Ben stood and shook Will's hand firmly, noticing that his rough, callused hands had tangled with hard work in the past. "Ben Daulton here and my wife Jo. Yes, we're just passing through. Here from Florida via Las Vegas, where we attended a convention. Here," he said pulling a chair from another table. "Sit and have your drink with us. I'll guarantee Jo will keep the conversation going with questions about the area and the Wort in particular."

"Be glad to join you and give you a rundown on the hotel. I was at the big opening in '41. Heck, over 2,000 people paraded through here just to get a glimpse of Jes and John Wort's monument, as we called it. Set 'em back $150,000 bucks, and that was a lot way back then. Lost most of it in the big fire in '80 though. Built it back good as new, maybe even better."

"Jo's fallen in love with this area. Matter of fact, we've been looking for a place for the summer months. Gets so blasted hot in Jacksonville."

"Mardie—she's my wife—keeps telling me we oughta buy one of those condos on the ocean in Florida for the winter, but I'm native and don't want to give up my favorite time of the year."

"You ski, Will?" Jo asked animatedly, thinking a person can ski no matter how old he is.

"Did for years but decided to give it up and just sell land to folks who want to ski."

"Oh, you're in real estate?" she asked. Ben thought, we're in for it now. He's got two suckers on his hook. Pulled the good-old-boy bit with us and knew just the right bait to use.

"It's just something I've got into these past few years. Got a spread over in Wilson and run a few beeves and also dabble in raising thoroughbred horses. Mardie likes to spend time in town, so while she's out with her lady friends shopping and all, I just sit in the Wort and sell a few parcels from time to time. She's upstairs. I'd like you to meet her…"

"Oh, we're just in for a drink before deciding where to have dinner," Ben hastened to say. Probably have to listen to another Mimi type, he thought. But Jo had other ideas. "We'd love to meet her. Perhaps you can suggest a restaurant that we can walk to."

Will nodded his grey head toward Greg, having picked up on Ben's apprehension and, answering Jo, said, "Greg will take care of you. He's got a stack of brochures that'd choke a horse, with lots of restaurants and maps and how to get to them. Me and Mardie keep rooms upstairs, and if you don't have time to visit now, well, we'll be around while you're here." He tipped his western hat and murmured that he was glad to have met them and that if he could assist them he'd be at the Wort.

After he left the room Jo looked at Ben questioningly. "Why did you behave like that? You were so short with him."

"Thought that you couldn't see that he's a bar hustler, hon. You know, the kind who hangs around and attacks the unsuspecting tourists. Next thing they know, they've bought hundreds of acres of rock for their dream house."

"I don't think so. Really I don't. He seemed so lonely to me, like he needed someone to talk to, to pass time with."

The waiter, Greg, approached with another round of drinks. "Oh, we don't want another round," Ben hastened to say.

"Mr. Wilson ordered them and paid for the lot."

Jo smiled and turned to Greg. "Who is this Mr. Wilson, Greg?"

He laughed. "He just owns a lot of the state of Wyoming, that's all. About the finest man I've ever known. Has a boys ranch up in the Wind River Mountains. You know, for troubled youngsters, and he and Mrs. Wilson do a lot for the local youth. Lost their only son in Nam. They keep a suite here all year. Mrs. Wilson isn't well and likes to stay close to the doctor.

Jo looked accusingly at Ben. When Greg left she chastised him. "See, he was just being friendly. He's lonely, hon."

"I should have known that you'd see that. Never knew anyone who could see only the good in people like you can, Jo. Now, I mean that."

"Don't start with that halo bit. This is our fun vacation, sir. I want to be wild and crazy and unpredictable. Besides, I haven't been able to see any good in Mr. Avery Bellin in years. Try as I might, I can't."

Jo took her hand away from Ben's and watched Greg approach a tiny older woman. He motioned toward Ben and Jo and the woman approached them tentatively.

"I hate to intrude, but Greg said that you might know where Will ran off to. Oh, I'm sorry. I'm Mardie Wilson, Will's wife."

Ben rose, took her hand and introduced Jo. Mardie was nothing like he had suspected. He had envisioned a brassy woman, half Will's age, wearing lots of silver and turquoise and western to her teeth. Mardie resembled any good Baptist lady from the deep south and wore a simple pale blue silk shantung dress with pearls. Her hair was silver and worn fashionably, and she tottered on very high heels.

"He didn't indicate where he was going, Mrs. Wilson," Jo warmly said.

"We're due at a party shortly and I want to make sure he's dressed. Maybe he went up to the office to visit Louise. Bet that's where he is."

They exchanged good-byes, and as she turned, Will came through the door. He softened when he saw her. They embraced and approached the Daulton table.

"See that you met my missus. Hope you have a pleasant stay in Wyoming and come back to see us…"

"Well, before you leave perhaps we can set up an appointment for tomorrow to talk about the local real estate," Ben said, surprising Jo.

"No problem. You set the time. I'm an early riser."

Ben looked at Jo and she nodded, pleased.

"Why not over breakfast? We're at the Snow King. Want to join us there about eight or eight thirty?"

"Rather treat you two to Jedediah's. It's on Broadway one block east of the square. Can't miss it and you'll feast on the best sourdough this side of 'Frisco. Maybe Mardie can join us?" he asked.

"Oh, hon, I can't. Have to see Dr. Adler at nine o'clock. I'm really sorry, really I am."

"We understand, Mrs. Wilson. Perhaps another time," Jo said.

When the Wilsons left, Jo reached for her wine glass, raised it and said in a low voice, "I love you, Ben Daulton."

He responded and clinked her glass. "I knew you were dying to question him about this place. Why not! It does have a special feel about it, doesn't it? I love the expansiveness. Don't feel hemmed in by the mountains out here."

They left the Wort singing softly, *Oh, give me land, lots of land under starry skies above. Don't fence me in…*"

FOUR

"You what?" Robbie yelled over the phone.

"I said that your mother and I've fallen in love with Wyoming and just signed the papers on a forty-acre parcel near the town of Bondurant about forty-five miles south and east of Jackson. It's in a place called Hoback Ranches. Never saw such a beautiful place, son."

Jo took the phone. "Now, Robbie, don't have a conniption fit. We'll spend summer vacations out here; then in seven years when dad retires, we can spend four or five months if we want. Oh, you and Julie will love it, and the girls will be crazy about it. Just wait 'til you see it. It's heaven!"

Pause...

"Neighbors? Oh, there are other people around. Some actually live there all year round. It's near the Hoback River. You can find it on your map. Will, our realtor, said that there is a doctor from Florida who owns the forty acres next to ours and has a lovely home on it, and there's a widow up the road from our parcel who owns 160 acres. The locals call her place Charlie's Mountain. Her late husband was named Charlie, I think he said. Maybe you've heard of her. She uses the name Irma or I. Fronk. You know, she's the famous naturalist photographer. Heck, you grew up with her photos in the *National Geographic*. How about that?"

Ben grabbed the phone from Jo. "Your mother is impressed about living next to someone that famous, but Will said we'd probably never even see her. Seems that she's very reclusive. What did you say?"

Pause...

Ben laughed and turned to Jo, "He said that she doesn't suspect how persuasive his mother can be and that you'd probably be taking brownies up to her house and having tea on top of Charlie's Mountain before she has you figured out. You know, he's right,

20

hon. You do have a way with you."

But Robbie was not right—far from it.

They built the house the summer of '86. It was another dry year. Not nearly the snowfall nor May rains needed to curb the drought that had plagued that part of the country. Ben had insisted that they build on a knoll overlooking a flower filled meadow instead of in the tall pines and firs that were abundant on their acreage. If they had a fire he'd rather be away from tall timber, he reasoned. The Wyoming Range and Gros Ventre Mountains surrounded them.

They selected a local builder and decided on cedar siding rather then the popular log construction. Jo had wanted a contemporary style with floor-to-ceiling windows to allow the breathtaking views to visit each room. "They seem to be striving to outdo each other, don't they, hon?" He agreed.

The construction company moved a small house trailer up to their site for them so they could supervise the construction for the month they'd be there. They quickly met Jack and Betty Sheffield, the doctor and his wife from Ocala, Florida, that Will had told them about. They were somewhat older than Jo and Ben, probably in their mid-sixties, and had summered in the ranches for over twenty years.

Their home "La Vista Grande" seemed unpretentious on the outside, but that was deceiving. It was log with two stories plus a full basement. Betty collected Indian art and had decorated the entire house with it. Jo could tell that money had been no object in her choices. She was particularly fond of a local sculptor, Lee Riley Cameron, and had several of his full-size bronzes prominently placed. Jo loved the Indian maiden, who practically greeted you as you entered the foyer. Betty had used stone floors and rough rock to contrast her beautiful lines. It was very effective. Everything was beige and earth tones. The only accent color was cobalt blue, and that used sparingly. Jo thought, I've a lot to learn from this woman. And she liked her. That was a plus.

They found that they had a number of similar interests. They all enjoyed bridge, and Jack golfed as did Ben. Betty enjoyed working with wool and had a number of exquisite wall hangings, rugs and even place mats. She also took painting lessons from a local artist, something that Jo had always wanted to do but had never seemed to find the time. Now she could. She could hardly wait for Liz to visit and had literally begged her to. But she was hesitant to leave Avery for any length of time. Scared to leave was more like it, Jo thought.

Their other close neighbors, the Kirchers, spent mostly the winter months in the Ranches. Usually came out in early December and stayed through January. They were, according to Jack and Betty, cross-country skiing and snowmobiling enthusiasts and usually came with other couples, so they seldom saw them.

When Jack spoke of Irma Fronk Barksdale he seemed rather sad, Jo said to Ben after their first evening with them. They'd had a very interesting time. They started out with cocktails on the wrap-around deck that was surrounded by the mountains, even the Wind River Range could be seen from there. She was glad that she'd taken a wrap. The sun felt good to her, and she had commented that it was in the 90s in Florida when they had called Robbie from town that afternoon.

"When do you think we'll be able to get a phone out here, Jack?" Ben questioned. He was getting a little tired of driving into Bondurant, the small town that was closest, to use the only public phone on the highway.

"At present it's cost prohibitive. As more people move in I'm sure it'll be arranged. We already have a number of residents working on it, but, don't count on it anytime soon, Ben. One thing you'll learn out here is patience."

Betty began to laugh, and when Jo joined her she went to Jack and patted his shoulder saying, "We've been coming out here for over twenty years and I've not seen any improvement in that department, Dr. Sheffield."

Ben was amazed at how many houses he could see from that height. He had no idea that there were that many in the area. "It's understandable why you named your ranch La Vista Grande. Is that Barksdale's, Jack?"

"Yep, and that's probably as close as you'll ever get to seeing it.

Irma's gotten so strange since Charlie died three years ago. Hell, they both got downright peculiar when Patty was killed. Only child, and those two worshiped her. Just about killed them. Hardly left the mountain after that."

Betty interjected. "Those two were the most fun-loving couple you'd ever want to meet. We used to have a standing bridge date every Wednesday at six o'clock sharp. We'd take turns going to each other's house. We were so close."

She looked lovingly at the barely visible log house on the hill. "I miss Irma. I really do. We were such good friends, and oh how she and Charlie loved to dance. Never missed a one. Would drive 150 miles or more if they took a notion."

"How was their daughter killed?" Jo asked.

"Hit head on outside of Albuquerque. Broke her neck. Was on her way here for Christmas. Irm had that house lit up like you can't imagine for a blooming week. Even had Charlie put a red bulb in the deer's nose over the mantle. We were with them when Joey Shiffar came up on his snowmobile to tell them. He's the local deputy, you know."

"Now don't get started on that, honey." Betty said, patting his back. "Let's get to the bridge table."

"Here, let me help you clear the table," Jo suggested.

"OK. That'll get us started that much sooner." When Betty got to the kitchen she told Jo that she really had rather not talk about the Barksdales anymore. Jack and Charlie had been very close, too, and it upset him. Jo said that she understood.

But Jack wouldn't let it go and seemed to need to remember and share their good times. Betty shrugged, shook her head and gave in to Jack's need.

"It's not going to do any good to try to steer the conversation away from Irma and Charlie, Jo. When Jack gets something in his craw, well, it just has to run its course. Guess that's why he's such a good doctor. He always has to find the cause."

So the Daultons heard a great deal about the Barksdales and the other owners of the Hoback ranches that summer evening. Jo and Ben didn't return to their trailer until after midnight, and Jo commented, "Do you realize that we played just one rubber? But wasn't it fascinating? Makes me want to sneak up Charlie's Mountain to meet the illusive Irma."

"Now, Jo, don't you go getting nosy. You know sometimes when people have had a truly traumatic experience like she did that they do get, well, a little peculiar."

"I was just teasing. I'd not think of invading her privacy. But, I'll have to admit that I'm more curious than ever." She slept fitfully and awakened before daylight.

The trailer was small. Jo heated the leftover coffee, trying to be quiet, and put her parka on over her robe and went outside. Her breath was visible. When she looked at the thermometer she was surprised that it was only seventeen degrees. Seemed colder somehow. The kids can't believe that it's below freezing in late June, she thought. She and Ben had waited until the basement had been finished before coming out. They had left their dog Maggie in the care of Andrea and Carlos and had flown out and rented a four-wheel-drive truck for the month.

She decided to walk down their driveway toward Elk Drive, the main road in their section. It was as the others, two lanes of gravel. As she came around the curve she heard a motor. "Oh, Lordy! I'm in my night clothes! Heaven's, it's only six o'clock. It can't be the workmen!"

She was about to turn back when she saw a figure beside the locked fence gate leading to Charlie's Mountain, although the name carved on the large log above the gate read "Altamonte Ranch".

Can that be the illusive Irma Fronk? I can't believe it! And she's on a four-wheeler. Jo ducked into the copse of aspens and observed. She's so small, she thought. I thought she'd be tall and thin for some reason. She couldn't see her face because she was so bundled up. She was putting a large package in the log shed or out-house, as the locals called it, beside the gate for Manny to pick up, no doubt. Jack had said that a not very bright man called Manny was the only one who knew if Irma was alive or dead and picked up her mail and deliveries every day. He also said that he didn't trust him, but Betty shushed him, so he didn't explain why.

Jo felt funny peeking at the poor old soul. As she turned to leave she heard, "Might as well come out of there. I can still see, you know!"

Oh, my, is all Jo could think. But, she is right. This is ridiculous.

"Good morning. I'm still in my night clothes and didn't want to be seen." She hesitated, then continued. "I'm sure you're Mrs. Barksdale. I'm your new neighbor, Jo Daulton."

As Jo approached, Irma got back on her four-wheeler and said loudly over the noise as she turned around, "I hope you and your husband treat the Hoback right. He's a nice looking man." And with that she was gone.

"How do you know?" Jo yelled after her. "Why, the old thing! She's been spying on us." She began to laugh. Wait'll I tell Ben. I'll hafta use the binoculars on Charlie's Mountain, that's what. Two can play that game, I. Fronk. Oh, I'm loving this.

"You what?" Ben said loudly. "Come on, Jo. It's not seven o'clock, and the men aren't even here. Riding a four-wheeler? I don't believe you!"

FIVE

Jo was so excited about seeing Irma Barksdale that Ben knew she wasn't teasing and would do just as she pleased first chance she got. After a light breakfast she dressed in her heavy long pants, long sleeved shirt, vest, hiking boots and called to him from the trailer door, "Going hiking, hon. Might be a long one." In her knapsack she had stashed the binoculars, bird book, wildflower book, note pad and a flask of cool water and headed for the highest part of their property. It was a difficult hike over and around fallen trees and boulders.

Winded, she could hardly wait to get to her binoculars. She was positive that she'd be able to see Barksdales' from there, but she couldn't because the lodgepole pines and Douglas firs were thick around Irma's house, like a barricade, she thought. She felt defeated. Well, you win this round Miss I. Fronk, but I'm as determined as you.

She resumed collecting the wildflowers that were abundant in the meadows: wild geraniums, blue flax, scarlet gilia. Later she told Ben that she hated to walk in the woods, the flowers were so thick. The deep blue lupine were a foot and a half high. No wonder Irma had no trouble finding subjects to photograph. It was a photographer's paradise.

Betty had said the wall-sized photograph of a field of blue flax and yellow arrowroot that hung in the hospital in Jackson was taken right there on Charlie's Mountain. Jo had seen the winter scenes she had photographed hanging at the airport: snowshoe rabbits nestled in the thick snow against evergreens with a buck fence in the background. The one she especially liked was the winter scene with moonlight shining through the pines on two pairs of snowshoe tracks leading up to a log cabin with a soft light shining through the windows and smoke rising from the stone chimney. The cabin looked so inviting and warm.

She had asked the Sheffields if they knew where the cabin was, and Betty said that it was Charlie's folks' homestead up at Cliff Creek north of Bondurant. It had won a tri-state award and was on the cover of *WYOMING MAGAZINE*. That photo truly kicked off Irma's career. She got her first big assignment from *NATIONAL GEOGRAPHIC* and her reputation grew rapidly. Charlie teased her unmercifully and said that his work of stuffing the largest Alaskan polar bear ever killed by an American, that stood proudly in the Smithsonian, would go unnoticed now, but he couldn't have been prouder, nor could the residents of that entire section of the state.

When Jo awakened early the next morning she got dressed quickly and headed down their rutted road to Elk. She stood drinking her coffee, but no 4-wheeler did she see or hear. She was surprisingly disappointed. Ben was still asleep when she returned. *Oh, it was a fluke that I saw her yesterday. We've got two and a half more weeks. I'll just be patient. But she seems so interesting.*

The next morning Jo repeated her walk to Elk, and when she was halfway up their driveway she heard what she thought was the 4-wheeler. She did an about face and she was right—it was a 4-wheeler. Instead of waiting in the Aspens to be discovered she approached the outhouse. Irma was so enshrouded in clothing that Jo could barely make out a human form. Her old red ski cap was missing one string, and her gloves lacked a few finger ends.

"Good morning, Mrs. Barksdale. Beautiful, isn't it?" Either she was being ignored or Irma hadn't heard her. "It's a beautiful..."

"I can hear as well as see. Didn't know you Easterners were early risers." Her voice was strong and crackled like an open fire, Jo thought.

"Always have been." Jo wondered how she knew she was from the East. *She might be reclusive but she's up on everything around here, I bet.* Jo wanted to say, "I'm not an Easterner. I'm Southern."

"You like flowers and birds, don't you?"

Well the old thing. Even knows I go bird watching and flower picking.

"Ben and I both love the outdoors. That's why I knew that we'd love it here..."

"But he doesn't go with you." She seemed to be chastising the sleeping Ben.

"He does sometimes but feels that he should stay around here while they're building…"

"He's just getting in the way! Billy Parker knows what he's doing, and so do Jeff and Andy," she said sternly and with no non-sense expected from Jo.

With that said and another large parcel placed in the outhouse, she virtually hopped on the 4-wheeler, revved it up noisily, and up the gravel road she sped, her long, grey, braided ponytail protrud-ing from the cap bouncing behind her as she bobbed along.

Jo could hardly wait to get back to the trailer to share the meeting with Ben. He was getting a kick out of their cat-and-mouse game but felt that he knew who the winner would be. Even though his Jo was persistent, he felt that Irma would win out. People seemed to get wily when senility crept in. He could remem-ber how clever his mother had become and how she cussed like a sailor in those later years. His brother and sister had been very upset by her actions and seldom visited her in the home, but he and Jo went every week. Half the time she hardly recognized them, but they went anyway. Jo had bought several books dealing with senility, so they knew that her behavior wasn't unusual. Even so, it was still hard to deal with. Boy, how she'd cuss Dr. Innes, but he said that he was used to it.

For the next three days Irma didn't show up at the gate. Jo was becoming concerned, but her fears were alleviated on the fourth day when she approached the Altamonte Ranch gate and saw Lyman Markos, or Manny, as Jack called him, waiting at the gate in his old truck. Jo had never met him but recognized him from Jack's description. He was older than she had imagined, early forties, she thought. He was unkempt, clothes grease stained, hands obviously those of one who worked on machinery, and he was a nervous sort—shifty.

He opened the conversation after tipping his western hat to her. "Miss, I'm Manny, Miss Irma's man. Now, I'm not known for cussing in front of ladies, but Miss Irma told me to say it just like she told me. So here goes. 'I don't want any goddamned Easterner sneaking around my ranch. So you mind your own goddamned business or you'll pay the consequences'. Them's the exact words, miss. Now, as I said…"

Jo heard little more she was so put out, but she knew a retort was called for. She pursed her lips and proceeded. "Manny, I want you to take this message to Miss Irma verbatim! I am not an Easterner! I'm a Southerner! I am also a lady and have not found anything or anyone interesting enough on her ranch to warrant poking around, as she has accused me of!" With that said she whirled around to return to their trailer, brushing the tears aside and tripping over the deep ruts.

When she opened the door Ben saw her contorted face and knew that something had happened regarding Irma. He did not inquire but let her calm down and be the one to tell him about it.

"I don't believe the old thing. Sneaking indeed. She's the one who's spying. Now, why did she have to say such a thing? I thought that the ice had been broken and that we could become friends, and…and…"

"Come here, honey. Come here." She felt warm and comforted in his slender arms, but her sniffling wouldn't stop.

"Do you remember Mama and how she became toward the end? Remember?"

"But, she's not old like Mama Daulton was. She's probably only in her mid-seventies."

"Age doesn't matter. Remember what Doc Innes said? Hey, don't let her get you down. We've got only two more weeks. Let's enjoy them."

"I know you're right, hon, but I was so in hopes that…"

"Jack and Betty told you that she's gotten peculiar. Don't you remember? He said that she called him on their CB radio, the one that Charlie had installed years ago. Remember what he said?"

"Yes, he said that she told him she was going to tear the thing from the wall and for him to quit poking into her business, calling her all the time. And she yanked it out, he figured, because he never got another response. But that was different, hon."

"How so?"

"Because I wasn't bothering her one whit. All I ever did was walk down our road—our road—to Elk. I can't help that that's where her old gate and outhouse are."

"Jo, this is the end of it! Do you hear? She doesn't want your friendship or anyone else's. Betty said that there are two clubs in the basin, and the little church is quite active. You'll have lots of friends out here. You don't need her. Let it go. Jo, are you listening?"

She nodded yes but all the while knew that Irma Fronk Barksdale was not going to best her. She didn't know why she felt that way—it wasn't in her nature, but she did. The planning began. But she should have listened to Ben.

SIX

The last two weeks of their vacation seemed to fly by. Jo made it a point to be down near the gate or digging up thistles beside Elk when Manny went to Irma's Monday, Wednesday and Friday. But she glimpsed Irma only once during that time. She had asked Betty and Jack at their weekly bridge game what on earth Manny found to do three days a week.

Jack replied, "Oh, she has him keep all three 4-wheelers in top-notch shape and even that old car of Charlie's mom polished and in running order. Hell, that thing hasn't left the mountain since Patty was killed, and before then they only used it for parades and such. Charlie kept it only because Miss Kate had loved it so, and of course Manny brings Irma's mail and what she might need from town. Doesn't need much food. Grows everything she needs. One of those organic gardeners, even when Charlie was alive."

Jo interrupted. "But she can't grow anything for most of the year, can she?"

"She cans and freezes everything in sight. Charlie built her a room off her darkroom to store all that food. Never figured out why anyone as smart as Irma would waste time with all that stuff. Even makes her own jam, scouring that entire mountain for wild raspberries and strawberries." He looked off in space.

"Jack, let it go! Let's play bridge." Betty looked at Jo, shaking her head in dismay. "He's concerned about Manny. Doesn't trust him. Jack worked in a psychiatric hospital while in college and thinks that Manny might go off the deep end one of these days. He seems harmless enough to me, but he's right. You never can tell about those people. Totally unpredictable."

Jo responded, "I'm sorry. I don't mean to pry but I honestly worry about her, too."

"No need, Jo. You know Irma had a life before she and Charlie moved back west and thinks she can move mountains all by herself

31

even if she can't.

Betty shrugged her shoulders and resigned herself to another evening of very little bridge and a lot of talk. She watched Ben as he stood at the heavy glass doors leading to the deck and wondered what he was thinking. He's a deep man, and it's obvious that he's concerned about his wife's obsession with Irma.

Jack continued. "You probably know that Charlie was born and raised right here in the basin. Grandparents were settlers here. He and his sister Pat and a lot of the other children were schooled by a teacher who lived with them during the summer months. The other ranches had the same set up, I'm told. Way back then there was no winter school. Heck, he said it'd get to 58 below many a day. The older children went to school in Pinedale and boarded with families. The school district paid for it with what they called isolation pay. Charlie said that they'd come home for visits periodically by horse and sled. We didn't get our Bondurant school 'til '51. Imagine that!"

"Charlie got a full scholarship to the University of Wyoming. Then he went to Indiana University and studied to be a pathologist. That's where he and Irma met."

"I didn't know that," Jo interrupted. "I just thought that they'd always lived here…"

"Oh no, he and Irm had a pathology lab in Indianapolis for years. Did very well financially. But a surprise package arrived when Irm was 42 years old. That's the year Patty was born, and it changed their lives completely. They started spending more time at Charlie's folks' spread, and Patty took to ranch life and horses. She was one of the best horsewomen this area ever had. And smart! Was out of high school by the time she was sixteen. Wasn't much to look at—some might say she was homely, but when she smiled or laughed—well, there was something very special about Patty, and Irm and Charlie knew it."

Betty interrupted Jack. "Why she wasn't spoiled, I don't know—had everything a youngster could want. But she wasn't. Those two worshiped her. That's why it was so hard on them when she was killed."

Ben had been patiently taking the conversation in and wondered why Jo was so curious about it all. He knew that it was her nature to be concerned about the poor and downtrodden, but this new wrinkle was unexpected. Maybe she's just bored—misses the kids and grands. I hope so. This is getting out of hand.

"When did they build Altamonte Ranch?" Ben inquired.

"Think Patty was about six or eight when they decided to sell their lab and move out here for good. That's the year Kraemer Wilson and his buddies bought all this land and started developing it. Charlie and Irm were just about the first to buy in here. There was no one else on Elk then. We built a couple of years later."

"Did you say that Patty was twenty-four when she was killed?" Jo asked.

"She'd just completed med school. Imagine! At twenty-four."

Betty added, "And Charlie and Irma had become pillars of the community. Never missed church in the summer months. You know that St. Hubert the Hunter is open only June through August. Then those of us who attend regularly go to St. Andrew's in Pinedale. You'll have to attend with us some Sunday. It is delightful. It's Episcopalian, but people from all denominations attend. We have several Catholics who always attend."

"Irma had established herself as a top-notch photographer, and Charlie's friend Lee Bryant, who owns the most prestigious art gallery in Jackson, had taken Irm under his wing and sold her work as fast as she could turn it out. Got a contract with a top New York agent, and she was on her way. Not that it changed her, because it didn't."

Ben asked curiously, "Did it change Charlie?"

Betty looked up at him and was amused by his question. "Of course not. He loved everything about Irma. It was Charlie who got her started in photography. Even built her a darkroom and matted the prints and made frames. They were a team. Besides, he had his taxidermy hobby and was very respected in his field, and that gave him all the pleasure he could tolerate, he often said. Charlie knew who he was and didn't have a jealous bone in his body. He was just happy for his girls, as he called them."

"Irma started photographing elk, bear, moose, deer and antelope for Charlie. He was quite a hunter. She hunted only with her camera, she said. That way he could mount the animals in a more lifelike pose. He'd study the photos, and his work was bought by museums all over the West. Even had some at the Buffalo Bill Museum in Cody. That's the one of the elk bugling, a full mount. Absolutely beautiful. So lifelike."

"It started out as a hobby for both. Charlie had one rule. He refused to work with a deadline. Didn't cut down on his orders though. Always had more work than he could finish every winter. When hunting season came in the fall he and Irma shut down everything. Hunted only in Wyoming and ate their kill. Our bridge games came to a halt in September. But by the first of May, when we returned to the ranches, it would be like we hadn't had that hiatus."

"Betty refused to snowmobile in. We'd get a call from Irma and Charlie in Ocala telling us that we could come on up, that the roads were clear enough and that the cards were hot. You can't believe the good times we had."

Jo sat at the bridge table smiling, picturing the four of them in better times. No wonder Jack is so sad. A piece of their lives is gone, never to return. I wonder if Ben and I will experience something like this when Liz and Avery are gone, or any of our other best friends. Probably not, because we have such a full life. They depended on each other for companionship. I guess this is what small towns are all about—that dependency.

The day that Jo and Ben were due to leave for Jacksonville arrived. Jo had had a restless night and knew that it wasn't because the coyotes had howled for half of it. She knew that it was because of her ridiculous obsession about one I. Fronk. Pulling on her sweats and grabbing her coffee she turned back to see if Ben was awake. His back was toward her but his breathing was steady, so she said nothing. Quickly and quietly she went out the trailer door. She was nervous.

I am going to miss this place, she thought. Oh, how I'm going to miss it. She heard the noise and knew that it was too early for Manny to arrive. I'll not be deterred, Miss Irma. I own this land and I'll walk it if I feel like it. Sure enough, it was the 4-wheeler hauling down the hill toward her, gravel shooting from both sides. Irma was carrying a package but instead of putting it in the back of the outhouse she opened the gate and walked straight toward Jo.

Now what! is all Jo could think. But before she could even say good morning, Irma spoke.

"A going-away present, Mrs. Daulton. I hope you like it." Jo knew that her mouth was open in astonishment while she stammered thank you.

Irma closed and locked the gate, climbed on her 4-wheeler and began her ride up Charlie's mountain. She didn't look back. Jo could tell that is was a picture or at least a frame about 16 x 12. She was apprehensive about removing the brown wrapping paper but knew that she had to before she returned to the trailer. If it was a photo of something awful she'd not tell Ben.

She ripped the paper off. Gritting her teeth, preparing herself for one of Irma's tricks.

Tears welled, then ran down her cold cheeks. "The old fool. She's been following me."

Jo had been collecting specimens of every type of wild flower she could find and placing them in a basket for drying. Irma had apparently followed and using a telephoto lens captured Jo with the early morning sun on her back, resting on a large boulder while holding the overflowing basket of flowers. The flower-filled meadow was at her feet, the early morning mist rising above it. The creek, edged by the willows, with the towering pines and firs framing the opposite hill was surrounded by an indescribable western blue sky hovering above. It was so beautiful!

"The old fool", she repeated all the way back to the trailer. But she was smiling through her tears. She had broken through. At last, she had broken through.

SEVEN

Reba Markos, Manny's mother, was a large woman in her early sixties. She had arrived at the Big Bear Ranch forty-three years earlier. It was the largest ranch on the Hoback River north of the small town of Bondurant. She was half starved and large with child. Eileen Stroebel took her in, asked no questions and assisted her when she delivered Manny. To this day no one knew where she came from nor who Manny's father was. And no one really seemed to care. It was her business.

She was housed in the small log house that had been the original homestead of the Stroebel family back at the turn of the century. To pay for her keep she assisted Eileen with her eight children. All knew from Manny's early days that he was not quite right, but there wasn't a vehicle on the ranch that he couldn't repair. He had a good nature and, unless he was drinking, he was a mild mannered man.

Reba had sent Manny to the new school in Bondurant along with the Stroebel children, but Manny couldn't keep up. She let him fish or help her around the ranch. He had learned to read and do his numbers a little, and he got along.

He was built large like his mother, over six feet tall and square. Carried about 220 pounds and was a homely man. Seemed to always be drooling and wiping the seeping saliva running down his chin. Charlie and Irma hired him on as their handy man when they built Altamonte Ranch. When Charlie's taxidermy hobby became a business, Manny was invaluable. He ran errands that the Barksdales didn't have time for, going to Jackson or Pinedale or even all the way to Idaho Falls.

Charlie'd drive to the highway and call in his orders using the Triangle F Restaurant's phone, and Manny'd pick up the order. It wasn't that Charlie didn't trust Manny with remembering; he just wanted to make sure that the orders were right. He was an easygoing man, never in a hurry, but was thorough. They paid Manny well, and Reba took his pay every two weeks and gave him a small amount for his personal use. She took part for the household and put the rest in the bank.

It was a big day when she told him that he had enough money for his own truck. Jamie Stroebel went with him into Jackson, and they came home with a bright red Ford pickup. He was still driving that same pickup twenty years later, but now it was painted blue and ran like a top, everyone said. Jake Fisher said that Manny could listen to any engine and diagnose its ailment. He'd won many a bet on being right.

Spending Saturday nights at the Elkhorn Bar had become a habit with Manny in the last few years. Bart Sikes had threatened to boot him out many times, but frankly, he felt sorry for him. The bar was a popular spot for the ranch hands and locals alike. It was just about the only entertainment offered in the basin except for the annual BBQ and the chicken supper that the Ladies Guild put on and the Christmas party at the church/ community club.

The juke box was blaring when Manny showed up the night that Jo and Ben left for their return trip to Florida. He was glad that they were gone. He didn't like foreigners, as he referred to the Daultons and everyone else in the Hoback Ranches. He asked Bart for a Bud and moseyed back to the room off the bar to watch a couple of young cowboys shoot pool.

Marthie, Bart's wife, noticed that he had cleaned up, even getting most of the grease from under his fingernails. She laughed at Bart's expression when Manny came in. "He's splashed on enough cologne to start a bloomin' stampede," he whispered to her. "Just hope he behaves himself. Don't want any trouble tonight. God, hon, I got myself a beaut of a headache. Be glad when haying is over. Seems to get worse every year."

"I'll get you an Advil, honey. If Manny gets too tanked up you're gonna have trouble with Elway. Last week I thought he was gonna deck Manny. Said that he was funnin' with Betsy Ann. Now, you know that Elway won't stand for that."

"I'll keep an eye on him. Go on back and get me that Advil. You might hafta take over if I don't shake this thing."

She went past the pool table and the men throwing darts to the small room off the main room. Mumbling to herself, she wondered why they were so dumb as to have Binge put down red linoleum. Showed every bit of mud those cowboys dragged in. It wasn't a big place. Only ten barstools at the bar as you walked in. The usual décor, baseball pennants on the walls and pictures of the local hunters with their kill. A wood-burning stove backed by a stone fireplace was opposite the bar and, of course, the usual beer ads everywhere you looked.

Marthie was kept busy just keeping those fellows full of pizza and sandwiches. That microwave was the smartest thing Bart and me ever bought, she said to herself. They made good money from the snacks and sodas, but since they started serving pizza their sales truly increased. They'd always done well on the beer. You know, maybe we can retire to Arizona one of these days. I ain't been warm since we bought this place.

"Here, hon, and you drink plenty of water with these. That Manny is bugging Lavon. If he keeps it up he's gonna throw a dart at him and we're in for trouble. Oh, oh. Here comes Betsy Ann and Elway, and she's got her sister with her. If those jeans got any tighter they'd split."

"What you complaining 'bout? Marthie, there ain't a gal comin' in here who has your ass. Why, honey, you've still got the cutest ass I've ever patted."

Marthie grinned up at him, took the tray of beers to the back room and set them on the juke box. Manny was the first to grab one. He reached inside his jeans pocket and threw the dollar and a half on the tray. Marthie could feel Elway watching him. God, he's just hunting trouble with Manny. Best get to Bart.

As Marthie was dodging the dart throwers she looked up just in time to see Heather and Jonsey McDonald saunter in, their butts bouncing with the tempo of the music. Oh, God! We're in for it now. Manny has seen them.

She got to Bart and whispered, "Manny's already had four beers. Cut him off."

The girls sashayed past the bar and headed for Betsy Ann and

Elway's table. Manny couldn't keep his eyes off them. "Gimme another, Bart. This is gonna be my night to howl." And he let out a wolf howl that rattled the bar glasses. That got the attention of every man there. Marthie saw Elway jump up and head for him.

"Not here, it ain't, Manny. I ain't gonna have any rowdiness goin' on here. You best get on back to the Big Bear before there's trouble."

Manny took in the situation as the back room emptied into the bar. "Ya all think ya so damn smart, don' ya? Well, ya don' know nothin'. Not a goddamned thing. If ya knew what Ah know then the lot of ya would be smart!" He knew he'd not be able to take on all of them so he turned and left. But not before he said, "If ya knew what they done up at Barksdales' like Ah do, then you'd know I'm smarter than any of you. Think you're so smart...think you're..." He slammed the heavy wooden door shut with a bang.

"What the hell's he talking about, Bart?" one of the men yelled.

Bart shook his head and said, "He's been saying the same thing for the past two years now, and I ain't got an answer outta him. He's just a little tetched, boys, that's all. Just calm down."

"If he eyes Betsy Ann one more time he'll be more than tetched!" Elway threw in. "And not only that, Bart. Me and the boys been talking, and we think you best see to it that he quits coming in here."

"Wait a good goddamned minute, Elway Saunders. This is my place, and it'll take more than the likes of you to tell me who can and who can't come in here. You got that?" Bart spoke low, jabbing his finger into Elway's taut chest. "Now get back to what you was doing and be quick about it or I'm calling Joey Shiffar to make you for sure understand what I mean!"

Marthie went up to him and stroked his back. "You want that I should take over, hon? I know that headache ain't got any better."

"I'm OK. They just shouldn't test me when I hurt. Fix me a pizza, hon. Just might be hungry. Why don't you go on upstairs and check the kids. Got a feelin' that these rowdies might be leavin' early tonight."

Manny didn't go back to Big Bear like Bart had suggested. He decided to go up to Altamonte Ranch and poke around there. "If I had a camera, then they'd believe me. I'd take pictures of that crazy old woman's goings-on." When he got to the outhouse he realized that he didn't have his key to the gate. He swung his truck around spewing gravel as he high-tailed it at breakneck speed over the curvy, steep road. Just missing a doe, he let out his wolf howl, jumped out of his truck and threw gravel at the frightened deer.

The lights went on at Sheffields'. "What on earth is that, Jack? Have they let wolves loose in the Hoback, too?" Betty called throwing on her robe.

Jack was on the deck trying to make out what was going on. "Hell no! That's that crazy Manny out there. Just made the hill by Buchos's cabin and driving like a bat outta hell! I'm going to speak to Irm about him. She's got to do something…"

He stopped, walked back into the living room and closed the door behind him, this time locking it. Betty went to him. "I do believe that Jo will get through to her, hon. Then it'll be like it used to be. Come on to bed. He's probably drunk and just showing off. Come back to bed."

Betty was restless. She thought, this is like waiting for the other shoe to drop. But the only noise she heard was a distant coyote's call to its mate. Neither slept the rest of the night.

EIGHT

"But don't you ever go anywhere? I mean to a movie or…?" Julie asked.

"We make it a point to go to Pinedale—that's our county seat, you know—once a week or Jackson, and if Billy wants us to make a decision about cabinets or wallpaper, then we go more often. But we go in mostly to grocery shop and have dinner out. And then some of the neighbors have had us over for dinner or a picnic. They're big on picnics. Everyone takes something, and the host usually provides the meat. Once Jack and Betty grilled salmon they'd caught in Alaska, and was it ever delicious! We picnicked up in Elkhorn Park out of Pinedale for that one. Great hiking there. The trails are well marked, but you do have to be careful about bears, I'm told.

"We have the church in Bondurant, and Dad and I went one Sunday, but we had got the time wrong, so we sat in the car until services were over. You know, I showed you the pictures of it. It is beautiful. Well, to me it is. Log, of course, and small, but the stained glass window above the altar of St. Hubert The Hunter and the pictures by Billy's wife Fern along the walls make it so homey. It doubles as the community hall, and that's where the two clubs meet. One is just to raise money for the volunteer fire department, and they call themselves Fyre SyWrens, and Fern designed the cutest logo for them, two perky wrens on a branch wearing fire hats. Just darling.

"The other club is the Ladies Guild, I think they call themselves. I plan to join when we return next summer. That way I'll get to meet the people in the basin. Oh, and there is the darling little log library next to the church. I can hardly wait for the girls to visit it. Some of the ladies have a story hour for children on Saturdays, and I usually check out a book every week. Dad does, too, and they have scads of magazines and newspapers. It has just about anything we

41

want. Dad goes into the post office almost every day, but frankly, Julie, I'm just content to stay at the ranch."

"So, it's now *The Ranch,* is it? Next thing, Dad, she'll be giving it a fancy name like your neighbors have theirs and having the entire town of Bondurant out for a BBQ. How many people did you say were living there?" Robbie asked enjoying teasing his mom. "Fifty? Or was it seventy-five?"

"I know you're teasing, Robbie, but it's a delightful, active community." She didn't tell him that she'd already selected a name for their place, Willow Creek Ranch. The meadow that led down to the creek edged with willows was covered with wildflowers, but she didn't want a flowery name. She had purposely not told Ben. He thought that she'd gone off the deep end anyway.

"And for your information, son, the highway signs that are erected on each side of the town say population one hundred. Of course in the summer it more than doubles with all the summer people in. That includes our Hoback Ranches and the Upper Hoback. They have a county road, and most live there all year because their road is plowed, unlike ours. That's one of the areas where there are the very large working ranches. That's where Dead Shot Ranch is located. You know the one that has a cabin built by a man named Bellin. Remember I wrote you about it."

"Do you really believe that Avery Bellin is kin to the man who built it?"

"When I called Liz and told her, she said that Avery said he had a great uncle who went to Wyoming and that the family had received only one postcard from him from a town named Kemmerer, and not another word had they heard. Bellin is not a common name, you know. Wouldn't that be something if he really were Avery's kin? You know, I think that he and Liz will be coming out next year, so he can check on it."

"Honey, you want a brandy with your coffee?" Ben called from the great room.

"No sir, I do not. But thanks, honey. Oh, Robbie, Liz also said that Avery has been going through his mother's old letters and papers, and he really is excited about finding out more about his father's family. He died when Avery was a baby, you know. She also said that his grandmother's sister was sending him more information on the Bellins. I'm excited about it for him. Must have been very difficult to grow up without a father."

"Jo, you didn't tell them that I have already joined the volunteer fire department. As dry as it is now they need every man and woman there. I hope that they have a good winter with tons of snow. Everyone is concerned. I called Billy last night, and he said there had been no rain. Can't even burn the leftover building material and have to truck it to the county dump in Pinedale. A real nuisance…"

"Did they find water yet?" Robbie asked. They were glad that he was concerned and not just inquisitive.

"Drilled 350 feet and not a drop." Ben laughed.

"What's so funny?"

"Billy said when they were drilling that got Irma Barksdale off Charlie's Mountain. Said that she came flying down that road, her ponytail straight out behind her. It's the first time anyone's seen her outside the gate in over three years, ever since Charlie died."

Jo thought, but didn't say, "Not so, Ben." Why hadn't she shown him the picture? Why did she feel that it was her and Irma's secret?

"What was she upset about? Did she think that we were stealing her water or something?" Robbie got up and poured himself another cup of coffee, asking Julie if she wanted more. She shook her head no, obviously bored by the conversation. But she did get herself another serving of peach cobbler from the sideboard, heaping whipped cream on top of it.

Jo had to refrain from saying anything to her or Robbie. She's going to get as fat as her mother if she's not careful. Such a dull girl. Never did see what Robbie saw in her. Well, she's given us two adorable granddaughters. For that I'm grateful.

"Billy said she started giving them a piece of her mind, and she told Jerry and Gordon to stop that drilling, that they weren't gonna find any water and that they were scaring all the deer away. She said that if the Daultons wanted water, there was a spring down at the bottom of the hill just waiting to be developed and that even in a drought we'd have plenty if we weren't wasteful like every Easterner she'd ever known.

"And, Robbie, Billy said that she pulled Jerry over and told him to get on the back of her 4-wheeler, and just like on a bucking bronco they rode across sage brush and rocks down that hill, Jerry holding on for his life. When they got back Jerry was shaking his head and mumbling 'She's right, Billy'. Jerry's like most Westerners, a man of few words." Ben began coughing while he laughed.

"See, I told you that cigars caused you to cough, Ben Daulton!" Jo called as he rushed through the French doors on to the patio. "I do wish your dad would give those things up. He scares me when he has those fits."

"He doesn't smoke more than a couple a week, Mom."

"That's what he tells us, but I bet he has several more every week when he goes to the University Club for lunch. I just bet!"

Julie looked off into space, continuing to eat. Jo sighed, silently putting another nail in her coffin, as Ben always reminded her.

Ben came back in clearing his throat. "Jo, almost forgot to tell you, Billy said that Irma told him to make the hallway about a foot wider."

"What? Why'd she say that?"

Ben chuckled. "She said, 'Just like an Easterner, wasting space. If the hall was wider you could actually use it instead of just using it for going from one room to another.' What do you think?"

Jo thought about it and replied, "Well, come to think of it, she's right. That pine washstand of your mother's would look great there." She didn't add that she'd like to hang her picture over it. The warm pine frame Irma had given her would be perfect with the washstand.

"Why don't I call him, hon? I think the old busybody has a good idea. He could take six inches off the stairway to the left and six more from the kitchen and bath, couldn't he?"

"You'll have to ask the expert. Go ahead and call him. It'll be two hours earlier, remember." He looked at the mantle clock. Only six-thirty there. I'm sure you'll not interrupt their dinner. They usually eat early."

While the phone was ringing in Bondurant Jo kept thinking. I've broken through. She really does need people. She really... "Billy, hi, this is Jo Daulton. How's Fern? Oh, hope she's soon over it, but guess she'll have to wait 'til after the ranchers are through haying. I've had hay fever and it's no fun. Ben said that Irma suggested—no, I really don't mind. Anyone who can photograph with such an artistic eye has more vision than I. Frankly, I think she has an excellent idea. But is it workable?"

Pause...

"That's just what Ben and I said. Six inches off the stairs and six inches from the kitchen and bath. I must drop her a note to thank her."

Pause...

"What did you say? I'm sorry I'm having trouble hearing you."

Pause...

"Ben has always said that, Billy. I've always loved people, and I'd like to be her friend."

Pause...

"Well, perhaps she's now over her grieving period and yes, if you see the Sheffields tell them that I'll write soon. Yes, they're very nice."

Jo hung up the phone and said to Ben, "Well, sir, it looks like we're going to have a wider hallway. Billy said that it would be no problem."

"Gotta go, Mom. Great dinner as usual. We were supposed to pick up the girls from Stewarts' by eight o'clock, and it's going on nine o'clock."

"I wish you'd brought them..."

"They need to be with kids their own age, Mama Jo," Julie interrupted.

Jo thought but didn't dare say, they're with kids their own age almost every day of their lives. She smiled and replied, "Of course they do, Julie. It's just that they're growing up so rapidly."

Ben and Jo stood in front of the double mahogany doors and watched Robbie and Julie drive off in their Ferrari.

"Why did he feel that he needed that tiny sports car? The girls won't be able to fit in it by next year. Actually, Julie won't either if she keeps eating the way she did tonight."

"It took me fifteen years to afford a car like that. Kids these days don't seem to want to wait for anything."

"But he said it was second hand and…"

"That car cost as much as my entire year's salary when I was his age, Jo, second hand or not!" He opened the door shaking his head in wonder with Jo patting his back.

Thanksgiving arrived, and the Daultons and their two children, spouses and four grandchildren celebrated. Jo was in her glory, as Ben said. Her babes were home. It was festive. She had made the table arrangement using the dried wild flowers from Wyoming, and everyone said it was spectacular. Andrea and Carlos had been given the holidays off so they could enjoy their own families.

Why do I have to stay busy? Jo thought. Mimi and Chet are having dinner at the Officers' Club at the navy base, and here I am slaving away and loving every minute of it. I wonder what Irma is doing today. Why do I allow her to invade my thoughts so often? She's not answered any of my letters, not that I believed she would. But then Billy said that she'd not come around the last few weeks they were working on the house, and she hadn't missed a day earlier…

I do hope that she's not ill. Why do I feel closer to her than I did my own mother? When I look at my picture I get so full. Why haven't I been able to show it to Ben? He said before we left Wyoming that I was obsessed by her. I guess I am.

"Mom," Ruthann called from the dining room, "do you want me to remove the tablecloth?"

"No, hon, I'll do it later. You go on out to the patio and enjoy this Florida sun. You'll not be getting it much longer."

"I miss it, you know. Especially the beach. I thought I'd die when we went to Acapulco. I couldn't believe it! Tan sand. I mean it! Light tan and coarse sand. You've met Michelle next door, haven't you? Well, she and Mike went to New Smyrna Beach and when they got back, those Yankees, who think they know every-thing anyway, were carrying on about the beautiful beach this and that. I just smiled and told them that I know beaches, that we kids camped in almost every state park along the peninsula of Florida, and those beaches on the Pacific are a zero in comparison."

Jo wasn't listening. She was so concerned about whether Irma was all right that she said, "That's nice, dear."

"Mom, are you OK?"

Jo reached for the phone as she nodded yes to Ruthann. "Billy, Happy Thanksgiving to you and Fern. Oh, you had two inches of snow. I bet the Hoback is gorgeous. I imagine that the Sheffields have left. Oh, all the summer people. Oh, by the way, how is our neighbor Irma doing? Been telling you how to run your business?" Jo laughed.

"You haven't seen her? I know I'm a worry wart, like my mother used to call me. Has anyone checked with Manny?"

Pause...

"And he can still drive in? Do you know if he snowmobiles in all winter?"

Pause...

"I'm relieved. I thought that he probably went in only once a week. Oh, three times, just like in the summer.

"No, it's just that Ben and I have our family around us, and I started wondering how a widow, or recluse as Jack Sheffield calls her, celebrates her Thanksgiving."

Pause...

"Yes, you're right about the phones. Isn't it great? I think that everyone in the Ranches signed up for one, except Irma, that is. Ben said Jack and Betty told him that they'd begin laying the lines the middle of next year, and we'd all have phones by '89.

"Tell everyone at the Triangle F hello for us. Oh, tell Monta that one of these days I'm going to duplicate that wonderful potato soup. Still don't have it quite right."

Jo was smiling when she hung up. She was relieved. I'll write her a note tonight, she decided. She had been writing ever since she and Ben returned. She didn't expect a reply. First, it was to thank her for the picture; then it became a habit.

Ben said that she probably didn't even read them, but Jo felt otherwise. She's just lonely, but like he said, if she's lonely why doesn't she allow visitors? Jack and Betty said that they'd not been inside her home since Patty's funeral. At first they thought that Irma and Charlie's grief had been just too much to allow them to be civil, even to best friends. But Manny had told them that Miss

Irma didn't allow him in the house either. They just chalked it up to another of her peculiarities.

But Manny knew better. They all thought they were so damned smart. He'd show those smart-asses. His patience was running out...

NINE

Liz pushed in the AT&T number, looked over her shoulder at Avery, who was already pacing, and smiled at the flight attendant, who was busily checking in passengers. Good, it's ringing. I hope John's home.

"Hello, John Bellin speaking."

"John, it's Mom. We're in Salt Lake and our flight for Jackson leaves in about twenty minutes.

Pause...

"How'd you guess? Yes, your dad's pacing."

Pause...

"What? I'm having trouble understanding you. There's so much noise here."

Pause...

"What? Oh, the weather is delightful. Cool but not cold. Oh, the reason I called is that we finally got confirmation on the hotel in Yellowstone. It was waiting for us here at the Delta office. We'll be in the Yellowstone Inn. You know, the Old Faithful Inn, the one Jo and Ben stayed at. They're meeting us in Jackson and will join us for dinner. We'll be at the park tomorrow through Thursday."

"That's right. We'll be at the Jackson Lake Lodge tonight and Friday. You already have that number. Then on to Bondurant."

Pause...

"Yes, he's getting excited. I just hope he's not disappointed. Gotta go now. He's waving at me. Kiss the kids and Debbie. Love you. Call you from the Lodge."

Pause...

"Yes, we should be home in about two weeks. I know we don't have to rush, but you know your father. Bye, love you."

Liz hung up the phone, put her address book back in her Valentino bag, grabbed her make-up kit and hurried toward her anxious husband.

"What took you so long? Everything OK?"

"Avery, I wasn't on the phone three minutes." She kissed his cheek. "I told John that you were excited."

"Why'd you do that? I'm not excited, just like to be on time, that's all."

"He asked if you were, and I said yes. Besides, why shouldn't you be? I am, even if you pretend that you're not."

The flight attendant called out rows one through twenty. Liz followed Avery, who had hopped up and rushed for the line. Why does he do that? There was a time when he had impeccable manners. Actually, he still does when we're around his law partners and their wives. But alone? You'd think he was raised in a barn.

He took her make-up kit and placed it in the overhead compartment above their seats and placed his neatly folded brown suede jacket on top of it.

"You want the window seat?" he asked.

"No, you take it."

He was still a good looking man. Worked out regularly every Monday, Wednesday and Friday at the club and played golf most weekends plus watched his diet. His medium brown hair was streaked with gray, but Grecian formula blended it nicely. He was tanned and fit and determined to live by his doctor's orders. His last check-up after the heart scare was good, and Murph said that if he relaxed more he'd live to be ninety-plus.

Liz had urged him to retire, but he said that fifty-six was much too young, but he did agree to a vacation. That in itself was a concession for Avery.

The young girl across the aisle was having trouble with her rambunctious little boy. He looked to be about four, same age as Jonathan. His western outfit was so cute. I'll have to get one for Jonathan, she thought. She smiled broadly at the child and his mother smiled back.

"I have a grandson just about his age back in Florida."

"Oh, what town? I have an aunt in Naples."

"We're southwest of Jacksonville in Orange Park. My husband's an attorney there." She could feel Avery bristle. He'd never understood how she could strike up a conversation with perfect strangers.

"I love the Gulf coast. Colt and I visited Aunt Judy last summer and we both came back to Utah with a wonderful tan. You going to be staying in Jackson?"

"We'll be there a couple nights. We'll go to Yellowstone for a few days playing tourist. After that we're going to a small town southeast of Jackson called Bondurant to visit friends. Also, my husband had an uncle, who was one of the old timers, and we want to find out more about him and that side of the family."

"I know where Bondurant is. Used to go to their annual BBQ with my folks. Best BBQ in the state. Have you been there before?"

"This is our first trip to Wyoming. We've been to conventions in Vegas and California, but actually haven't seen a great deal of the West."

"Colt, be still! We'll be there in a little while." She turned back to Liz, "I take him to see his dad every year. We're divorced but have a real good relationship. He liked Jackson and I liked larger cities. Jackson is all right, but it's so small, and if you don't care for skiing and snowmobiling and all those things it's a real bore. But Colt loves it. 'Fraid his daddy spoils him to death when he visits. My folks still live there, and I stay with them."

The stewardess came by with the cart filled with drinks and snacks. Liz asked Avery if he wanted anything. He declined, so she got an orange juice and gave it to the girl for Colt.

"My name's Cindy Frye."

"Oh, I'm Liz Bellin, and this is my husband Avery."

Avery nodded to the girl and smiled his practiced smile at Colt who by now already had the chocolate from the covered raisins and nuts all over his face and hands.

"Here, Cindy, I have extra tissues in my purse for him. Colt, take these. He looks about four…"

"He's only three and a half, but he's big for his age. His dad's over six feet, so he'll be tall," Cindy said with pride.

Liz squeezed Avery's hand. "Doesn't he remind you of Jonathan?"

He whispered, "Not really."

She whispered, "Don't be an old poop. Oh, Avery!" Liz

exclaimed. "Are those the Tetons?" He didn't have to answer. The captain informed them that they indeed were.

"This is Captain Smythe again. For those of you who haven't seen the majestic Tetons, there they are, and you're in luck. The sun's on them, and they are still snow-capped.

"Avery, aren't they gorgeous? I've never seen any mountains that beautiful. He's right; they are majestic."

"They are beautiful." She could feel his restrained enthusiasm when he took her hand. *I hope this is a new beginning for us. We have a lot of living left, and I just hope it's better than these past fifteen years have been. I know that he's not seeing her anymore and that it's all over, but I wonder if we can recapture that feeling we once had. I'll never understand what went wrong. I'm going to do my best, but he'll have to do his part. I intend to make darned sure he does. I don't like who I've become.*

The plane's wheels touched down, and Colt let out a war whoop. Cindy tried to quiet him and smiled at Liz as she shook her head in resignation. The seat belt sign went off, and everyone scrambled for the aisle. Avery slowly unbuckled his belt and said, "No need to rush, Liz."

"You're the one who could hardly wait to get on board, sir." He was drumming his fingers on the arm rest in between them. "Have a nice visit, Cindy. Goodbye Colt. Have fun!"

"Why do you do that?"

"You mean be friendly? I enjoy people, Avery. I always have. That's one reason Bently wants me to put people in my paintings. He has said for years that I have a special warmth, and my work reflects it. Besides, hon, I cause no harm. I'm just being friendly."

He shook his head in disbelief. "Liz, you probably offend people with this…this attitude."

I'll ignore him. He's picking a fight and wants me to defend my actions so he can play the big lawyer. She looked at him and smiled sweetly. "If you want to fight, Avery, you'll have to find another adversary."

"Fighting! Who's fighting? I'm not fighting, just making an observation."

Liz got up, opened the overhead compartment, removed her

make-up kit and walked down the aisle. She smiled at the attractive attendant and said, "Lovely flight. Thank you."

She turned around in time to see Avery give the young girl his come hither smile. Won't he ever change? Why does he do that? Does he really think that a twenty-something-year-old girl is interested in him? Probably does. At most, she's possibly interested in the security she sees written all over his Ralph Lauren outfit. I'm not going to let him ruin this vacation. Not this time! Son-of-a-bitch! It felt so good that she thought it again. Son-of-a-bitch!

She stretched to her full five feet seven inches, held her head higher and almost pranced down the commuter plane's stairs.

Jo and Ben had arrived at the Jackson airport early. She wanted to see the paintings by Fern and the photographs by Irma that were displayed in the lobby. Ben went to check with Budget Rent-a-Car to make sure that Avery's rental car was satisfactory. He knew how fussy Avery could be. They planned to accompany Liz and Avery to the Jackson Lake Lodge for dinner then return to the ranch.

The lobby was crowded with tourists going and coming, but some had paused to view the artwork, too. Jo couldn't believe that she actually knew such respected artists. She overheard the others' comments and couldn't help but tell a very friendly woman who gawked beside her that she knew the artist and photographer.

"Yes, Fern Parker is our builder's wife, and Billy's so proud of her." A crowd gathered and Jo continued. "She grew up on a ranch on the outskirts of Bondurant, the small town near us, and had never had a painting lesson. Billy loves to tell about her first paint brush. Said that after they'd been married a few years, she talked him into letting her order a set of paints. They lived way up in the hills, and a trip to town was quite an excursion, so they had to order a lot of things from catalogs. But when the paint set arrived, there was no paint brush with it. So being industrious by nature, Fern had Hartley, their son, go to the barn and clip some of their mule's tail hairs. She then took a lid of a tin can and wrapped it around the bristles with a heavy twig for a handle and that's how the famous Fern Parker got her start."

Someone murmured, "Sure, she did."

"I'm not kidding. That's a true story as unbelievable as it seems," Jo added.

"Are her paintings for sale in Jackson?" the woman asked.

"Her works are in most of the galleries in Jackson and other galleries throughout the state, I'm told."

Ben called to Jo. "They're on the runway, Jo."

"I didn't hear them announce it."

"You were too busy spinning your yarns, young lady. Think you've gone western on me. Whoa! I'm only kidding. I heard Billy tell you that story, remember?"

He hooked his arm in hers and they rushed toward the large window to watch the small plane taxi in. The anxious people rushed down the stairway. Jo at first thought that Liz and Avery had missed their flight, but then she saw Liz. "There they are! Last ones off. Wouldn't you know." She's a beautiful woman. I can't imagine any man with any brains at all treating her like he does. Liz was quickly in Jo's arms. Ben went past them, shook Avery's hand hard and asked if their flight was good.

Jo and Liz talked rapidly while the men searched for the luggage.

"I've never seen so many western hats in my life. I'll be out of place out here, Jo. Look at you. You've even gone western." She was animated, flushed. She didn't notice the man behind her observing the crowd. His western hat was not a new one, obviously well worn, and his boots the same. Typical jeans and western shirt opened at the neck. He left his place by the wall and approached two men who were picking up heavy equipment from the pile of luggage.

"Cam! How about getting the cameras? Over there in the big black bags," one of them said.

"No problem," he said brushing closely by Liz.

"Sorry, ma'am." He tipped his hat.

"That's OK. I shouldn't have been standing in the middle of the room," Liz responded. Laughing at Jo, she whispered, "I wouldn't mind being toppled over by him any day of the week."

Jo looked at her, "Why, Miss Liz, I do believe you're on ready. What's come over you anyway?" She was laughing when Avery and

Ben approached them.

"What's going on, you two?" Ben asked.

"I do believe Mrs. Bellin has got her second wind." Jo responded in a low voice. "At least, I hope she has." Ben's expression was quizzical, and it told her that he had no idea what she was talking about. She decided to not inform him. She was enjoying this new Liz.

Liz saw the man who had almost knocked her over easily lift the large black bundles, then join two other men also dressed in western garb who she could tell were not the real thing. They're playing cowboy, she thought. She felt herself staring at him, trying to avert her eyes, but was not unhappy when their eyes made contact. Abruptly turning she could feel him watching her, following her as she lagged behind Avery.

I had hoped for a new beginning, but not this. I've got to get hold of myself. I've been strong for so long. I'm sure he's still watching me. Maybe not. But when she turned around, he was and he tipped his hat once more. He was smiling slightly. Oh, God! He even has dimples, or are those laugh lines? What's come over me? This is not like me at all...

"Liz," Jo called back to her, "These are the paintings I was telling you about. You know, by Fern Parker, Billy's wife. Aren't they spec..."

Liz saw him and the others, loaded down with equipment, walk past her. She had heard Jo, but her thoughts were not on Jo's chatter nor on Yellowstone nor on the Bellin heritage. Her thoughts were on who is this man and why am I drawn to him? I haven't even looked at another man since I met Avery. Heavens! I was only twenty years old. Has it been that long?

TEN

"Ben," Jo called. "Can you hear me?"

She heard him rummaging down in the basement and reluctantly went down the long stairs. "I don't know why I insisted on a multi-level house. My calves are going to be a large as Arnold Schwartzenegger's if I keep having to go up and down these blasted stairs."

"You designed the house, my love."

"Don't be a smart drawers with me, Ben Daulton. You approved it."

"What's up? You get another dressing down from Miss Irma?"

She ignored him. "I'm out of sage! That's what! And we're an hour away from town and no time to change my menu even if I could get to town."

"You mean we're in a catastrophic situation."

"As far as I am concerned, yes! Who's ever heard of cornbread dressing without sage? It's bad enough to have to use their terrible cornmeal. I'm going to bring my own from home next year. This western stuff is so coarse it looks like grits."

"Replace the sage with another herb. Try rosemary like we had on the chicken Betty fixed the other night. I liked it."

"It's just not the same…"

"I didn't say it was the same, Jo. I just said try something different. What does it matter, anyway?"

"It matters to me, sir. It's my favorite dressing recipe, and I wanted to show off for these Westerners—that's what. Some good old southern cooking for Billy and Fern. We've had their beans and jerky and…"

"You are kidding, aren't you, hon?" He could tell that she was upset, but knowing Jo as he did, he knew that it was something else that had kicked this off.

"Yes, I'm upset but it'd take more than a lack of sage to get me this angry. I could borrow some from Betty, if that were all it is. You know that Avery has decided to cut their vacation short! Can you believe that man? Gordon just drove up and gave me a note from Billy. Liz called him from Jackson after they drove up to the Upper Hoback to interview the Earles. You know, the people who own Dead Shot Ranch, the place where the Bellin cabin is. We went to the Samuel Parker party there."

"Yep, I remember it very well. Had one helluva good time as I recall, and they didn't serve just beans and jerky either. Seems to me that they had buffalo."

"I was just kidding. But not finding the items I'm used to is one of the infuriating things about being out here. To get back to that jackass Avery, Liz wrote that the Earles had referred them to someone in Kemmerer, and Avery didn't see the need to drive all that way, so he wanted to leave for home immediately. Can you imagine? Coming all this way to find out about his long lost uncle and he wouldn't even give it a chance."

"You mean that they're not going to come for a visit with us?"

"Yes, sir, that is what I mean!"

"Damn! That does it! I'm going to call their hotel and give him a piece of my mind. No, don't try to stop me. I'm going to the Triangle F to use their phone and tell him what I think of him. I mean it! You and Liz have been planning this visit for a year now, and it's just not fair, Jo."

"Oh, Ben, do it! Say it just like that. I'll be so glad when our phones are in. If I could have heard her voice, then I'd know how she felt. I know she's devastated."

"If you'd not been so excited about finding out about your uncle, I could understand, Avery. Really I could. But the very first set back and you're ready to throw in the towel. I didn't think lawyers enjoyed losing their cases."

"Why did you say that? There is no comparison. None whatsoever! Sure, I wanted to find out about him, but it isn't a life-or-death matter, Liz. It would have been interesting, that's all. Imagine, they called him Moose. That's hard to believe."

"Why? Why is that hard to believe? Sam Earle said that it was because he was a very large man and tough as they come. It was necessary to be tough out here in the early part of the century. He said so. And he said Moose with great affection, Avery. It's not something that you should be ashamed of.

"And what's wrong with working for the railroad? How many jobs were there out here? So he lived up in a cabin away from everyone. Yes, it's one of the few built with logs squared off like railroad ties. Sam was proud of that. It's unique, Avery. Can't you see that? The man built it with his own hands. And what's wrong with being a trapper? What do you think the people did out in this wilderness for a living, anyway? For heaven's sake, where is your sense of humor? There was a time when you would have loved the history and a name like Moose. What the hell has happened to you, anyway?"

He looked at her like he was seeing a stranger. Softly he said, "I don't know, Liz. Really, I don't." His head was in his hands.

The phone rang. "Yes," she answered. "Hi, Ben. I guess you got my note."

Pause…

"Here he is. It won't do any good. Mister Bellin has made up his mind. It doesn't matter what I want. He has this tremendous NEED to return to Florida. He says it's business. That's a laugh! Here, Avery, it's Ben."

Avery listened, gulped, composed himself and said, "I can understand your disappointment, Ben. Especially Jo's. But, I'm feeling very weary and feel the need to go home. No, it's not the altitude, though I'll admit that it has bothered me."

Pause…

"Here, you speak to Liz."

"Hi." She sniffed.

Pause…

"Frankly, I had thought of that, and the more I think of it the more I'm inclined to take you and Jo up on your offer. I didn't come all this way to miss seeing your place, and I, too, need to escape. Do I ever! It's enough that we seldom see you in Florida. Mr. Bellin is too busy. Yes, I'll be packed and ready when you get here. Better yet, I'll drive Avery to the airport so he can go home and sulk or whatever he intends to do, not that I care anymore, and

I'll drive out to the Hoback myself. All by myself. Boy, does that sound good.

"No, I mean it!"

She helped Avery pack, and joy set in, she told Jo later. I felt like a burden was lifted. I could breathe. I felt this...this tremendous relief. I wanted to shout. I wanted to dance. I wanted to go to the Cowboy Bar and dance with every cowpoke there. I wanted to be ME, ELIZABETH MARY LAINE! Remember that girl, Jo? Do you remember me? I liked who I was, and, by gum, I'm gonna like me again! To hell with Mr. Charles Avery Bellin! To hell with that flat tire—that stuffed shirt—that...

"I love it, Jo! It's you, it really is."

"As I told you, we didn't want the typical log house. They're really attractive, but Ben and I aren't hunters, or into all these outdoor activities, even though we both enjoy fishing. Most of the houses here are too rustic for my taste and his, too. Don't you love all the windows?"

"I wouldn't want it any other way. You can see the mountains clearly, but they don't...encroach is the word. They're there but you don't feel smothered by them. Remember Virginia Stokes? They built a house in Colorado, and I thought I'd die before we got out of there. I've never had claustrophobia before."

"I do worry about the fires though. They're already having their share in Yellowstone. It's probably just as dry here. I'm glad Billy talked Ben into removing the sage and the aspen close to the house. Oh, Liz, they're so beautiful in the fall. I wish you could be here to paint them. Do you think you can come back?"

"I've made up my mind, since I talked to Avery the other night, that I'm going to do more things that I enjoy doing. Without him, if necessary. He was noncommittal when I told him. Guess what he asked me?"

"What?"

"He asked if I wanted a divorce?"

Jo gasped. "What brought that on?"

"Guess it's the first time that I've stood my ground. Should have done this a long time ago, Jo. I told him that I haven't made up my mind. But that I've certainly thought of it."

"What'd he say?"

"Nothing. He didn't say a word. What could he say? Guess he figures that I've got the goods on him and I'll take him to the cleaners financially."

"You could, you know."

"Oh, yes, I could, and if push comes to shove, I will. I don't want to be put in that situation though. As long as I can be me, get in some traveling without him tagging along, have my friends. And paint…I'll have to paint, Jo. I need to paint."

"What has taken you so long, Liz? Why didn't you act when you found out about the other…women?"

"Guess I was so devastated that I believed I was thinking of the children. I truly didn't want them to find out about their father, especially Laine. It would have killed her. You know how they dote on each other. It hurt so much. You'll never know…"

"Oh, honey, come here. I didn't mean to bring all this up again. Here…"

"I'm all right! I've cried all the tears that I'm going to. He's not worth it. I now know that there is something lacking in Avery. I don't know what, but he's minus some ingredient. What kind of a father, who loves his children, would treat his son like he's done Chuck? Just because he dropped out of college and took the job as manager of Sonny's, you'd have thought he'd robbed a bank or murdered someone, the way Avery turned against him."

"Try compassion, Liz. Maybe growing up without a father and with his mother and aunts doting over the only boy in the family, maybe that's it. Maybe he's just spoiled. I remember when you first saw him. Remember? You called me all excited and said that you'd met Mister Right. Remember?"

"What does a twenty-year-old, innocent, naive girl know, Jo? What?"

"I'm the one who lucked out. I think I'd die if anything happened between Ben and me. I mean it."

Jo hesitated to continue but did, anyway. "Liz, do you love Avery? Is that why you stayed with him?"

"Goodness knows I've had a long time to think of that. No, I don't love *this* Avery. I'll always be in love with my Avery, the Avery I knew for twenty years, Jo. But this man I don't even know. We did have twenty fantastic years, though. We were so well matched, I guess you could say, sexually. We were passionately in love. He's the only man I've ever known, you know, intimately. And as good-looking as he was and with all the girls falling over him, he had had very little experience. We found out how to please each other by reading a book. What are you laughing about?"

"I bet we read the same book. No, I mean it. I think it was called *MAN AND WOMAN*. Was that it?"

"I'm not sure. After the children started arriving, I think I put it in the garbage. How naive we were."

"I'd rather be that way than like the young kids are today. No, I mean it. It frightens me how wise they think they are. We were better off, Liz."

"Liz, do you know that we have only another week? How fast the time's flown! I wish you could have at least got a glimpse of Irma. Oh, I know that she's watching us like a hawk when we walk. I left a note in her outhouse and asked her to join us, but there was no reply, not that I thought there would be one. But you can bet that she's up on all our doings."

"I hope she wasn't watching yesterday. I thought I'd die!"

"You thought! What about me? I'm the one who suggested walking over there. I felt like a naughty teenager. You know, I couldn't even tell Ben. I've gotten so secretive. We were in the house for two weeks before I had the nerve to drag out the picture that Irma took of me."

"What was his reaction?"

"Typical Ben. He said, 'Jo, I love it', not, 'when did you get this'? Just, 'Jo, I love it.' And he brags to everyone who sees it that Irma gave it to us. He's a true love."

She and Liz had a morning routine. They'd get up early and walk. The first day they walked to Rim Road and went east. They decided that they'd try to walk a couple miles each day in every direction. Jo took along a bag and would stop to collect wildflowers. She intended to make wreaths for the August sale at the little church. The clubs needed to raise money for repairs on the church and library.

Liz had been visiting for a week, and on this particular morning they decided to walk all the way to the end of Mountain View and back. Jo and Ben had brought their Springer Spaniel mix, Maggie, out with them this year since they planned to stay longer than usual. Maggie walked with them for protection, Jo said. Actually it was the two of them who had to protect her. The porcupines were of particular interest to her, and Ben had warned them that he'd spent the last dollar taking her to the vet. She was so fascinated by them that even Jo had no success in stopping her from sniffing them and removing their quills that ultimately became imbedded in her muzzle.

It was a gorgeous day. The Wyoming-blue sky was not to be believed. "If I painted a sky that color, people would say that I had used too much blue in the paint. Look at that view of the Wyoming Range! Spectacular! No wonder they named the road Mountain View." Liz commented. Jo already had her bag full of flowers by the time they got to the dead end of Mountain View. They had turned around to begin their trek back when Maggie started barking.

"If you get more quills in you, young lady, your dad is going to tan your hide. Come here, Maggie. Now, I mean it! Come here!"

"I'll go get her, Jo." Up the driveway she trotted, over pit run and brush. Whoever lives here doesn't visit often, Liz thought. Jo had put her basket of flowers down and followed Liz. "Liz, wait up. I'll get her. She'll come to me."

They could see a small log house on top of the hill and a truck parked beside it. "I wonder who lives here?" Jo asked. "Maggie you come here immediately! You hear?"

About then Liz's mouth flew open, and so did Jo's. "Dear Lord!" is all they could think to say. Flashing before them was a man as naked as God made Adam. No leaf! No nothing! But Liz recognized his face, when she could take her gaze off of the rest of him. They did an about face, and Maggie soon followed.

When they got to the bottom of the hill Jo asked, "Who was that? Dear Lord in the morning!"

"I don't know, but I intend to find out," Liz responded, not believing she had thought it much less said it.

They could hardly wait to get to Betty Sheffield's to ask her who lived at the end of Mountain View. "I know she'll know who he is. She and Jack know everyone in the Ranches. And, besides, I've wanted you two to meet ever since you arrived. Wait 'til you see her collection of Indian art."

When Liz entered the foyer she stood gaping at the Indian maiden sculpture. "It's beautiful! Who did it? Jo was telling me of your collection and especially the sculptures, but this is …well, I'm awestruck!"

"You'll meet him tomorrow at the program at the church. You are going, aren't you?"

"We plan to. Jo showed me a brochure that she'd picked up at the visitors center in Jackson. His work is very special. You can tell that he has a definite affinity for the Native Americans."

Betty went into the living room and gathered some brochures and handed them to Liz. "Here, these are his newest ones. Handsome devil, isn't he?"

Liz looked at Jo, and they both looked at Betty. Finally Liz spoke, "I believe we've already met. Just didn't know who he was."

"I wonder if Mr. Lee Riley Campbell will recognize us at the program. I'm going to have a heck of a time keeping a straight face, aren't you?"

Liz didn't mention to Jo that she'd already had an encounter with Cam, as folks called him, at the airport. And it was the most unusual encounter she could imagine. He was the only man she'd ever seen, since Avery, who started her heart pumping, and to think that he lived in the Ranches. Uncanny! Jo, I've gotten secretive, too. Maybe I'll extend my vacation…

ELEVEN

It was Marthie Sikes who saw the sisters Heather and Jonsey McDonald when they opened the heavy log door to the Elkhorn Bar that Saturday night. Her intuition told her immediately that there'd be trouble. Manny had already had a near altercation with Lavon over whose turn it was at the dartboard in the back room. She had told Bart about it, but he just shook his head as if to say not to bother him with this. His headaches had gotten worse instead of better, and they had an appointment with an allergist in Idaho Falls the following week.

He had already told Manny that he was not going to have any trouble with him, and Manny mumbled something unintelligible when he grabbed his brew and headed for the back room. The usual Saturday night crowd was there and all were excited about the poker ride the next morning. Manny had planned to get a horse from Miss Eileen at Big Bear so he could be a player in the game. He'd promised to repair that old Chevy that Jamie had near 'bout totaled up at Dell Creek just to avoid hitting a stupid coyote. She dearly loved that old car, which had belonged to her late husband Harve. That would give him enough money plus a little left over.

But everything changed when Elway and Betsy Ann got all lovey dovey while dancing to Dolly's latest hit. That got Manny in the mood, he said, when he pulled on Jonsey's arm trying to get her cute little behind out of the booth.

"You might be in the mood, Manny Markos, but you can plainly see that I don't wanta dance. Now let me be!"

Didn't take more than that for Elway to disentangle himself from Betsy Ann to make sure that Manny understood just what Jonsey was saying was what she indeed meant.

Marthie made a beeline for the bar and Bart, but by the time he'd put down the glass and towel, the chairs were being thrown.

He grabbed Lavon's shirt, trying to yank him off Manny, and yelled at Elway, "I told you, Saunders, that I wasn't gonna have my place torn up and I meant it!"

Marthie ran for the phone to call the sheriff's office. Seemed to take forever to get an answer, and a sleepy sounding young man answered and slowly said, "I'll get Joey over there, but it won't be soon. He's down on a call at the Green River Camp Ground. Some crazy woman's naked as a jaybird throwing beer bottles at the campers up at Warren Bridge. What a night!"

"Well, if you wanta see tomorrow's sunrise, you'd sure as hell better get someone up here, you hear?"

"Don't hafta get sassy with me, Mrs. Sikes. We do the best we…"

She slammed the phone down and ran back to make sure that Bart was all right.

Before she got there she heard Betsy Ann yell, "Watch out, honey, he's got a knife!"

Marthie was a small woman, but when she heard that, she jumped in swinging the bar stool. Hit Manny hard on the side of his head. He staggered backwards, landing between the booth and table. Bart stomped hard on the hand that held the knife. Manny let out a moan, then a grunt, and yelled at Bart, "Ya broke my hand, you son-of-a-bitch! Ya broke my hand!"

"That ain't all I'm gonna break, Markos! If you ever set foot in my place again, you won't even have a hand! Who the hell you think you are? No one brings a knife in a place of mine! And I mean no one! You boys hear that? Marthie, get Joey!"

"I already did, honey," she said, sniffling while picking up the chairs and bar stools. "You, there, Jonsey! Help straighten this place up, seeing as how you started it!"

"What you mean? I didn't start a thing. All I said was that I wasn't gonna dance with that dumb ass. And that's my right!"

"Don't be gettin' on her, Marthie," Elway chimed in.

"I'll be gettin' on every one of ya, Elway. You just been hankering for a fight with Manny, and you all know it. Her sashaying in here every Saturday night, swinging her ass in Manny's face. What'd she think he was gonna do? Ignore her near 'bout shoving her pussy up his nostrils?"

Bart came over to her, "Now, honey, I know you're upset, but it's over now. Calm down and get me that belt I keep back of the bar. Gotta get Manny subdued 'fore Joey gets here. Come on now, Marthie."

She glared at Elway and Jonsey, backed up toward the bar but had to have just one more parting shot. "I told Bart over two weeks ago that we'd have trouble with you, Jonsey. It's gals like you who give a place a bad name."

"Just one good goddamned minute, Marthie! I been coming to the Elkhorn for a long time, and ain't nothin' ever happened before. You had no business lettin' that dumb ass in here!" She started crying, and Heather told her to come on, that they'd find some place else to give their business to.

"Good! I hope to hell you do. I feel sorry for the next bar you cause a ruckus in. And I hope to hell that they make you pay for the mess you make," Marthie shouted.

Elway grabbed Betsy Ann's arm and said, "Come on, honey. We don't hafta put up with their mouths. There're plenty of places we can go to."

"Yeh! You'll hafta drive all the way to Pinedale or Jackson, mister! We sure don't need the likes of you in our place! Look at this mess." Bart shook his head when he realized all the work they had before them.

"Hey, boys! Help me pick up this place 'fore Marthie gets on all of us. Hey, Jay, you ever see Marthie wield a stool before? That's some kinda woman I got, huh?"

"Whew! You right on that one, Bart. Come on, Lavon, give us a hand. Bart, think you're gonna hafta replace that Coca Cola clock. Even the hands are bent."

Bart had Manny secured to the side of the bar with his hands belted behind him, chin bent down to his chest and saliva oozing down the side of his mouth. He was barely conscious.

Joey Shiffar came stumbling in. "There're some nights that I'd gladly throw in this billy club. I swear that this is one of 'em. Ever see a fat, old naked woman chase a whole park of campers off? Well, sir, I just saw it." He looked around to see if there were any women around then continued. "Now, if she'd been pretty with a good figure, then I think I might have enjoyed cuffing her. But you can't say that this one fit any category you could've come up with. No sir, even the Lord would've thrown her back and shouted 'good riddance.' Whew!

"Her sagging titties hung near 'bout to her belly button and those rolls of fat ripplin' down her back looked like the force of gravity had taken over, and they were approaching her tail crack at avalanche speed."

"Joey, I'm glad you're here. We had us a..."

"Bart, what's this all about? Melvin said that your missy got downright sassy with him."

"She had every right to, Joey. You know I don't allow any violence in a place of mine. I'll tell you all about it while you get Manny into the squad car. He began wielding a knife. I got it over there on the counter, and goodness knows we got plenty of witnesses. It all started..."

Betty Sheffield turned into Daultons' driveway and honked her horn. Jo called to her, "Be right there, Betty!" She closed the dark turquoise door and yelled to Ben, who was in the basement, "We're going, hon. Should be back by three at the latest. Oh, I made extra Mexican salad, and it's in the aluminum bowl in the frig. Ta, ta."

She and Liz had talked into the night. They both felt like teenagers. Ben asked her the next morning, before Liz had joined them, "What were you two giggling about?"

"We weren't giggling. Or, maybe we were. I'll tell you one of these days. Oh, honey, I'm having such a good time. It's almost like old times."

"Has she made up her mind about Avery?"

"What are you talking about? Made up her mind about what?"

"Hey, this is your husband you're talking to. About staying with him. That's what I'm talking about."

"Well, for the time being, yes, she'll keep the marriage going, playing the game, so to speak."

"Is that fair?" He saw her bristle. "I mean, is it fair to Avery to not level with him? It's a marriage, Jo. There are two people involved in the contract."

"I can't believe that you're thinking that, much less saying it."

"What do you think a marriage is?"

She caught her breath, letting it out slowly. "There was a time that I thought I knew what a marriage was and the responsibilities that went with it, but, I'm not sure that I know any more."

"What does that mean that you don't know anymore?"

"Since all this business between Liz and Avery came up, I've had a lot of time to analyze. I've tried to put myself in her place, but I've not been able to. I mean that I've not been able to visualize you doing what Avery has done. Maybe I'm naive, maybe I'm not realistic, maybe it's that I've trusted you for so long that..."

"Whoa! Number one, I'm not Avery Bellin. I know, and you know, or you should, that our relationship is the most important thing in my life and, I hope, in yours as well."

"Honey, listen to me, please. I have always thought that. Until Liz and I had this chance to share, that is. It makes me see that people change. She never thought that anything like this would happen to her and Avery. She said that if anyone had told her this, oh, sixteen years ago, that she would have laughed in their face. She, too, was sure of Avery."

"I don't like the way this is affecting you. Hey, girl of mine, I really don't."

"Maybe I'm preparing myself in case something..."

"Stop it right now! I think you have too much time on your hands out here. Too much time for your imagination to take over..."

Jo looked up and saw Liz in the hall. "Hi, Liz! Betty should be honking for us any minute. You want a cup of coffee before we go?"

Ben excused himself and headed for the basement. "Liz, you want me to make a birdhouse for you and Avery?"

"I'll think on it. Thank you, Ben."

She looked at Jo. "Anything I need to know, little sister?"

Jo shook her head no. She heard Betty's horn.

Betty talked non-stop for the twelve miles to the church/ community hall. The community club had prepared a month-long arts program open to the area's weavers, painters, sculptors and other craftsmen. Today's program was to be presented by the acclaimed sculptor Lee Riley Cameron, Sublette County native, past professor of Art at the University of Wyoming and owner of Pine Ridge Studio in the Hoback Ranches, Bondurant, Wyoming.

Liz and Jo sat in the middle of the small room with their brochure in hand. The table in the front of the room was covered with small bronzes, all beautiful. One of the board members handed out the various brochures and greeted everyone. The room needed more space and certainly more chairs.

Why am I so excited about this? I'll not act on these impulses; at least, I hope I won't. Liz turned toward Jo, grabbed her hand, and whispered, "I need you, my friend. I mean it." Jo nodded, understanding.

His back was toward the audience. People were lined against the walls of the church. There was no movement, just expectancy, almost a hush. He turned toward the audience, searching, found Liz and smiled. They knew. Somehow they knew that they were on a precipice. Do we jump? Do we surrender? What do we do now?

"There's lemonade, Liz. Do you want some?"

She barely heard her. She heard no one, only her heart pounding loudly. She couldn't take her eyes off him. She saw him move among the crowd, fielding their questions, smiling but not truly listening. She felt Jo's arm circle hers, and Jo said, "Are you all right?"

"What? Oh, Jo, I don't think so. I really don't. Do you think that Betty is ready to go home? No, I mean it. I need to go home. Jo, I mean it!"

Jo could see how flushed she was and knew that she was having trouble. "I'll go ask her, but she's helping serve. Might take a while, so hang in there," and she left.

Liz didn't have to see him to know that he was working his way toward her. When she allowed herself to turn he was there, smiling, his dimples and the twinkle in his eyes evoked a hesitant smile from Liz, and then he tipped his hat and said, "I believe we've met before, miss...?"

Jo managed to excuse herself and weaved her way through the crowd to where Liz was standing. She was grinning. "Liz, what did he say?"

She repeated Cam's cliché about having met her before, then began laughing uncontrollably. "I can't believe that I said it! Jo, I said, 'Surely you jest, sir!' That's what I said."

"You didn't!"

"Those are the exact words. Tacky, wasn't it?"

"What'd he say?"

"He cracked up! I mean it. He almost had a laughing fit, and the two of us stood in the midst of all those women who were practically fondling him, laughing and making fools of ourselves. I don't know when I've had a better time."

"I'm so happy for you. You've always had such a crazy sense of humor...until these past years."

"He asked if I was interested in art, and I had the good sense to say 'I, too, am an artist, Mr. Cameron.' Then someone grabbed my arm and said that she'd like to have me meet someone who is also a painter. She said that you knew her work."

"What happened to Cam?"

"He didn't leave my side, walked me over to what's-her-face—I don't even remember her name—literally pulled me aside. I'm not kidding. He whispered that he had to see me again. When I questioned him, he laughed and said that the next time he'd be wearing clothes. I almost said 'Frankly, my dear, I don't give a damn.' I really did, Jo."

Liz slowly walked over to Betty's car, opened the back door, snuggled in and relaxed. He was the most gorgeous man she'd ever seen or hoped to see. His voice was as resonant as Gregory Peck's, his eyes intense but with Rhett Butler's sense of mischief, and Liz Bellin knew that she'd have to know more about him. Avery's image did not surface. Leaning her head back against the seat, she sighed. When she turned, she saw him get into his truck. He tipped his hat to her. She smiled. It lasted until he was out of sight.

Betty asked if they wanted to go to the Triangle F for bread or milk, and Jo said that they planned to go to Jackson after church the next day to shop and that she'd be glad to get anything that she might need.

Betty continued to chatter. "I had forgotten that Cam was such an engaging speaker, but why not? After all, he taught at the university for years and guess he'd still be there if he and Caroline hadn't got divorced."

Liz asked, "Did they have children? Seems to me that he referred to Riley several times."

"That's his, I mean, their son. Don't know what happened to the two of them. They were certainly in love. Robert, Cam's father, said once that she couldn't take to the West or our ways. She likes city life and, last I heard, was teaching art at a small college somewhere in the Northeast. But Riley spends every summer at the ranch in Pinedale. He's like Cam and western through and through. Looks just like him, too. Dark brown, curly hair, same dimples and is as tall if not taller. He and Cam used to ride up to see us, but since Cam's been going on those location scouting trips for the movies they don't get up as often. I miss having the young folks around. So does Jack."

Liz realized that she was pumping Betty but couldn't seem to help herself. "How old is Riley? I mean, is he a teenager yet? Divorce can be difficult for youngsters when they're that age." She was thinking of her own children.

"Must be sixteen or seventeen by now. Think Cam mentioned that he was looking at colleges. He wants him to study archeology at the University in Laramie, but Caroline might have other ideas. She no doubt will want him to attend one of the Ivy League schools. She's very social, I've been told. New England blue-blooded type, summers at Newport, etc."

Jo interrupted. "He met her at the university, didn't he? Seems that Fern told me that."

"I believe you're right. She was working on her doctorate and he was teaching. He was almost thirty when they married. Robert was afraid that he'd never have a grandson, he said, but Cam surprised them all when he brought Caroline home. They got married by a

71

justice of the peace in Laramie, but her family, the Rhode Island Masseys, insisted on a big shindig in Newport that summer.

"I remember that Robert and Sarah were having some kinda fit, according to Cam, planning what to wear and hoping that they wouldn't embarrass their only son. When they returned they both said that they had had a delightful time. Toured Boston and even went to New York City. I told Jack that the Camerons could probably buy and sell those Masseys. They own a tremendous ranch passed down from both families. And, of course, Cam will be the sole beneficiary, he and Riley. They're an old Wyoming family all except his great grandfather, who came over here from Australia as a youngster, before the first World War."

"Betty, let us out by the road. No need to drive into the driveway. Ben needs to have Gordon haul in some more gravel. Thanks for the ride. I want you two to come over for dinner before Liz goes back. What night would be best for you?"

"We haven't got any particular plans for this week. I had planned to have the members of the art league over before everyone gets too busy. Would you two be interested in joining us? Ben, too, of course."

"Sure, just let us know when. I want Liz to look at the Simpson house over on Mountain View. It'd be perfect for a studio. Just small enough, and the loft has that wonderful window facing north, but I haven't been able to talk her into considering it."

Liz smiled and added, "Jo thinks just because she and Ben have fled west that Avery and I should, too."

"It's the best of two worlds, Liz. Really, I mean it. Jack and I have never been sorry that we took the plunge. I love Florida. I really do, and so does Jack, but I'd truly miss this place if we had to stop coming out."

"Is that Irma hauling down the road? Look at her go, would you!"

"Ben says that she's acting up because I've been ignoring her since Liz arrived. Once earlier in the week I found a note on the little blackboard I keep beside the front door. She had written that my friend was pretty. Can you imagine? And oh, another time she wrote that I should watch Maggie because the coyotes might get her. She ended that one with, 'She's a sweet dog.'"

Betty just shook her head. "Poor thing. Look at her! What's she doing with that package? Oh, putting it in the back of the outhouse for Manny. Jo, I know you've broken through, but what's going to happen to her when you return to Florida?"

Irma pretended that she hadn't seen them, hopped back on her 4-wheeler and spewed gravel doing wheelies up her road. "I'll write her just like I did last year. Just newsy letters mentioning what's going on in the outside world. Manny mentioned that she had a radio, so maybe she keeps up more than we thought. Betty, I truly believe that it helps her loneliness. Billy said the same thing recently."

"I hope so. Don't want to tamper with a fragile mind that's been damaged though. Jack mentioned that the other night. Never know when she might be set off. Be careful, dear. I'll ride the 4-wheeler down to let you know what night is best for us after I speak to Jack. Liz, go look at the Simpson cabin. Won't hurt."

It might hurt more than you think, Betty. But aloud she said, "Probably not, but Avery would never consider it, I'm sure. He had a heart scare a few years ago, and the altitude does bother him."

Jo wanted to say, "Do what's best for you, Liz. To hell with Avery Bellin!" But she said nothing.

TWELVE

"Someone's gotta go up to the Ranches to tell Irma Barksdale that Manny won't be going up there any time soon," Joey told Bart.

"You know as well as I do that they'll probably get shot if they try."

"Well," Joey answered, "Guess I've done got myself elected. What's the poor old soul gonna do without Manny to do her fetching and carrying?"

"Why don't you stop by Billy Parker's place and ask him to go with you? Someone said that she'd been down to the new place he and the boys were building next to hers to give them some of her expert advice. Only time anyone's seen her off of Charlie's Mountain since Charlie died."

"Dr. Sheffield used to be a real good friend of theirs. Maybe he'll go up with me," Joey remarked.

"Hell, he was in not long ago with a friend of his, and the two of them sat there and had a couple beers, and I asked him about Irma. Said that she got more peculiar by the day. Don't think he's the one to go with you, Joey."

"Well, I ain't going 'til tomorrow morning anyway. Probably have to scale that gate to get in. But maybe Manny has the key on him. If not, I'll be able to get it out of him where he's stashed it. Tell him that he'll be in jail a helluva lot longer if he doesn't cooperate."

"He can be as stubborn as a mule, Joey. Once he's made up his mind about something there's no budging him."

Joey laughed, "Bart, this little old billy club does come in handy sometime. Better yet, I'll threaten to put him in the cell with that ugly old woman I picked up last night. That'd get Lucifer himself to turn good. Wish you could have seen that commotion. I really do." He left laughing.

Joey got to the jail in Pinedale near about noon. He was still dead tired. When he got to Manny's cell he could see that Manny was in no condition to tell him much. That smash to his head that Marthie gave him left him groggy. Joey told Mosely to keep an eye on Manny, that he could have had a concussion. "And Mosely, check for a padlock key." But Mosely had already gone through his pockets and the only keys Manny had on him were his truck keys.

"Go ahead and see if you can rouse Doc Ryels, Mosely. Hate to call him on a Sunday, but we'd better cover our butts. Hell, if he has had a concussion, dumb as he is, he might just sue us. Some starving lawyer will get hold of him, for sure."

Mosely shook his head in disbelief. "Hell, these prisoners get better treatment then we do, but I'll call him. You see what that crazy old woman did this morning?"

"No, what?"

"I had Sally bring one of her housecoats over so I wouldn't hafta look at that pitiful thing, and when I gave it to her and told her to put it on, you know what she said?"

"What?"

"I don't wear hand-me-downs, mister! So she began to tear that thing in as many pieces as she could, singing *Shall We Gather At The River* to the top of her lungs. Bet she knew six or seven verses. I do wonder sometimes what the Lord has in mind when he makes one like her. Makes me almost lose my religion, it does."

"I'm going over to Barksdales' and don't know when I'll get back. I just hope Irma doesn't have a loaded gun handy. That Manny was carrying on last night about how he knew things that would grow hair on a bald man and how we were all dumb and that he was smarter than we think. I told him that was funny, seeing as how he was the one headed for jail and I was the one driving the car that was taking him there."

Mosely chuckled. "He ain't done much talking since you put him there. Mostly in and out of consciousness. I'll call the doc, though. Wouldn't it be a trip to put him in with that naked old bag? That'd sober him up!"

Jo and Liz were returning from their walk when Joey arrived at

Charlie's Mountain. They had steered clear of Pine Ridge, Cam's studio, and walked up Rim Road to a field of blue flax off of Fisherman Creek Road.

Maggie began barking, and Jo tried to hold her back. "Maggie, stop it! It's just a car. Stop it this instant! She barks at mailmen and UPS trucks. Don't know how she differentiates, but she does. That's a police car. Wonder what has happened?" Jo began to panic but Liz held her arm and said that she'd go ask. But Jo couldn't be stopped.

"I hope that nothing's happened to Irma! How would he know if something had?"

"Good afternoon, ladies," Joey said, tipping his hat to them.

"Is anything wrong with Mrs. Barksdale, officer?" Jo managed to ask.

"No ma'am. It's her handyman Manny. He got himself in a little scrape at the Elkhorn last night and will be out of commission for a while. Thought I'd better let Miss Irma know so's she can make arrangements to have someone else do her shopping and all that. You wouldn't happen to have a key to her gate, would you?"

"No, and I don't know anyone who has. She's reclusive. You know she just lets Manny in to do her chores, according to Dr. Sheffield. He might have an old one. Have you asked him?"

"Don't think he does but I'll go over there to ask. You know if they're home? Seems to me that they're church-going folks."

"You know, you're right. We had planned to go this morning, too, but my friend awakened with a sinus headache. Probably hay fever."

"Lot of that going around this time of year. Never been bothered with it myself, but my missus has it something awful. Eyes water so much she can't even see her soaps. She's a real bear if she misses *As The World Turns*." Joey chuckled, shook his head at the situation and said, "I've got two witnesses if Miss Irma comes at me with a gun. Don't forget that I have to do this. Don't know any other way to get the word to her. Someone said that she ripped that phone out that Charlie was so proud of. Poor old soul must be mighty lonesome."

"I can get my husband to boost you or go to the garage for the ladder, if you'd like," Jo offered.

"Oh, I'll just drive the squad car close and climb up on the hood. That should do it."

Jo and Liz watched him maneuver the car up, and in no time he'd scaled the gate. He waved to them as he slowly walked up the gravel road. Soon he was around the tall trees and out of sight.

"Liz, why don't you go on home and have lunch? You hardly ate any breakfast, and it's after one o'clock. And tell Ben what's going on and that I'll stay here until the policeman returns. He might be needed if Irma decides that she doesn't want the policeman around. She's unpredictable, you know."

"Do you want me to bring you a sandwich and something to drink?"

"Don't think so. I doubt if he'll be there long. Take Maggie along with you, please. She's bound to be thirsty. If we don't get some rain soon this whole place is going to blow away."

Irma was on the deck waiting for Joey. Now, how did she know I was coming up here he wondered. There ain't no way that she can see through those thick trees. I'm not sure if she's got a gun hidden inside all those clothes or not. God, why doesn't she burn up wearing all that stuff. She must have five layers of clothes on.

He tipped his hat and said, "Good morning, Mrs. Barksdale."

"And what's so good about it, Joey?"

"Well, actually it's afternoon and…"

"I do believe that you didn't come all the way up here to alert me as to the time of day, Joey. What is your business? You know that I'm a busy woman."

"Yes ma'am, I know that for sure. Well, your handyman Manny got himself in a bit of trouble at the Elkhorn, and I thought that you should be told so you can make other arrangements for someone else to do your running around for food and…"

"Joey, the only thing I need Manny for is to keep my vehicles running and to go to the post office for me. That's all I need him for. I'll have Eileen get one of her boys to take care of that 'til the fool gets out."

"Mrs. Barksdale, do you want that I should go see Miss Eileen to ask her?"

"That would be fine, Joey. When do you think Manny will be let loose?"

"Don't rightly know, 'cause he pulled a knife on Elway Saunders."

"Elway needed a knife pulled on him. He's been mean all his life."

"Well, the law don't look fondly on such as that, Miss Irma."

"It'd save a lot of taxpayers money if it did. That should do it, Joey. I'd invite you in but the place is a mess. I've been jamming and haven't had a chance to clean up yet."

"That Manny's passing around a lot of rumors, Miss Irma. Think you'd better have a little talk with him."

"What kind of rumors?" She began to fidget, repeatedly shoving her hands in her pockets and nervously taking them out again.

"Well, you know, like folks wouldn't believe what you got going on inside your place and..."

"Joey, what the hell you talking about! You think I've got a still in here?" she gestured toward the log house. "Well, if I did I'd guarantee not much would get off the place what with that Manny liking it the way he must." She started laughing.

So did Joey. "You might be right on that one, Miss Irma. But he's saying things like how smart he is and how dumb we all are, and that there's something unbelievable going on up here."

"I don't think he means that I'm running a whorehouse, do you, Joey? Now, that might be kinda interesting but..."

"Miss Irma, I'm just telling you what he's saying so's you can have a little talk with him, that's all. No ma'am, I don't rightly think you've got any girls up here giving away their favors."

"Giving away their favors! Now Joey, Manny might be right about all us being dumb. If I allowed my girls to give away favors, then I'd know for sure that I was dumb. If I did run a whorehouse I guarantee you men would pay a pretty penny for their favors. Hell, I doubt that you and the other men on the force could even afford my girls on what Sublette County pays you, now could you?"

"You said it, Miss Irma. We could sure stand a raise. Been over two years already. Didn't mean to bother you. Good day to you. I'll let you know what Miss Eileen says about one of her boys."

"And Joey, I don't think that your superiors would take kindly to it if you mark up their squad car with those boots just so you can climb over my gate. I'll leave what I need to in my outhouse for Eileen's boy. Good day. Say hello to Bruce Lee for me. He's a friend of mine, you know."

How the hell did she know that I had to climb up on my car? That old woman is spooky. Friend of the sheriff's is she! God, that old woman's gonna have my butt in a sling. Whew! Maybe Manny is right about something going on up here that isn't quite right. Maybe I'd better have whichever Stroebel boy Eileen sends up to keep his eyes open. She was acting a little nervous—more than a little nervous. Wonder if she had a pistol inside one of those pockets? Wonder what she's got going on in there?

Jo was waiting beside the gate when Joey returned.

"Is everything all right?" she questioned.

"Seems to be. But can't say yes and can't say no. I'm gonna have one of the Stroebel boys take over for Manny 'til he gets out. Miss, have you happened to see anything peculiar going on up there?" he gestured toward Irma's house.

"Like what? No, can't say as I have. She does have this uncanny ability of knowing everything that goes on around here, though." Jo laughed when she said it. "My husband and I think she's got a telescope on top of the mountain. It's a joke between us," she smiled.

"Well, that Manny is passing around rumors about how we're all so dumb and that there is something strange up in that house."

"Manny isn't quite right, you know, officer. I haven't seen anything at all. What could there be?"

"Well, she sure was nervous. Keep your eyes open for me, please. I'm beginning to think Manny just might be right. I'm gettin' bad feelings about this whole thing, and when Joey Shiffar gets bad feelings, then there's usually some reason. Yep! Haven't been wrong many times."

"I don't think there's anything going on. Besides, what could be amiss? She lives alone, and Manny's the only one who ever goes up there. I can't imagine what he's referring to. Oh, and my dog Maggie goes up almost every day. She's taken a liking to her. You know dogs have a sixth sense, I've been told."

"Maybe you'd better be watching your dog, miss." Joey left shaking his head. I'm going to put on my thinking cap about this. Maybe I'll just interrogate Mr. Manny Markos to find out more. Yessir, I'll just give this billy club some exercise. Been a long time since it's banged a hard head, and that Manny sure has got himself one.

So she knows Sheriff Lee, does she? I wonder if the old biddy's telling the truth or if she's trying to pull the wool over my eyes? Well, she'll hafta get up mighty early to do that. Others have tried and...

He stroked his billy club. I'll just wait a little while before I give you a workout. So she knows Sheriff Lee, does she...

THIRTEEN

The phone rang in Orange Park. Liz knew that Avery would still be home at ten o'clock on Saturday morning. Adelle had the day off and his golf date wouldn't begin until ten thirty as usual. It was a ritual that he'd established years before. It rang and continued to ring. Well, maybe he left early, she thought. The answering machine picked up, and when she heard his voice she got the strangest feeling. It didn't sound like Avery.

She and Jo had met the realtor at the Simpson cabin the day before. She didn't know how to explain her decision to Avery, but she knew that she was going to buy it. After all, it was her money. Her mother had left a sizable amount to her and her sisters, and she'd invested it wisely. At least, that's what Avery and his broker had told her.

Ben had joined them at the cabin, gone over it with the realtor and told him that he'd like to have Billy Parker, their builder and a man whose opinions he trusted, check it out. Liz was exhilarated. She'd never owned a thing in her life. Here I am fifty-four years old and I've never even owned a car, much less anything else. She was also frightened. They had taught their children that ownership meant responsibility, and she knew that this transaction would be hers and hers alone.

It is just large enough to be considered a cabin, she thought. Not liking everything about it, she still understood that the changes she wanted to make were cosmetic and not costly. I didn't take all those art courses for naught, she thought, buoying her reserve.

Again she called home, let it ring four times and hung up. Well, maybe there's something going on at the church. Vestrymen do have to make an appearance, she rationalized. If she were still working in the church office I'd be concerned. No, I'd not be concerned! He's rubbed all the salt of the Dead Sea in my wounds, and

I'll not allow any more pain to destroy me. Thank you, God. At last I'm free. I think it was Martin Luther King who said, "Free at Last." Well, that's how I feel. But will I feel that way when I return to Orange Park?

"I'll give him until Monday, Jo, and if I can't get him at home or work, then I'll call Rory and tell him to transfer my CMA money to my personal account, and we'll sign the contract. No, don't protest! This is my decision and I need to start making them. It doesn't matter if Avery and I stay together or not. I need to learn to take care of myself financially."

"Why do women of our generation have such a terrible time learning that we're able to stand on our own? It has taken me years of studying to figure that out. Our daughters know how. What happened to us?" Jo wondered.

"You know that in every magazine you pick up there's an article on just what we're talking about, survival. But do I read them? No, I flip over to another article about some movie stars we've grown up with, ones we identify with because of an age thing, and read that dumb article believing that these unpleasant occurrences will not be a part of our lives. How dumb! Guess we think that we'll never be put in that position. You know, being left alone, and who should we turn to, and has our financial advisor been honest or...?" Liz stopped short. I've known Rory Morgan since high school, but so has Avery. I know that they're buddies. Should I be concerned? I'll not mention this to Jo. She and Ben know him too.

The door bell rang. Ben left the dining room table where they'd just finished lunch and called Liz. "Liz, Dwight Amarand is here."

What on earth is he doing here? There's no way I'll be able to make a decision until I get in touch with Avery. Sometimes realtors are just too pushy.

"Yes, Dwight. I've not been able to get in touch with my husband, and I can't make a decision until I talk to him to see if he approves the transaction. If the sellers have another offer I need to know about it. No cat and mouse game will I entertain."

"Mrs. Bellin, I don't mean to make you feel that I'm trying to rush you, but..."

"I like the cabin, but there are plenty of parcels of land in The Ranches for us to purchase to build that dream cabin on."

She looked at Jo and realized that the ball was in her court. I can't believe that I even said that. "I don't want to appear rude, but I'm not ready to sign anything, and as I told you, I've not been able to get in touch with my husband. I'll call you when I do. Yes, thank you for driving all this distance. Not having phones is a real bother, isn't it?" Dwight gave her his best realtor smile, shook her hand and left in his jeep.

"Whew! He was not that aggressive when we were at the cabin. I wonder what's up?"

"The Simpsons are due to leave for Germany for their new post and probably want to have everything settled before they leave. At least, I imagine that's why the rush."

"That's probably it. But I don't like to be pushed. Am I being obstinate?"

Ben piped up, "Not in the least, Liz. You're being sensible. And like you said, there are plenty of other parcels for sale around. It's just that the cabin is close to us, and it is a good buy. Underpriced, I'd say. I do want Billy to go over it, though."

Liz and Jo finished the dinner dishes and decided to take a walk to the cabin. They still had several hours before dark. "Ben, you want to tag along?"

"Don't think so. Maybe I'll join you later. Take Maggie with you, though."

When they turned on to Mountain View they spooked a doe and her fawn. "Stay, Maggie! Don't you move, you hear! Good girl," Jo said, rubbing her neck. "She's doing very well with deer but doubt that I'll ever get her trained to leave porcupines alone."

"Or naked men!" Liz chimed in laughing.

They could see dust coming from Aspen Drive. When the dust cleared a pick-up truck emerged. Jo grabbed Maggie by her collar and pulled her to the side of the road. "Is that who I think it is? Now, aren't you glad we decided to walk?" She was teasing Liz about Cam. They could see that there were also others in the truck. Cam slowed down, put his head out of the truck's window and said, "What are two lovely ladies doing out this close to dark?"

Liz was feeling frisky, just like she would have years ago. "We were hoping that some handsome, intelligent, world-traveling gentlemen would come along and ask us to take a ride. Would any of you qualify?"

The man beside Cam was one of the ones that Liz had seen at the airport, so she knew that they were the movie scouts. The one in the jump seat answered first. "You're in luck. We're at your disposal, aren't we, Greg?"

"Hey, wait a minute, you two. I'm the one who stopped and inquired."

"Cam, you Westerners are too slow on the draw. It takes city slickers who've been around to know how to handle fillies like these."

At that point Maggie decided to start barking. "See, even their dog knows that you're just on the make. We Westerners are quiet and slow, but honest in our approach. You guys are just flashes in the pan, whereas we are forever true. Even their doggy knows that."

The girls began to laugh then. "Actually, we were going over to the Simpson cabin. Liz is interested in buying it for a studio. Isn't that right, Liz?"

"I'm thinking about it…"

"Do more than think, Liz. It's perfect for a studio. Ron approached me about buying it, but I'm too lazy to have to move right now. There is a good spring there, and, as you know, water is a real problem here. Greg and Pollard have been giving me a rough time about spit baths. But my cistern holds just so much, and it's hard to get anyone from Rock Springs to come up here to fill just one cistern. I was cleaning it when you surprised me that day. You do remember that day, don't you?" He had that Rhett Butler glint in his eyes.

"Even Maggie remembers that day, Cam," Liz answered blushing.

"What's going on here? Greg and I thought we had a chance with you two."

Jo could see Ben coming toward them. So did the men. "Help arrives, methinks," Greg said with a wide sweep of his arm. "Simon Legree has been foiled again. You've been saved, my ladies."

"Ben Daulton, this is Cam Cameron, and I believe he said Greg and Pollard. I think they're either from New York or L.A. Am I right? At least we know that they're city slickers," Jo added.

Cam turned the motor off and got out of the truck. He extended his firm hand toward Ben and introduced the others. "We're on our way to the Triangle F for dinner. You want to join us? At least, I hope that Monta's still open."

"I doubt it. She usually closes early on Sunday night. What do you think, Jo?"

"Hate to say this, but the sidewalks of Bondurant have been rolled up. If you don't mind leftovers or an omelet, I can reopen the Daulton restaurant."

"Don't want to put you to any trouble, Jo."

"Hey, speak for yourself, Cam. He's been trying to starve us ever since we got here, hasn't he, Pollard?"

"Hey, guys, if it's an omelet you want, I've got eggs. I really don't want to..."

"No more is to be said. Just give us a head start, and Liz and I'll have something fixed up in no time. Honey, why don't you take the guys over to Simpson's and get their opinion on the cabin? I know Cam likes it, but I'd like the opinion of the others, too."

"Don't ever argue with the missus or you'll loose, gentlemen. It's just over the hill and around the bend alongside the willows. Maggie and I'll lead the way."

Jo and Liz talked non-stop all the way back to the house. They were planning the menu when Liz said, "This is like old times, isn't it Jo? I mean after you and Ben were married Avery and I'd pop in to see you and Ben, and you'd insist on whipping up one of your specialties. Avery was so impressed. Oh, my, what laughs we'd have. I've missed that kind of camaraderie for so long. Do you and Ben still have friends you can share fun with? We no longer do. Our life has gotten so dull."

Jo was dicing leftover ham and veggies for the omelet. "Liz, get out the big iron skillet and lid, please. Oh, those leftover baked potatoes will be fine for steak fries in the other large one. Here, I'll finish these veggies and you fix the salad. And I have Italian bread in the freezer. Oh, I know, we'll scoop out the insides and fill the loaf with scrambled eggs and the other ingredients. I used to do that for luncheons. I have good sharp cheese to top it with and we can put it under the broiler to melt. Sounds yummy, huh?"

"Jo, you're a wonder! I'm not the least hungry, but I'm salivating."

"Now, don't you dare let Avery spoil our fun tonight. They sound like they'll be very interesting. Who needs a dull life, Liz? Certainly we don't.

"Grief, I think I hear them now. Hand me that bread so I can nuke it in the micro. That'll speed things up."

They were laughing when they came into the living area. "Hey, Jo," Cam said animatedly, "This is nice. Now, that's a loft! Look at their view, boys. That's Wyoming. Not only the Wyoming Range like you can see from my cabin but the Gros Ventre as well. See, you can clearly see the Hoback Canyon." Pollard handed Ben his jacket and got closer to the large picture window.

"Look, Greg. That's what I was talking about. The rosy and gray colors over the mountains to give that fire and smoke look we need to roll the credits over. Our film has the Wyoming fires in it. You know, the ones in Yellowstone."

"They are getting bad. We feel so removed from them out here, but we could be in the same situation," Ben added.

"I'm glad to see that you kept the sage brush and trees from your place, Ben. I've got to take down a lot of trees around my cabin too. Got the sage out last year. It's just so hard to find anyone here who'll do that kind of work, and I've not had the time. My dad has loaned me some of his hands, but he's having trouble, too."

"Boy, does that smell good," Greg remarked when Liz put the hot platter of bread filled with scrambled eggs and ham on the kitchen bar. "The plates are on the table, and we'll have the potatoes and salad on in a minute. Here we are. No sooner said than done. Jo was a home-ec major and is still practicing." They all laughed.

"Which wine do you want me to serve, Jo?" Ben asked.

"Ask the fellows, hon. We have both red and white and the white is already cold. Oh, I also have a rosé in the frig."

Liz reached in the overhead cabinet for the wine glasses, selected the larger ones, and found a tray in the cabinet by the frig. "I'll do the honors, Jo. What'll it be, boys? Red or white or that rosé Jo mentioned?" She could feel Cam following her with his eyes. I can't let this happen, she thought. But, God, I'd like for it to.

"If you have a cold beer, I'd prefer it," Pollard answered.

"We New York boys like our beer. As a matter of fact, Jo, I have an egg and beer recipe that is out of sight. Remember that one, Greg?"

"Yeh, as I recall it turned green. Is that the one?"

"You ate every bite and asked for more, pardner. It's the recipe Lucy gave me. You loved it."

"It was better when she made it, as I recall."

"I think you two enjoy each other," Jo said teasingly. "Liz and I have that same kind of relationship. It's great to have a best friend, isn't it?"

Cam asked, "How long have you two known each other?" He took the glass of red wine from her, their hands barely touched, but she caught her breath, exhaled quietly and tried to appear relaxed none the less. "We'll not tell! Since kindergarten. A very long time. That's one of the reasons I want her to move out here. What did you guys think of the cabin? Think it'd make a good studio for our fabulous artist, Elizabeth Laine Bellin?"

"I saw some of your work in Florida! I don't believe it! We were in Jacksonville shooting a pilot for a television series and stayed at the Hilton. You do use your full name don't you?" Greg asked with his mouth full.

"Yes, I do. I did some watercolors for the lobby. Seascapes, I believe."

"Hey, I can't believe it! Cam, you're not the only famous person here."

"I certainly am not. Irma Fronk lives just up the mountain. She's the naturalist photographer I was telling you two about. Had a spread in the June issue of *National Geographic*. Did you see it?"

"I didn't know that!" Jo said excitedly. "We have been having trouble getting our magazines, so our son has been picking them up in Florida. Why hasn't anyone said anything about it? Not even Jack and Betty Sheffield mentioned it."

"I just got mine this morning. They probably haven't even gotten their mail."

"What was it on? I mean was it flowers or hummers or what?"

"Actually, it was on badgers and their habits. If I'm not mistaken she has a great shot of Maggie with her nose in a badger hole. Haven't had a chance to read it yet, but did glance at the pictures. They were talking about it at the post office when I got there. Must have had six or seven people all standing around discussing it, and that's a crowd for Bondurant."

"Hey, Ben, if she didn't get a release from your dog you might be able to sue her," Pollard said jokingly. "I had something similar happen once when I was in Arizona. An old guy was on his donkey and I took some stills, and you know what? The old fool tried to sue me when we used them in some pre-publicity. Said that I didn't get permission from his donkey. Had a son who was going to law school, I believe."

"What happened to the suit?"

"Hell, didn't even bother with it. Turned it over to the studio so they could settle it. Doubt that anything happened, though."

"Mrs. Daulton and Mrs. Elizabeth Bellin that was delicious. I'm glad Monta's closed early on Sundays. In more ways than one," Cam added, literally staring at Liz.

Ben picked up on Cam's obvious interest, then looked at Jo, and she was glorying in Liz's attention. *I'm going to have to have a little talk with her,* he realized. *She will fight me, but I don't want to see this happen. At least, I don't want Jo to have a part in it. I know it's been hard on Liz, and Jo, too, but it's just not right, no matter what Avery did. So this is why the interest in the Simpson cabin. I'll be damned. I should have known that Jo, the romantic, had a hand in all this.*

FOURTEEN

Pollard and Greg had been ensconced on the built-in bunks in the small loft of Cam's cabin. The large, slanted, tempered glass window above them allowed the light to plummet down and across to the studio below. "How the hell can he sleep up here with all this moonlight?" Greg whispered to Pollard. He had made himself a makeshift blinder out of black cloth, but it wasn't satisfactory. Kept falling off during the night.

"All artists gotta have that north light, dunce! You'll have to admit that it's unbelievable when the stars are so close that you can almost reach up and grab one."

"I'll take the street light on Deloney street in Brooklyn any day. Remember when we were kids how we'd knock them out about once a month and how that fat Mahoney would chase us yelling 'youse kids gonna get me canned' and he'd haul his fat ass after us? Don't know how he lasted on the force so long."

"Didn't his oldest boy, Jimmy, join the force, too? Seems to me Ma wrote that he was killed in some kind of shootout with a Puerto Rican kid."

"Don't for Christ's sake say that those were the good old days. They were not! These are the good days. Wish ma had lived long enough to see what I'm doing. Don't give a good goddamn about Pop. That son-of-a-bitch would've said, 'what the hell kinda job you call taking pictures?' and probably would've cuffed me."

"If you'd showed him your check book he'd 've quit laughing. Don't be so hard on him, Poll. He just didn't know any better. Keeping your ma pregnant was just about all the fun he could tolerate. What ever happened to Harry? You never did say whether he got out of drug rehab. I think that's what finally killed your ma. Why is it that the baby of the family always turns bad?"

"Remember Johnny Stoltz down the street? Same thing happened to him, and he was the baby. Then there was Frankie Polaski, the same thing. Hey, there's a movie in that. One of those social issue themes that the kids eat up these days. You know, with lots of violence, car chases…"

"We oughta mention that to Steven. It's the kind of thing he'd latch on to. When's he getting in to Jackson? Did you say Thursday? God we'd better get to Yellowstone and shoot some of those fires before then. All this mountain scenery won't fix it for him. He thrives on the macabre."

"Hope he can keep it together this trip. I'm not going to be put in the position of buying the stuff on the street out here. Doesn't bother me in Brooklyn, but I don't know anyone here. God, remember what a close call we had in the City! Never again!"

Cam yelled up to them. "You two come on down. Got those sweet rolls from Faler's in the toaster oven. Now, don't start giving me this lip about how they can't compare with your bakeries in New York. I know it. Been there, done that, remember? It's the best I can do."

"Hey, Cam, how the hell do you sleep when it's daylight all the time out here? Finally put the pillow over my head and thought I'd suffocate before morning." They carefully executed the narrow log stairs.

"Get used to it. Better than what you're gonna put up with at the Park. You'll be tenting it there. Did you get that confirmation from the Department of the Interior? Hey, Pollard, did you hear me? You did, didn't you?

"Steven's gonna have your asses. Both of yours! You're not gonna be allowed to go in there, you know. Thursday is just around the corner."

"Maybe they'll forward it. You know anyone with a fax?"

"Hell, we don't even have a phone! Get a move on and we'll go into Jackson. When you gonna shoot Fremont Lake? Shit!"

"All right, tell you what we're gonna do. We'll go to Pinedale, fax the Interior, wait for their reply then drive on up to Elkhorn State Park. Those rocks and terrain on the way up, alongside Lake Fremont, look just like a moon shot. Hey, Poll, I'm not kidding. Unbelievable terrain. Ice age stuff. You know. Surrealistic. Awesome!

"Took my ex-wife up there and thought she'd flip out. She couldn't believe it. We went for one day and ended up staying an entire week. She painted the most fantastic stuff of her career. The shading on those boulders and rocks gave you the feeling of outer space. You could feel the hush on your skin. When she had her showing in Laramie, art critics from London, Paris and, of course, New York were there. I think that's when she felt that she didn't need this old boy from the West anymore. She'd arrived. They're still the best things I've ever seen her do. They actually showed that she had a soul."

"That Liz is quite a piece of work, Cam. You got designs on her? I mean up-scale, class. Skin like a Georgia peach that ignores the sun, those red high-lights in her hair when the sun's on it and a stride like a pedigreed race horse…Wow! Did you watch that ass move? Just like a yacht taking gentle waves on its way to Bermuda. I'd sure as hell like to ride her waves." Poll gestured going through the motions.

Cam got a far away look. "She is a class act all right. I lean toward the arty types, you might say. She's no Caroline, thank God. She's sensitive, not just beautiful. I seem to have a thing for the hurt ones. Think she might be having problems with her husband, and she might need a shoulder to lean on or an ear to listen to her southern moaning, or someone to make her feel like she's a real broad. Now, that's the part I'm interested in fulfilling. You keep your image of a yacht riding the swells, but I'd like to see her sit a horse. A beautiful woman being one with the rise and fall of a horse's gait; now, that will bulge my jeans instantaneously.

"Plus, I'd like to see her work. Is it really good, Greg?"

"I don't know about good. I just know that I liked 'em enough to remember her name. Hey, maybe it was the name that attracted me. Elizabeth Laine Bellin. That's a sophisticated handle. Hell, I grew up with Rosie O'Donahue and Franny Salvatore and…"

"How old you think she is?" Poll asked.

"What difference does it make anymore? Madonna, Liz Taylor, Barbra and all those are lots older than their husbands or lovers. In Europe that's the norm, I'm told." Greg responded.

"I'm not Lolita hungry. God! You see that movie? Made me

almost puke. I could see Rebekah, my little sister, with that pervert. Hell, I've seen enough of that on set. Remember that last director, Greg? What's his name? Oh, Igor something or other. Never saw anything like him. And all those mothers of those would-be stars practically shoving their little darlings on top of his prick, and him pulling them on like a goddamned Wellington boot. God, made me sick. He had the busiest trailer on the lot. Know he was pilling and shooting 'em. Almost quit the business."

"Why didn't you?" Cam asked.

"I got back to New York, and damned if the same thing wasn't going on there. My sister, you know Beverly, Poll, well she told me what she was asked to do in order to get a raise in that dress house on Seventh Avenue. Poll, if we'd been there longer, I'd have bashed that Jew Boy in the face! Naturally he was married to his big-nosed wife basking in the sun in Miami Beach, and those darling little ones going to summer camp in the Catskills, and he was challenging my little sister, threatening her, about how she was gonna loose her job if she didn't give in to his sexual needs."

"What'd she do, Greg?"

"She picked up the phone right in front of him and said, 'Hey, Sal, Beverly here. I got a live one you can eat all by yourself! He ain't got the balls of your pit bull Harry. He needs fixing, and I mean right now. Get the word to Luigi!' She hung up, turned to Schwartz and said, 'pick out your funeral coat, Mr. Schwartz. I know where you can get one wholesale! You might need it by as early as tomorrow night. Hey, Schwartz, better call your wife down in Miami Beach and your other kin. Don't bother counting your days, you don't have that many left.'"

"You're kiddin'!"

"Hell, no. She grew up in Brooklyn and that twerp was an up state New York Jew. What'd he know, already! If he'd been from Brooklyn he'd have known how to deal with her smart mouth."

Cam laughed and had to ask, "Greg, what happened to Schwartz?"

"Who the hell knows? He's gone and Beverly is still there, has two kids and is married to Sal. Hey! We know how to get along in Brooklyn. Not only that, she's now the assistant to the head designer. How about that for Brooklyn mouth?"

Liz rolled over, pushed her dark hair out of her eyes and wondered how she had gotten through the night. *I've never heard nor seen a storm like that! And I thought Florida had storms!* The lightning and thunder had started about five o'clock a.m. Not being able to sleep, she had pulled on her wrapper, and wandered barefoot through the living area of the multi-level house. She could feel the electricity in the air and all she could think was, *I hope this dry lightning is not attacking Yellowstone. They've had enough problems already.*

Finally, the rain started. *Glory be!* She was so excited that she dashed out the front door and let it spray her. *I've never been so dry in my life! How do the women out here stand it? They look like dried up brown prunes. I wonder if they think that it's appealing to men, this outdoor look? Yuk!* as the grands would say.

If—and I'm no longer sure—if I do buy the cabin, I might start a skin care program the likes of which Elizabeth Arden has never heard of. Hey, maybe I can begin another Red Door Salon, or maybe a string of salons. I remember when Avery paid for me to go to the one in Palm Beach. Wow! I've never been so pampered. Those were fun days. What happened? I've gone over and over it and still don't understand. Enough of that! About then a lightning bolt zigged and zagged across the sky, skirting the top of the Wyoming Range, and the thunder quickly followed. She bolted inside.

Shower day! "My turn," Liz called as she dashed into the bathroom downstairs. The water was so low that Ben had decided to have a water tank buried beside the pump before they left this year. Flushing the potties and shampooing were limited. They did the dishes in a small bowl, even though they had a dishwasher. Everyone did it. Putting her head back she felt like she was underneath a waterfall even though there was only a meager stream. She sighed as the trickling water sent rivulets over her soft body.

As she lathered she wondered what it would be like to have Cam bathe her. *His wonderful hands stroking her body gently.* Avery had enjoyed it when they were first married. She had loved it. It was so sensual having him soap her down, cup her breasts, bend down and suckle her. Why am I thinking this? He's lost interest in me. I still need that thrill of acceptance by a man. But is it wrong? I'm a married woman. Jo says not. She said that Ben reminded her that when adultery occurs that the marriage, in God's eyes, is dissolved. I haven't had the nerve to ask Pastor Tom. It does make sense. When vows are broken, there is no marriage.

"What's that? Oh, a truck!" Jo exclaimed. "Ben? Where are you?" He's in the basement as usual. Who could it be at this hour? Hope it's not news about the fires."

She tossed her dish towel onto the counter, removed her sweater from the back of the chair and headed for the front door. The blast of cold air took her breath away. When does it warm up, she wondered. And to think that I actually pray for it when in Florida. She didn't recognize the young man riding up.

He got out and before she could say good morning he spoke. "I'm Jamie Stroebel. Joey Shiffar sent me to tend to Miss Irma, you know, Manny's boss. Said she needed a man to do her chores. He said that I should check in with you so you'd know who I was." Jo thought, gosh, he looks like the Marlboro man and has a rich, deep voice to go with it.

"Yes, Jamie, he did say that you were replacing Manny until he was released."

"He should be getting out in about a week."

"I hope that Joey gave you a key to the lock because we don't have one."

"Yes Ma'am, he did. You suppose that Miss Irma knows that I'm coming? I don't want to…"

"She knows, Jamie. You can rest assured that she knows."

Jo decided to walk alongside him as he drove slowly down the Daulton driveway. He looked at the foreboding gate and reluctantly made his way up to it. Slowly he removed the key and inserted it into the lock. He seemed disappointed when it turned and the pad lock almost fell into his hands.

He turned back to Jo and said, "I'll be back in a minute. Will you be here?"

"I hadn't planned to, but if you want me to, I will."

He inhaled deeply, shrugged his heavily muscled shoulders and hopped into his truck. Jo decided to wait for him. She was glad that she'd brought her sweater. Maggie came rushing up to her. "Where were you, young lady? You down in the basement with your master? Was that where you were?"

She waited and waited. She was getting a little worried. What should I do? If he doesn't come back in a little while, I'm going to have Ben go to Jack's and use his cellular phone to call Joey. He's been gone over thirty minutes.

She saw the dust before she saw Jamie. Beside him was Irma, and she was hauling it. "Thought I'd kidnapped him, Mrs. Daulton?"

"No, I thought you'd eaten him for breakfast, if all those rumors are correct, Irma."

She threw her head back and howled. "That's what I almost did, he's so handsome. Reminded me that I had once been his mother's best friend. Now, what kinda person would I be to eat my friend's youngun, huh?"

Jo had to laugh. "You'd become a blood relative, I believe, Mrs. Barksdale."

"That's what I like about you, Mrs. Daulton. You have a sense of humor. That's more than I can say for most around here.

"Jamie, you mind what I told you, you hear?"

"Yes Ma'am. I will."

She wheeled around and parted, giving Jo the finger. "Where in the world did she learn that? I can't believe that she did that!"

"What happened, Jamie?"

"It was really nice. We sat on the deck and she gave me some homemade bread and wild strawberry jam, and she told me about the first time that she ever saw my mom. It was really cool. Then she went inside the house and brought out this gift for me. It's an album with pictures of my mom and papa in their courting days. They're really nice, Mrs. Daulton. My mom was surely pretty. I never saw my mom that pretty."

"Didn't she give you any chores to do?"

"I'm supposed to come up day after tomorrow to see if she has any parcels for me to mail or any other chores to do. She's not scary like everyone made me believe. She's really great! She asked me if I was interested in learning how to take pictures. Imagine! Me taking those beautiful pictures like Miss Irma."

Jo smiled. Patted him on his sturdy back and said, "She's great, like you said, Jamie. You tell the others. They need to know, too. See ya!"

Liz and Jo were the first customers at the Triangle F. Monta brought them coffee and said, "The sweet rolls aren't quite ready to go into the oven. If you can hang around a while they'll be done in about half an hour."

"Might take that long to get through to Florida, Monta. Liz you want to wait on them?"

"It's ringing, Jo. Hi, glad I caught you. Avery, there is a cabin out here very close to Jo and Ben that's for sale. Has a perfect loft for a studio and frankly, I'd like to buy it. What do you think?"

Pause…

"No, it's just a cabin. Has a large living area, smallish kitchen, but with plenty of cabinets, full bath downstairs. Oh, also a bedroom that's, I'd say, twin sized, then a large loft with storage. No, no bath up there. Well, I'd only use it for my studio, so wouldn't need a bath. Right now they have built-in bunks but they could be taken out to allow…What?"

Pause…

"With the money Mama left me there should be enough with plenty left over. It's being sold furnished."

Pause…

"What? Oh, the furniture is that lodgepole furniture that's popular out here. Goes well with the cabin, but that's not…

"I want to call Rory, or have you call Rory to ask him to transfer the money into my personal account…

"What?"

Pause…

"I don't think you understand what I'm saying, Avery. I said that I want to buy the cabin. I do not expect you to invest in it. You know, with the money that Mama left me."

Pause...

"I do believe that we're having a problem communicating. I'll call Rory myself, and I'll have Ben speak to him. It really is none of your business whether I decide to spend my inheritance to buy a cabin or a condominium or a beach house or a..."

She hung up, and not gently.

Jo was sitting at the small table in the corner writing postcards to the children and listening to Liz. If she needs me, I'm going to by gum speak up. Don't care what Ben says.

FIFTEEN

The *Jackson Hole Guide* was spread open on Jo's lap. She and Liz had come into the Smilin' S Motel to ask Eva and Bud Young if Liz could use their phone to call Avery. Eva called from the kitchen, "Anyone want coffee?"

"All coffeed out, thanks, Eva." Jo really liked those two. They had bought the Smilin' S so their children would have summer jobs and to get them out of Kemmerer, which was having a drug problem. The decision had worked beautifully according to Eva. There was fishing in the Hoback River, hiking right outside their back door and picnicking almost anywhere.

The motel had only a dozen cabins, but the laundry and cleaning took up most mornings. Bud came into the lobby, just a small room with a tall bar used to register guests and a beautiful stone fireplace and two worn leather chairs. The usual animal heads and antlers hung on every wall. Bud and his sons were avid hunters and, as did all the hunters Jo and Ben had met in Wyoming, ate their kill.

Bud had the soiled sheets draped over his shoulder. "Aren't those fires in Yellowstone something, Jo?"

"I'm just reading about them. I had no idea. Ben and I stayed at the Inn when we first came out. I hope they can save it. One announcer on the radio said that if it is destroyed they'll never be able to replace it. The matching burl logs just aren't available anymore. We plan to get a TV dish installed next year. Do listen to the radio to try to keep up, though. But one picture says so much more."

Liz had finally caught Avery at work. "I called Rory, and he said that he'd transfer the funds. Ben said $65,000.00 was a very good price. Avery, the land alone is valued at $25,000, and there is a wonderful spring on the property. They had already signed up for a phone, and that was, I believe he said, $2,000. So you can see that the price can't be beat."

Pause…

"The realtor said that they were being transferred to Germany and would be gone at least four or five years. So that's the reason for the rush."

Pause…

"The driveway is pit run and gravel, and it's not a real long one, so the maintenance won't be much. No, I haven't thought of everything, I'm sure. Another thing, it's only about a half mile from Jo and Ben. That's a real big plus."

Pause…

"On Mountain View. If you hadn't been in such a hurry to leave you'd have seen it. The view is not as spectacular as others I've seen", she was thinking of Cam's, "but it is beautiful. I particularly like the sloping hill to the south of the cabin down to the stream with all the willows and aspen. Dwight said that the Simpsons see a lot of wildlife down there."

Pause…

"I'm sorry that you don't share my enthusiasm, but then I have enough for both of us, don't I? You can spend your summers in steaming Orange Park and I'll be in cool, gorgeous Wyoming. And who knows? You just might see how much fun I'm having and decide to join me." She laughed and hung up without even saying goodbye.

Jo looked up at her. "Are you all right?"

"Have never been better! Let's go to town. I want to shop for my new home. Well, not yet. I'm happy, Jo. I'm so happy I can hardly stand it."

Eva overheard her and smiled at Jo. "Are we going to have a new resident? We need more exciting people, Liz. I hope that you become active like Jo, even if it's only for a month or two."

"Oh, I plan to. I can hardly wait. This has been a long time coming, I can assure you. Too darned long." She grabbed Jo's arm, turned to thank Eva and Bud and asked if they could use anything from town.

"As a matter of fact, we can. I forgot to get butter. Just a pound will do. The kids have requested potato rolls, and they're not worth much without butter. Thanks."

"Grief! Things are so expensive here. Think I'll wait 'til I get back home to shop. I'm being premature, aren't I? First, I sign the papers, then I shop, huh?"

"Shop if you want to, Liz. Lets go to the Wort for lunch, and if the Wilsons are there you can meet them. They are the nicest people on earth. He's our realtor, remember? He and some associates developed the Ranches."

Jo had bought Casey her birthday present, and Liz had invested $5 in a magnet for her refrigerator. It was a moose with a silly expression, and she couldn't resist it. It made her laugh. They were crossing the square headed for the Wort when Liz saw Pollard and Greg. If they were there, then Cam couldn't be far behind. Grabbing Jo's arm she slowed her down. Jo followed her gaze, and sure enough Cam came out of a sports shop with a bundle in his arms. He looked up and saw them and yelled, "Hold up, boys!"

Dodging the noon traffic was a challenge in itself, but he was beside them without even huffing. "God, how'd you do that? You'd make a great New Yorker, Cam!" Greg called, huffing and puffing. "I don't think I'll ever get used to this altitude. God!"

"Takes a while, old boy. I'll buy lunch. Where do you two beauties want to eat? Have you done Billy Burgers? Just the most awesome experience you'll ever…"

"I've been wanting to, but Ben likes the Wort. That'll be fun, huh Liz?"

"Sounds good to me. I'm celebrating, Cam. I'm an almost cabin owner."

"You didn't!" He swung her around with his free arm, put down the package, lifted her up and kissed her hard. The square was packed with tourists, and they stopped to watch, clapped loudly while Liz brightly blushed.

"I guess I shouldn't have done that," he said softly. "It's just that I'm so glad that you'll be living here. I also shouldn't have said that."

"I'm glad too." When she looked up at him, she later told Jo, she felt like a teenager having had her very first kiss.

"Hey, Cam, we gonna eat or not! Gotta get a move on. Those fires aren't gonna wait for us, you know!"

"Wait up, you two. Or better yet, go see if you can get us a stool. It's always jammed. I'll help the girls across." He took Liz's arm and Jo grabbed the one with the package and he adroitly weaved them in and out of traffic until they were right in front of Billy Burgers.

"I think I'm going to have to take lessons, Cam. That was a high-wire experience. Whew!" Jo disentangled her arm but she noticed that Liz didn't. I hope that this doesn't get too serious. She needs time to think. What am I thinking! He didn't think of her when he romanced the other women while she stayed home and played the good wife. To hell with Avery Bellin! She needs to be loved and cared for.

Greg had corralled three extra stools and was wildly motioning to them when they walked in. Squeezing Liz's hand tightly, Jo whispered that she loved her. Cam mouthed to Jo, so do I. There were smiles all round the counter. The art deco bar and loud music was as different from the Wort as it could possibly be, but she liked it. I'll have to bring the kids here when they come out next summer.

Greg called to Cam, "Was that a Billy Burger you had the other day?"

"Yeh, with fries. You'll have to be carried home on a stretcher. Might be the last filling meal you have for a while. Think we'll be on K rations, if what they said was correct."

"You won't actually be fighting the fires, will you?" Liz asked, worried.

"We'll be very near in order to photograph them. Even with a telephoto lens we'll have to be close. The big boys want the flames approaching the Old Faithful Inn. Depends on how the winds blow when they'll get there. Of course, the fires might skirt it if the winds are from the opposite direction. We'll just have to be there to find out. Are you worried about me, Liz?"

She sighed, looked at him and softly said, "Yes, I am." He squeezed her hand underneath the counter. Why can't I feel this way about Avery? Has he hurt me too much? Has he hurt me for too long is a better question.

Cam could see that she was fighting her feelings. I wish

Caroline had had her empathy, her gentleness. She was always trying to second guess me, trying to come out on top. She never let down her guard, never allowed an honest emotion. This is a beautiful woman, but I'll have to be patient. I wonder what happened between them? She's been hurt and is probably afraid to take another chance. I don't want to screw this one up.

It was the end of August and Liz had signed the final papers for the Simpson cabin. She should have been exhilarated, but she wasn't. There had been no news from Cam and the others. She was worried, and so were Jo and Ben. She had called Avery from Jackson the day before and said that she had decided to stay another week so she could get some things done at the cabin. She had been only partly truthful. He actually said that he missed her. She did remove the old slipcovers from the living room furniture and bedspreads from the twin beds in the bedroom and taken them into Pinedale to launder; it brightened them up considerably. I'll be able to live with these for a while, at least. Don't particularly like the colors they used, but for now I can live with them.

Jack and Betty Sheffield had invited them up to their home on several occasions to see their TV, and tonight the pictures of the fires were more frightening than ever. The North Fork Fire, driven by gale-force winds, arrived at the Inn September 7th. Nineteen structures were destroyed. Liz was so afraid that she'd see Cam, but they couldn't distinguish who the photographers were. The flames were spectacular, and the eighty-five-year-old building stood tall, seemingly defying them. There were tears in everyone's eyes as they sat, not moving, staring at the TV, praying, and joyful when the commentator said that the old girl seemed to be laughing at the fire's persistence.

Jack called into the kitchen to Betty, "Honey, come in here. That can wait. They had to evacuate the Inn just in case. The first time since the park's founding in 1872. They said that they brought in 120 soldiers to remove deadfall and trash from the cabin areas. Remember when we stayed in one of them back, heck, over twenty-five years ago? The commentator said that those soldiers were the heroes. And it was a result of what they did that saved the building."

Liz sat on the edge of the grey leather chair. "Who are those men on the top of the Inn? They have cameras! Is that Cam? Jo, can you tell? Dear Lord, how can they stand the wind? Looks like they're going to be blown off!" The commentator only said that there were two photographers who had volunteered to use infrared cameras to track the movement of intense hotspots. Don't let it be Cam, please, dear Lord.

"There's no saving the storage shed nor some of the cabins, folks. Stay tuned for the latest news on Yellowstone. This is the evening news from…"

Liz heard no more. She had to get control of her emotions. Walking out to the deck she could smell the smoke. It was heavier than before. The air was dry, and she realized that the Ranches were just as vulnerable as the park. What have I got myself into? Almost all the money mother left me is tied up in the cabin. Maybe Avery was right. I'm a foolish woman and need to come down to earth. What possessed me?

She heard the French door open and Jo call, "Are you all right? That probably wasn't Cam, you know. Betty wants to know if you want coffee and pear torte or do you want a drink?"

"A drink, and make it strong." She whirled around and called to Jo. "I know I'm probably foolish, like Avery said, but I'm very concerned about fires here in the Hoback. What kind of protection do we have if we do have them?"

"Volunteer fire departments, and they've had a lot of training fighting fires in Washington State, Yellowstone, the Tetons and you name it. Don't have second thoughts, Liz. You know and I know that you did what was right for you, buying the Simpson cabin. You had to buy it! Don't you see?"

Ben stuck his head out of the door. "Hey, what's the answer, Jo? Betty wants to know. Torte or a drink?"

"I'm coming, hon. Liz wants a double scotch and I'll take a large glass of wine. Just as many calories as the torte, but makes me feel a heck of a lot better," she laughed.

"Get that worried look off your pretty face. It'll all work out, believe me. Can't you see that you've broken free?" Just like Irma, Liz. You both were imprisoned. Inch by inch Irma is coming out.

But your insecurities will take longer to heal, I'm afraid, my friend.

Liz, accompanied by Maggie, had walked over to her cabin. "Maggie, I'll have to think of a name for it. It's the type of cabin that needs a perfect name. Something with haven. It is a haven, of sorts. Yes, haven has got to be in it. Maybe Haven on the Hill. That says it all."

She had brought rags and detergent from Daultons' and set about cleaning. The windows need it the most. Now, why didn't I think of vinegar and newspapers. Mother always said that there was something in the newsprint that did the trick. I'll bring them when I return after lunch. It was hard to stay in one room. She was so excited that she wandered in and out of the few rooms, poking in this cupboard and that closet, going from one large window to the other. I can say this for the Simpsons, they realized that a cabin without large windows would not have any resale value.

She was humming to herself when she felt someone's presence. Abruptly whirling around, she gasped. He grabbed her and when their mouths met, his opening hungrily, hers responding, she knew that she had to put a stop to this run-away, uncontrollable emotion. When she pulled back, gasping for breath, she saw the soot on his face.

"I took a chance on you being here. Didn't even go home to shower."

"Doesn't matter. This can't be, Cam. No, I mean it. I'm married, as you already know, and…"

"And you don't love him. That's obvious, Liz. I wouldn't be here if I thought you did."

"I…I'm not sure if I do or don't. Really, I'm not. There has been so much strife in my life for so long that I can't seem to come to terms with it."

"I have been without love for a long time. Actually, I have been without a woman in my life for…seems like forever. I'm not a man grabbing just for the sake of sexual satisfaction, Liz. I need to truly care about a woman before I commit myself. Maybe that's not the way things are done today, but that's how I am.

"There are three people in my life; my son Riley and my

parents. They're all I have, and until I saw you at the airport I really thought that I'd go through life with just us. Something totally unexpected happened to me when I saw you. Now, I know that this is supposed to happen in sappy movies and soaps, and just doesn't in real life. Wrong! Wrong! I saw you and I knew instantly that I wanted you. I wanted you next to me. I wanted to make love to you like I've never made love to a woman before. I wanted to take care of you. You are a very vulnerable hunk of woman. And I want to kiss you again, take you up to the loft and, as sweaty as I am, remove your clothes slowly and bask in your beauty..."

"Mrs. Bellin, Dwight here. I knocked but guess you didn't hear me. Mrs. Daulton said I'd find you here. Oh, Mr. Bellin..."

"No, wrong you are. I'm a neighbor and just stopped in before I went home to change. Been out fighting the fires in Yellowstone. Excuse me, Mrs. Bellin. As I said, if you need me, just holler. I'm just over the hill. Bye."

Liz was still flushed. She was sure that Dwight knew that something wasn't quite right. "Cam saw Maggie, so he knew that I was here. He's been a great help to Jo and me. Now, what was it that you wanted, Dwight?"

"The insurance papers. You forgot to sign them, and I need to get 'em off to Cheyenne. Was up showing the Schuelers' place, so thought I'd take a chance on finding you home."

"I'll be leaving next week. I'm glad you caught me."

Maggie's barking alerted Liz that someone was coming. She had not had time to clear her head after Cam and Dwight left. Working furiously, dusting the window sills, scrubbing the kitchen sink and lavatory, anything to keep from thinking.

He crossed the room in giant strides and before she could think what to say he held her. "Where were we? Don't struggle, my Liz, your man is clean, shaved and hungry. Also the door is locked."

"Cam, I'm not sure that this is what we should..."

"This is exactly what we should be doing. I'm not going to take you forcefully like a crazed cowhand. This is going to be gentle, unhurried, measured, and we're going to savor every minute of our being one, like we were meant to be. No, don't say a word. I just want you to feel every nuance of our being together. Every rise and fall of our bodies in unison..."

"Oh...oh...this can't be...Cam, please, please, my sweet..."

SIXTEEN

The early morning fog lifted slowly. There had been a little rain close to dawn, and Liz had been awake ever since. *I don't know what to do. I wonder if Jo suspects. What have I got myself into? Maybe I should leave immediately and not wait 'til next week, but that would be running away. I can't do that to him. He's too important to me. Should I go to Pinedale with him? He wants me to meet his father and Riley. If I do, then the commitment will have been made, and there'll be no turning back.*

She heard Jo stirring in the kitchen. *She'll know something has happened if she sees me like this. I'll wash my face and ask her if she wants to walk. If she questions me, then I'll have to tell her. How did Avery handle his guilt? Maybe to him it was just a conquest and not guilt at all. What we did was wrong. I don't care what scripture says or our interpretation of it. Ben told Jo that Avery and I had a legal marriage only, that our covenant with God was broken when Avery committed adultery. I know he's taken lots of bible classes, but I feel guilty, and that's what counts. I really need to get back to Orange Park.*

Jo called toward the bathroom. "Liz, the coffee is down, and by the time we've had some the fog should be almost gone. Let's go for a walk after we have a cup. What do you say?"

Liz stuck her head out of the door and said, "Sounds like a winner to me. I had such a restless night that think I need a good brisk walk just to clear my head."

"Not enough rain to do any good, I'm afraid. But some is better than none." Jo went to the door to the basement and called Maggie. Bounding up the steep stairs, wiggling all over, following close behind Jo's heels she dashed out the front door barking and chasing whatever was there. Jo hadn't expected to see anyone on the driveway, but when she saw Maggie's tail wagging, she knew that it had to be Irma.

"Now what is she up to, I wonder?" She pulled her robe closer and went out onto the porch. Seeing nothing, she turned back to open the door and saw the note Irma had written on her chalk board. Shaking her head and laughing, she called to Liz. "You've got to see this, Liz. The old fool!"

Thanks for the sweets. You're a good cook was printed on the board.

Jamie had begun visiting them when he went to Irma's Monday, Wednesday and Friday. He was a nice young man in his late thirties. Jo tried to bake extra when she knew he'd be around and always shared the goodies with him. Actually, she was pumping him trying to find out more about Irma. Deputy Shiffar had planted a curious seed in her, according to Ben, but she also enjoyed finding out more about the area and ranch life in particular. So the invitations were not just to check on Irma and what she was supposedly hiding, according to Manny. The last two visits she had given Jamie some cupcakes and sweet rolls and asked him to share them with Irma. So guess he had.

Jo called to Maggie. "Maggie! Maggie, come back here. You've not even had your breakfast!" I might as well save my breath, she decided. She'll not show her face 'til near noon as usual. She was glad that Irma had taken a liking to Maggie. It's good for her, she had told Ben. She remembered when her mother had been in the home, the humane society would take puppies and kittens to the home for the patients to pet. Did them a world of good.

"Liz, it's damp and cold. Better take a jacket. Probably by the time we come back we'll be pealed down to our tee shirts, though."

Jo went to their loft to dress. "Ben, we're going for a walk. Maggie ran after Irma, and if she…"

"What do you mean? Ran after Irma? Was she down here?"

"Yes, you sleepy head, she was. I saw her practically running down our driveway, and of course Maggie had to follow. She put a note on the blackboard thanking me for the sweets. The old fool!" She said it with affection.

"What did you two eat? Are there any biscuits left? I could eat a horse. Don't know why I'm so hungry out here?"

"You're always hungry when you first awaken, Mr. Daulton. I

read an article in *Good Housekeeping* just last month saying that people with a high metabolic rate are hungry when they first wake up. So, that means you." She reached down and kissed his cheek. "And, yes there are biscuits left. Liz and I will eat cereal or toast when we get back. Oh, Hazel sent a jar of that wonderful strawberry-rhubarb jam over by Betty, and there is still a little cane syrup in the cupboard. Just wish I could find good syrup out here. The only kind they seem to know about is maple."

The sagebrush was sprinkled with the morning dew as they walked down the gravel road. "This is my most favorite time of the day out here. Every thing is so fresh. The pine scent in the air and that dab of moisture. The dryness does bother me as does all the dust. I've stopped dusting everyday, though."

Jo expected a response but got none. "Is anything the matter? You've been so quiet."

"I don't know how to respond to your question, Jo. Nothing is the matter, and yet everything is. I mean…"

"If you can't share with me, your best friend, who can you share with, Liz?"

"I feel so guilty. It's my fault. I didn't have to allow it to happen. I could have stopped him…"

"Why don't you just come out and say what you're talking about, or trying to talk about?"

"When I was at the cabin yesterday Cam came by, and we, well, we became intimate, and I know it was wrong, and I'm having a helluva time dealing with it, and…" She began crying, heaving, trembling.

"Stop it this instant! Do you hear me? Stop it! Now, I'm not going to tell you that what you did was right. It probably wasn't. And the fact that Avery has had numerous affairs for the past fifteen years does not make what you and Cam did right. I don't believe the same way that Ben does. But, Liz, I do feel that Ben is right about one thing. Your marriage to Avery ended a long time ago, and you've hung on only because you thought that it was the right thing to do for the children. Isn't that right?"

She continued to sob and shook her head yes.

"All right, let's look at this event, for want of another word, logically. If you had divorced Avery you would be a divorced woman, and no one would think a thing about your having an affair with Cam or whomever. Would they?"

"Probably not, but why do I feel so bad about it?"

"Darned if I know. You should have kicked Avery's rear end out a long time ago. But you didn't because you're a fine woman, and it isn't in your nature to hurt anyone. That's what I've not been able to understand. You didn't get angry enough! You were too hurt to get angry. That's too bad. If Avery had thought that you would've booted him out and exposed his lecherous side to his fellow lawyers and the church vestrymen, he'd probably have behaved himself and not put you through all that hell. Over and over again he thumbed his nose at you and your marriage. You have no reason to feel guilty."

"I know you're probably right, but two wrongs don't make a right, as my mother used to say."

"Two wrongs! Really liz, how many affairs do you know of? How many? And how many do you only suspect? You've told me of at least three, and you suspect several more. He's sick, Liz. The man has a missing ingredient, and I think it's called decency. I can understand why you don't want your children to know about them. I really do. But he's held that over your head all along, and that gives him the go ahead to behave as despicably as he has. I know that you think that they're all in the past, but are they? Do you want to be kicked in the head again and again?

"If Avery truly loved you, he wouldn't have behaved that way in the first place. Oh, he has a great love affair with himself. What Avery wants he goes after. Anything to please himself. What's the popular saying now? If it feels good, do it. Has he ever thought of the children? Has he?"

"I know he loves the children, but…"

"There are no buts. Does he love Chuck? If he truly loved Chuck, why would he treat him the way he does? Just because Chuck dropped out of college he's treated as an outcast by Mr. Wonderful."

"He was just so disappointed…"

110

"Disappointed! What does he think his children would think of their dad if they knew about all the bimbos he's messed around with for the past fifteen years? What?"

"I think you're right, Jo. No, I know you're right. But I was taught to forgive, to turn the other cheek. It's just hard for me to behave any other way."

"Accept his infidelity, my dear friend, and get on with your life. Your life counts too. Cam is a fine man. He's a **Man**, Liz. He's highly thought of. Betty and Jack were talking about him the other night when you were on the deck. He's talented, a fine citizen, a wonderful son and father, and has a great personality and sense of humor, a giving person. Those are the qualities that Avery Bellin is lacking. He had a good personality and sense of fun in his early life, but when he made it big he changed, Liz. Avery is not the man you married. I don't know who he is now, and all your old friends feel the same about him."

Liz stopped walking, hugged Jo and said, "You've helped me more than you know. I've known all you've said for a long time but didn't dare put it into words. I needed to hear them said out loud. I haven't really loved Avery for a long time. I guess I have trouble making change, but maybe I've broken the pattern, Jo, by buying the cabin and feeling the way I do about Cam. I know that I'm in love with him and probably love him, as well. And I know that I've broken free to a certain extent. But the final break, a divorce—that's a toughie."

"Oh, damn! Liz, I think I've twisted my ankle. Hold on to me, please. I should have been looking where I was going. Ohhh..."

"Here comes a truck. Do you know who it is?"

"No, but maybe they'll go for Ben and he can bring the truck to take me home. I need to get this iced and soon."

"Hello," Liz called while waving her free arm. "Please stop!"

The red pickup slowed and stopped. A handsome young man in his late teens called to them. "Is anything wrong?" *He doesn't sound like he comes from round here. Probably just visiting. I remember when John tried to grow a mustache at about that age. Just not quite enough facial hair.*

"My friend has twisted her ankle and we want you to go to her house to tell her husband. They live just up Elk and around the bend in the new house. Do you know which one I mean?"

"I know where Charlie's Mountain is. Is it near the outhouse? Think my pop said that there was a new house there."

"That's the one. We'd really appreciate it. She's in real pain."

"Here, Jo, sit down over here. I'm sure Ben'll be here in a minute. Do you want me to rub it?"

"No, but I do want to elevate it. There are some smooth stones over there. Do you think you can lift them and maybe make a stone pillow? This is ridiculous! I'm furious with myself."

"It was my fault. You were distracted because of me. I'm so sorry."

"Don't be a dunce, Liz! I can walk and talk at the same time."

They both began to laugh. "Remember when we went to Atlantic Beach and we saw that cute lifeguard? We were juniors in high school, I think. Well, we both tried to outdo each other doing cartwheels in the sand and trying out the school cheers and I fell head first in the deep sand practically breaking my neck and he came scooting off his tower yelling, 'Are you all right?' and I got up feigning dizziness so he could pick me up, and it wasn't 'til after he left that I realized that I really was hurt and ended up missing the big dance? Remember that? Well, this isn't like that. I ache. Where is Ben?"

"He's been gone only a minute. He'll be here soon."

"I hope that nothing's broken. I've had a sprain before, and it took longer to heal than if I'd broken it, according to the doctor. Where is he?"

They both heard the truck before they saw it. It was Ben's rental. He was hauling it, and the young man was behind him in his truck.

"Don't move, Jo! We'll make an arm chair and lift you. What the hell are you laughing about? You are hurt, aren't you?"

"I'm sorry, honey. Yes, I'm hurt. It was just your expression, that's all. You had the same expression when I went in labor with the kids. It's your I'm-concerned-about-my-wife expression."

"You are one strange girl, isn't she, Liz? Laughs when she's in pain and cries when she's happy. You're a peculiar one, Miss Pierce."

The young man and Ben made their arm chair and lifted her into the back of the pickup. Liz sat beside her, holding her foot in her lap.

Ben got in his truck and the young man followed. The gravel flew as they sped up the rough road.

They hopped out of the cab and went to the back of the truck to get Jo. Liz helped her down. Ben said, "I've already got a pan full of ice. It's on the porch waiting for you. Here we go. You know, I didn't even ask you your name, young man. We really appreciate your help."

"It's Riley. Riley Cameron. My dad lives over on Mountain View at the very end. I'm here for the summer but stay at the ranch in Pinedale with my grandpa."

I should have known. The same easy gait, uncontrollable curly hair springing out from under his western hat, same crooked smile. They placed Jo on the park bench at the end of the porch and Ben took her hiking boot off. The ankle was already swollen. "You've got a beaut here, honey. Hey, Riley, we don't have phones in yet. Would you mind going up to Dr. Sheffield's for help?"

"I'll go with him, Ben, since I know where he lives. But maybe you're in a hurry."

"No ma'am, I was just going to leave this package for Miss Irma for my dad. My grandpa said that it belonged to her late husband, and he wanted her to have it. My dad's a sculptor and has an assignment that he has to finish, and I said I'd run it up to her. Besides, this way I get to drive the truck."

"I know your dad. I'm Liz Bellin and met him recently. I just bought the Simpson cabin. Do you know where that is?"

"No ma'am, I mostly stay at the ranch when I'm out for the summer. I live in Rhode Island with my mom and her a...um, boyfriend. My folks are divorced."

"A lot of that going around, I hear," she said smiling.

"That's what I'm told. This is where I turn, isn't it?"

"Yes, it's the house at the top of the hill. Has a glorious view." She almost said like your dad's does.

"We're in luck. They're home, or at least one of them is. Let's hope it's Jack."

Liz quickly got out of the truck, rang the doorbell and Jack answered.

"Thank goodness! Jo's twisted or sprained or broken her ankle. She's at home, and Ben is worried. Can you come have a look at it, Jack?"

She heard Betty calling to him to see what was going on. "It's Liz, honey. Seems like Jo hurt her ankle. Wanta come with me? You might be of help."

"Sure, just let me get a wrap. It's damp this morning."

"Well, I declare, Riley, is that you? Where on earth did you come from? Cam didn't say you were coming out. How're Robert and Sarah? This is a nice surprise." She reached inside the truck's window and pecked his cheek. "You'll have to come over for supper while you're here so I can hear all about life back east. Jack, look who's here! Riley. Didn't you see him?"

"Betty, get a move on and we'll do our visiting after I get a gander at Jo's ankle. Howdy Riley. Catch you later."

Jack diagnosed Jo's ankle as sprained and said he'd go back home for a boot. "They're a lot better than an ace bandage. I want you to stay off it, young lady, except when we play bridge and you get so riled up that you prance around the table. You ever see her do that, Liz? She sure loves to win."

"You should have seen her when she was younger, Jack. Then she did cartwheels. Just joking, Jo. Anyway, that's an inside joke."

The Sheffields left with a promise from Riley that he'd tell his dad that they were invited for dinner, and Jo and Liz could hardly wait for all of them to leave so they could talk.

"Riley, tell your dad that Liz Bellin says hi. He's a wonderful artist."

"He sure is. Did he tell you that he got the contract for the Mountain Man for the museum in Pinedale? That's gonna be awesome! That thing's gotta be seven or eight feet tall. Awesome!"

Jo called Liz over and whispered, "Liz, God's on your side. I mean it. He knows the hell you've been through and now he's going to give you beauty and peace for the rest of your life. I just know it. It's not fair that I've been the lucky one. Not fair at all..."

SEVENTEEN

A week passed before Reba Markos was able to get Manny released from the Pinedale jail. His injured hand was still bandaged, and he was bitter, bitter at Joey Shiffar, bitter at Bart Sikes, bitter at Jamie Stroebel, who had taken his job with Miss Irma, to his way of thinking.

Reba knew that she was going to have trouble with Manny. He ranted and raved the entire trip from Pinedale about how that Jamie Stroebel was no friend of his and how he had stolen his job. When Reba reminded him that it was Jamie who had gone with him to the bank in Jackson to help him fill out all the papers at the bank so he could buy his truck, and it was Jamie who had... "Whose side you on? Whose?"

"Do not yell at me, Manny! I'll not stand for it! You've no need to be upset with Jamie. That's all I'm saying. Miss Irma needed someone to do the chores, and Deputy Shiffar came up to the ranch to ask Eileen if she had anyone she'd recommend. And that's the way it happened, 'cause I was there. So get off your high horse with me. I'll not allow you to take your problems out on any of the Stroebels. They've been good to us." Too good, she thought quietly.

She opened the heavy wooden door, put her groceries down on the kitchen table, removed her hat and wrap and sat down. She was weary. She remembered when Eileen Stroebel brought her into this cabin forty-four years earlier. She had been large with Manny and so hungry and weak that Eileen had to help her to a chair. "I'll get you some leftover supper, missus, but I want you to get some rest first. There's water at the pump and pails to fetch it in. Here, sit, I'll get you some. You look all in. When's your due date?"

She remembered saying that she didn't rightly know. Probably next month. "You'll not go that long, I'm thinking. I've midwifed before and can do it again. You'll be taken care of, don't you fret." She decided to not ask about the baby's father. It was none of her business. To this day no one knew, not even Manny. He hadn't seemed to care.

There was only one room in the cabin plus the sleeping loft with a narrow ladder leading up to it. A bed built in and a clothes rack for Manny's few hanging clothes were all there was up there. Reba had the bed downstairs with a quilt draped over a rope to separate it from the kitchen table and two chairs, and there was a long wooden cupboard on the wall next to the door.

She was thrilled to have two windows. They weren't large, but she could see the mountains out of one and the meadow down to a stream out of the other. They both gave her a lot of pleasure. She loved her flowers, and there wasn't a person in the basin who didn't know of Reba Markos's green thumb. Eileen often said to the ladies at the Guild, "If you want flowers for the altar, just let me know. Reba has enough for every church in the state." They were her pride and joy. She wished that she could say that about Manny. But she couldn't. He was her cross to bear.

"Here he comes!" Irma said aloud. "I'm going to have trouble with him but don't know just how much." She was dreading the confrontation with Manny but was also excited about it. Frankly, except for his ability to fix the vehicles, she'd much rather have Jamie around. He wasn't nearly as curious, nor surly and didn't reek of alcohol or smell like he hadn't bathed or changed his foul smelling drawers in weeks.

She went down the front log steps, felt the heaviness of the revolver inside her skirt pocket, and confidently said, "Well, well, if it isn't Wild Bill back from the dead! How'd they treat you in the great Pinedale dungeon, Manny? Joey Shiffar get to use his billy club on you, huh?"

He shuffled his big, dusty boots, the saliva drooling down both sides of his mouth. Still has grease underneath his nails, Irma noticed. Probably hasn't had a bath since he was incarcerated. Might not ever again since Bart won't let him inside the Elkhorn. Won't be any need to get all spiffed up for the gals. Doubt that Daphne will let him at hers.

He finally looked up and with that surly smirk on his homely face said, "Now, Miss Irma, no need to get cute with me. I was rail-roaded, and anyone who says I wasn't is telling one big lie."

"What are you wanting up here, Manny? I hired Jamie Stroebel to take care of my needs. He doesn't get into barroom brawls, he doesn't drink, he's dependable and he smells good. What do you have to offer a poor old widow?"

She could see that he was ready to burst he was so angry. He sputtered, "He…he don't know nuthin' 'bout snowmmobiles, and he don't know nuthin' 'bout four-wheelers, and he don't know nuthin' 'bout…"

"And he doesn't run around the basin spreading rumors about poor old widows, either. Manny, where do you come off telling folks lies about me? Huh? Hell, you had that deputy thinking I got a still in my basement and whores selling their favors on account of your rumors. Everyone knows that you're not quite right, Manny, and they aren't going to believe anything you say. So, tell me, why are you making a bigger fool of yourself than you are?"

He was beet red. His feet started pawing the dirt just like a raging bull about to charge, but Irma stood calmly with her hand on the revolver waiting. "I asked you a question, Manny. Why are you telling lies about me? Why should I hire someone who tells lies about me?" She was calm; she was unafraid. She was loving every minute of it. Gosh, I wish Charlie was here for this. Better than any hunt he's ever been on.

He started to back up kicking the dirt furiously. "You'd better go now, Manny. If I can use you to fix any of my vehicles, I'll get word to you. You are right on that. You were given a gift, but your drinking and your lies have cost you your job. Good day to you."

She turned around, then remembered that he still had her key to the padlock. "Oh, Manny, I need the key to the gate, please."

Throwing the keys at her he yelled, "Here's your goddamned key you old freak! And what I know ain't lies, and I mean to prove it, too! You just wait! I'll get you for this! I'll get you…"

Since Jo was unable to walk with her, Liz spent the next day at her cabin, Haven on the Hill, just to enjoy, remembering, trying to decide how she was going to handle her and Cam's situation, but no conclusion would come to her without hurting the people she loved. Am I prepared for the consequences?

Cam drove over to check on Jo the night following her injury. At least that was his excuse. Riley was with him but planned to return to the ranch the next morning. Liz was glad. She and Cam had had no time together since Riley arrived.

They had a delightful evening, and Liz and Riley concocted banana splits. The evening had turned cool so they sat in the living area with a fire in the wood stove. Jo had wanted to play a board game, but Cam said that he simply had to get back. He hated working with a deadline, but the movie scouting had taken a chunk—even if the results were lucrative—out of his summer.

Liz liked Riley. He was smart and intelligent. When she asked him what his college plans were, he demurred, looked at his dad and finally said, "My mom wants me to go to Brown University in Providence 'cause it's close to her and an Ivy League school, but…I want to go to Wyoming."

"Do you have any idea what you'd like to study, to major in? My children didn't at your age."

"I was thinking of animal husbandry or agriculture. I wouldn't mind geology, but what I really want to do is become a rancher. Grandpa understands, and Dad does, but my mom…well, she doesn't."

"Well, you've got some time yet. You're going into your senior year, aren't you?"

"Yeh, and I'd like to graduate, come out to the ranch for a year, then enroll at the university. But, guess my mom and dad will have to work that out."

"Our middle son, Chuck, dropped out of college in his junior year and was made manager of a Sonny's restaurant in Jacksonville. It's a chain of barbeque restaurants and very popular in the South. His dad still hasn't gotten over that. He now owns a franchise with two partners and is looking into acquiring another one, is married with two small children, and his wife doesn't have to work. That's a plus these days. But the great thing about it is that he loves his work. He is very personable, loves people, and plans to go back to college in a few years just because he loves to learn.

"I'm very proud of him. His father still doesn't understand his decision. So, Riley, maybe you'll have to go with your gut instincts. We parents certainly don't know it all." She patted his broad back, hugged him to her and smiled at Cam.

"You are one smart lady, Liz Bellin. Isn't she, Riley?"

"She sure is. Hey, Dad, maybe I can hang out around here for a few more days. You know, I could run your errands and help with the cooking..."

"I've already had a sample of your cooking. Beans and franks two meals in a row are not my idea of gourmet meals, son. And besides, I've got a deadline on that piece for the museum in Laramie. Riley, it's not that I don't want you around, it's just that there is not enough for you to do to keep you occupied."

"I could use his help, Cam," Ben interjected. "I've got a lot of sage that needs grubbing and..."

Jo saw Liz and Cam's expressions and said, "Ben, for heaven's sake. The young man had rather be riding or fishing on his vacation, certainly not doing backbreaking work like grubbing up sage."

"No ma'am, that's not true. I need to build up my biceps and shoulders for the varsity swim team. That'd work out great, Mr. Daulton."

Cam shook his head and looked at Liz. "I'll call your grandpa from Bondurant in the morning, son. If he says it's all right, then a few days more would be great. If I can get the piece done early, then we can wet a few flies in the Hoback. I'd like that. Haven't been fishing all summer. Want to come along, you guys?" He was addressing all of them.

"We could take a picnic and make a day of it," Liz said excitedly. "And, Jo, it'd be no trouble for you. We can take folding chairs and a foot stool for your foot and..."

"I'm sold on the idea. These four walls are getting a bit confining." Good for you, Liz. You have only a few more days, and I want you to be sure of your feelings when you get back to Orange Park.

Jo awakened later than usual. Hobbling downstairs, holding on tightly to the banister, she managed to get to the kitchen in time to look out the window and see a shadowy figure go past Ben's truck, which he had neglected to put in the garage the night before.

At first she thought that it was a deer or maybe even a young moose, but when she opened the front door and peered outside she saw the familiar figure of Irma Barksdale bundled up as usual. She was walking and not on her 4-wheeler. She looked on the blackboard beside the front door, but there was no message. Wonder what on earth she was doing down here this early? Just snooping around, I guess, but when she turned to open the door she saw something on the park bench at the end of the porch.

She was chilly but decided to retrieve it rather than return to the mud room for her wrap, which she kept just inside the front door. Hobbling, she bent down and picked it up carefully. It was a large bundle. Old Christmas paper enveloped it. Jo was apprehensive about opening it. Irma had not shown her erratic behavior in a long time, but Jo wasn't sure that this time wouldn't be one of her get-even days. After all, she hadn't paid much attention to her since Liz's arrival.

Liz had gone into the kitchen to start the coffee when she heard Jo gasp. Thinking that she'd fallen or hurt herself in some way, she dashed out calling her. "Jo! Are you all right?" She saw her in the mudroom, her face damp with tears. "What's the matter?"

"I can't believe her. Look at these, would you. She's been out picking wild flowers for me. Listen to this. *Since you will be unable to pick these beauties for a while, Maggie and I decided we'd present you with a bouquet to cheer you.* She didn't sign it. That's one of the nicest gifts I've ever had, Liz." She brushed the tears away and sniffed while trying to find a vase large enough to hold them.

"How on earth did she know that I sprained my ankle? You suppose that she has our house bugged?" She laughed when she said it, but Liz wondered the same thing.

"I know, Jamie must have told her."

"No, he didn't get up yesterday, remember? She's a wonder. I wish I could sit down and talk to her. Jack and Betty said that she has a keen wit and a fantastic sense of humor. She and Charlie were always pulling some kind of practical joke on them. When Betty turned sixty-five she found a large plastic pink flamingo on their doorstep, you know, like all those retired people have in their front yards in Florida. With it was a note saying, *Welcome to the club.* They thought it hysterical. Betty said that they've passed the same flamingo around the ranches for years. It's become a Hoback Ranches joke."

"What's going on around here?" Ben questioned. He was still in his pajamas.

"Look. A gift to me from Irma and Maggie." She showed him the note, and he began to laugh.

"What's so funny?"

"She used the back of an old Christmas card to write it on. Didn't you see what the other side of it said?"

"No," she took it from him and began to laugh.

"Look Liz. It's an old card from President Johnson and Lady Bird. Can you imagine? They're thanking them for doing such a good job on the antelope. I imagine that Charlie mounted it for them. This is priceless. I doubt that the Barksdales were Democrats—she's too conservative, but I bet that she's an independent. See, there's so much that I don't know about her that I'd like to know."

"Don't push your luck, my sweet. Is the coffee down?" Rummaging around in the frig, Ben asked Jo where that leftover creamed tuna was. "That'd be good on English muffins, hon."

"Yuk! You're as bad as Robbie. That child would eat anything he could find for breakfast. One morning I found him eating a COLD HAMBURGER sandwich. Didn't even bother heating it."

Ben decided to not say, I think they're great. When Liz looked at him, they both started laughing.

"What's got into you two?"

"I think cold hamburger sandwiches are yummy, and I think Ben does too. Right, Ben? Jo, you're too sophisticated for the likes of us. That was one of my favorite breakfasts in the dorm. I'd get two for dinner but save one for breakfast so I could sleep late in the morning. Worked out wonderfully."

Cam worked at breakneck speed to finish his bronze for the Laramie Museum. He would send it either to Oregon or Denver for casting. Riley decided to help Ben with the removal of sagebrush so he wouldn't be in his dad's hair, he told them. So, for two days Liz got to know Bruce Riley Cameron. She also got to know a lot about one Caroline Cameron, although she was now using her maiden name of Massey, a very social and political family in Rhode Island. There was no doubt that the family had political clout, and they expected their grandson to be a part of their predictable lives. Caroline had even added Massey to his name, not legally, but he was enrolled at an exclusive boys school as Bruce Riley Massey Cameron.

Liz was amazed that Riley was as normal as he was. They were strict with him, he said. Most of his friends already had a car of their own and spent their vacations in Europe. He said some were envious of his time on the ranch. When they bragged about their cars, he told them about his thoroughbred horses with his own brand and said he was going to be the owner of one of the largest ranches in Wyoming. Some had even hinted about coming out to visit.

"Have you had any out?"

"No, because I doubt if they'd understand the workings of a real ranch. They think of a ranch like a dude ranch. Grandpa wouldn't stand for that. I mean, when I'm out here I work just like any other cowhand, and I like it like that. How else am I gonna learn?"

"You're right on that, Bucko!"

"Why'd you call me that?"

"It's one of my pet names for John, our oldest. Just a term of endearment, as they say."

"Mrs. Bellin, I hope you don't mind if I ask you, but are you sorta…are you and my dad sorta…"

"If you're trying to ask am I and your dad interested in each other, yes, we are. I didn't know that it was so obvious. I don't want you to leave here with the wrong impression, Riley. We have no commitment to each other, mainly because I'm still married. I use the word still because I am not divorced. I never thought that I'd be divorced and I actually haven't asked my husband for one. I'll be direct with you. If I had not met your dad, I probably would not even be entertaining such a move. But I did meet him, and I did fall in love with him, and I do plan to get a divorce.

"My husband and I have not had a good marriage for the past fifteen years, and I thought I'd be able to ride it out until one of us dies. Now, that's not possible. Our children are grown with lives of their own, and I believe I need one of my own, too. I've been through a great deal. I'll not burden you with the details. Our children don't know anything of what I'm telling you. I believe I've been a very accomplished actress, but I, too, need some happiness, and I truly believe that Cam and I can give each other the love we both need."

"I hope so. I worry about dad. He seems so alone. Oh, I know that he gets a lot of pleasure from his work, his artwork, and I know he has lots of friends, but there's just gotta be more to it than that, don't you think?"

"You bet, Bucko! Let's get back to the house so I can help Jo with dinner. Your dad is coming over, isn't he?"

"I sure hope so. She's fixing just about my favorite dinner, roast chicken with dressing and gravy. I get tired of eating everything with watercress and bean sprouts like Mom fixes. She has to watch her weight, you know. I keep peanut butter and crackers in my dresser drawer so I won't die of starvation."

"Good move!"

When they got to Daultons' Willow Creek Ranch, as the new sign read, Cam's truck was already there.

"Liz, I was just headed over to your place to fetch you two home. I could smell that chicken all the way to Pine Ridge Studio. Yummm."

"Did you finish your piece?"

"Already packed and ready to send to Denver. You can get the fishing poles out when we get home. And, Liz, the picnic's on us. I found all kinds of goodies in the cupboard that Pollard and Greg bought and left. I mean good stuff! Snails, frog's gizzards…"

"If you're not teasing, Mr. Cameron, you can feast by yourself, huh, Bucko?"

Cam looked at the two of them and realized that they'd got very well acquainted these past two days.

"Come here, woman. I've been wanting to do this for two days, and I don't care if Bucko sees or not!" She didn't hesitate.

Riley stood and watched, a wide grin spread across his young face. When Cam released her, Riley put his arm around her, too, and the three walked up the steps. All were grinning.

But their timing couldn't have been worse. Liz saw the look on Jo's face as she handed her the note that Billy Parker had brought just ten minutes before. Her hand found her open mouth quickly. "Oh, dear lord…"

EIGHTEEN

"John, Mom. What happened?"

Pause...

"Did Adelle find him? Was he alone?"

Pause...

"What does Murph think his chances are?"

Pause...

"But why can't you see him? Oh, he's in intensive care?"

A long pause...

"Did you get in touch with Laine?"

Pause...

"I'm in Bondurant at the Smilin' S Motel. No, our phones won't be in until next spring. At least, that's the prognosis now."

Pause...

"I'm going to call the airport in Jackson as soon as I hang up. I'll get home as soon as I can but doubt that I can get a flight out tomorrow. It's a small airport, and it's still tourist season, you know. Wait a minute, son."

Cam whispered, "I can drive you to Denver tomorrow morning early, and you can be on standby, hon. I have to go to Laramie and Denver anyway. That way I can take my piece to be cast, and that'll hurry things up for me."

"John, there might be a chance that I can go to Denver and be put on standby. I'll look into it and will call you back when I find out. Jo sprained her ankle, and Ben is busily taking care of her, so I might need to either rent a car or rely on someone going to Denver.

"And son, if you are allowed in to see your dad tell him that I'll be there as soon as I can. Hang in there. Oh, write down this number. Area code (307) 733-3457. That's the motel number. I love you."

Eva and Bud assured Liz that they'd get word to her if a call came in.

"It's my husband. He's had a stroke. I'm just glad our maid was there at the time. I'd planned to leave in three days anyway. He was so healthy. Did have a slight heart attack, but our doctor told him that it was just a warning. Both our sons live nearby, but our daughter is in Seattle. She's with Greenpeace…"

Cam held her arm and let her rattle. "Can I get you a glass of wine or anything, Liz?" Eva asked.

"No, thank you. I need to call the Jackson airport. Cam, what do you think?"

"I think you'd be better off packing tonight, leaving early in the morning for Denver and going on standby. The airlines are great about helping people out during emergencies. What do you think, Bud?"

"That's a safer bet than trying to get a flight out of Jackson. They'd probably get you to Salt Lake, then Dallas, then who knows where. You'd be going to Jacksonville, wouldn't you?"

"Yes. I think you're probably right. I'll just wait 'til I get to Denver before calling the kids. Thanks, you've been a big help. You know, I'd planned on going home last week, then Jo hurt her ankle, and there were a few things I needed to finish up at the cabin, insurance papers and all that stuff…"

"Liz, don't get down on yourself." Cam chastised her.

"It's just that I could have been there, that's all."

Cam turned back to Eva and Bud and thanked them. "We'll keep you in our prayers, Liz," Eva called to them.

"Thanks," then Liz went back to the front door and hugged her. "I appreciate all you have done for me. Honest I do." She was crying.

"But Cam, Riley didn't need to go back to the ranch. Why'd you let him? He'll think I'm…"

"Hey, woman mine, Riley is the one who brought it up. He, not I, is the one who insisted on it. He knew that the fishing trip would be out of the question, and besides, he saw that we needed to be alone. And we do."

"I can't think…"

"Don't start a guilt trip, Liz! Now, I mean it! This is not something God is throwing at us to make us feel like we've done something horribly wrong. He has given us both a chance for happiness, and I'm not going to let you go. I mean it!"

"But things have changed now. Don't you see? John said that they don't yet know how much damage was done, but there was definitely some paralysis, according to Murph. If he's incapacitated, what kind of person would I be to leave him... to divorce him?"

"Liz, you have not told me what happened between you two, but I'd bet a mint that it involved another woman or other women. Am I right?"

She bit her lower lip and began to sob. Cam pulled the truck over onto the grassy knoll and took her in his arms.

"Shhhh. Jo indicated that you had been hurt repeatedly but gave me no details. So I assumed. I'm sorry. How any man with any brains could want another woman when he had you, I'll never understand. You're the most desirable woman I've ever known, and I've known a few. No, shhhh, I mean it. I'm not saying that so I can get in your britches, lady, I'm saying that because I care for you, deeply.

"Some men have to constantly prove their manhood. They're usually insecure and don't have the moral character of a rutting billy goat, as my dad would say. They're self-serving men, Liz. I've known more men of that caliber than I'd care to admit, and I've seen the damage they do to entire families."

"And what about the women who pursue the men? What do you think of them?"

"The same. But most times they're after financial security. The sex part is only a means to an end. But there again, they're self-serving without any concern for the people they're hurting."

"I don't understand, Cam. I can't imagine how they can knowingly hurt other people. As you said, entire families are ruined by their despicable acts. How can anyone behave that way?" She sniffled, wiped her nose on the tissue and said, "We need to get back so I can tell Jo and Ben what's going on. I know that they're worried."

"See. That's why I love you so. Well, one of the reasons. You think of others and their feelings. Oh, by the way. Riley said that he really likes you and hopes that we'll get married. How about that? Barely knows you and, like his dad, loves you."

The lights were on outside the house when Liz and Cam pulled up. Ben came out immediately to greet them and Jo was right behind waiting on the porch.

"What's up?" Ben asked as soon as they got out of the truck.

Liz answered, "Avery's had a stroke, but John was unable to tell me the extent of it. Murph did tell him that there was some paralysis, and he is in the IC unit with no visitors allowed. They got in touch with Laine, but she doesn't know how she can get home because of the expense and I don't know what all."

"Here, Liz, you come in here this instant. I bet you're freezing. Bet it dropped twenty degrees since you two left. Oh, Cam, Riley said he'd try to get out later in the week."

"Thanks, Jo, but I'm going to drive Liz to Denver first thing in the morning to get her on standby. She'd probably not be able to get out of Jackson for a couple days."

"We were just talking about that. We can drive her, Cam. Think Jo needs to get away anyway."

"I was going to send my piece to Denver for casting anyway, Ben, so it'd not be any bother. Need to go to the museum in Laramie and that's on the way. Will work out fine. I'll drop by the ranch to tell Riley on our way."

Ben looked at Jo questioningly. What's she know that I don't, I wonder. She smiled, took his arm and whispered, "I'll tell you later."

"The chicken is barely warm but I can put it in the micro. Liz, you need to eat something, and I'm sure Cam does, too. That is, if Riley left you anything." She laughed heartily. "I'd forgotten how much teens can hold. It was a delight having him here, Cam. Someone's doing a great job on that young man."

"Think you can say that it's mostly his grandpa. Those two are thick. I'm not saying that Caroline isn't trying, because I know she cares about him and loves him like we all do. But it's Mister Robert who has had the most influence on Riley, and I'm grateful."

"Here, Liz. Sit down and eat. I'll help you pack later. Your cabin will need little winterizing, and I'll take some old sheets over to hang on the windows. I'll ask Billy to tend to it when he does ours. The winter sun is brutal, I'm told, and everything in the cabin will be faded by the time you get out next summer."

"Oh, I can't think that far ahead, Jo. What if Avery is paralyzed and is confined to a wheel chair and needs constant care? I know that he'll not come out here, and I certainly can't leave him..."

"Whoa...young lady. You're jumping the gun, aren't you?" Cam asked, his brow furrowed.

"Cam's right. You need to think positively. If that is the worse scenario, then there are homes for people in that condition, and they can take care of him better than you could anyway. You have sons who live there and will see that he is getting the best care."

"But he is my responsibility, and it wouldn't be..."

"Liz!" Cam almost shouted. "You're letting your imagination carry you away. Wait 'til you get to Orange Park, talk to your doctor, talk to your sons before making an assumption like that. Please, hon."

Ben now knew that there had been some kind of liaison between them. He knew that Jo knew what had transpired and would tell him later, but he didn't have to wait for her explanation. Cam took care of it.

Liz and Jo had gone to the guest room to pack, and Ben asked Cam if he'd like a drink.

"You bet! Make it strong. Oh, bourbon will be fine. Ben, I think that you can tell that Liz and I have something going. I don't want you to get the wrong impression."

"I, and Jo, want to see her find some happiness, and if that is with you, then all the better. She's a wonderful woman and Jo's best friend. Actually, she's like a sister to me, too. Avery has not treated her right, and it's been very hard on us seeing her pain."

"I haven't said this to her, but I want her to get a divorce as soon as she can and move out here permanently—I mean, to become my wife. Riley even told me before we left this evening that he'd like for us to get married and..."

"You don't know Liz like I do, Cam. You've only known each other a short time. I can tell you right now that she will not, and I mean will not leave Avery if he's incapacitated. She couldn't do that to their children. That's why she has stayed with him through all his cheating. She thinks of others before she does herself. That's the way she is, and that's the way she'll always be. No matter how many times Jo has tried to change her, she can't change."

"That's ridiculous! The man has kicked her over and over again, and she just takes it. I don't understand."

"Guess you'd have to be a woman. That's the way some women are, so I'm told."

"Hey you two, want a drink?" Ben called.

"Yes, make it two glasses of Chardonnay. We're almost finished." Jo hobbled over to Liz. "Liz, you have a great thing going with Cam. I know you feel an obligation or a duty, whatever, to Avery, goodness knows why, and you don't want the children to think less of their father. But you have an obligation to Cam, too. He is a man who wants to marry you, take care of you, watch you grow as an artist and person, become an important part of Riley's life and…"

"How on earth do you know all this when I don't." Jo could tell that she was getting put out with her.

"We had a chance to have a little conversation before you and Riley came back earlier this evening. He told me that if you'd have him, he wanted to marry you. He's so in love with you…"

"Avery was, too, remember?" She sat down on the side of the twin bed. "Avery promised to love and honor me. What makes you think that it'll be any different with Cam? Maybe men can't stay in love with me. Maybe I've got this…"

"Liz, don't. Why are you doubting yourself? Why are you throwing this…"

"Jo, you've not walked in my shoes, as they say. You're my best friend, but you don't know everything about me or everything inside of me. I think that I love Cam, but I know that I have a duty to Avery. No matter what he's done, I have that obligation, and I don't want to hear any more about it. I simply can't make a decision right now. I simply can't."

She got up, went to the living room and told Cam that she

needed to talk to him, in private. He looked at Jo hoping her expression would give him a clue, but it didn't.

He walked over to her and asked, "Do you want to go to my place? Would that help?"

"Yes, it would. We really need to be alone. Jo," she called to her, "Cam and I are going to his place for a while. We need to talk, to work out some things. See you in a little bit."

They drove the dark, bumpy roads in silence. The stars were putting on a show for them but Liz barely noticed. A deer and fawn suddenly appeared and Cam had to slam on the brakes; they bounded off into the night. Up the steep road, over pit run and gravel the crunch of the tires invaded the still of the night. Liz had been able to put her mind on hold, but Cam had not. His would not stop racing. *I can't let her do this to us. I can't.*

"Here we are. Wait here 'til I get the door unlocked." He took a flashlight out of the console and its beam flashed through the silent darkness. Fir, pine and spruce trees were thick along the split log walkway. Liz noticed that he had placed a large carved wooden figure beside the door. She couldn't make out what it was. She closed her eyes tiredly and was startled when the truck door opened.

Cam took her arm gently and soon his arm was around her back helping her execute the rough walkway. A tree limb brushed her and she reacted. "Hey, I've got you. It is difficult to manage this unless you know the uneven parts. I'm not real good at sidewalks, I guess."

Large leather furniture with animal skins draped over the backs filled the room. There was a wood stove in one corner and a TV in the other. He turned on the tape deck, and Ravel's Bolero filled the room. When Liz looked up through the slanted tempered glass above the studio she felt his presence. She relaxed, closed her eyes and gave in to his being there, finally allowing him back into her life. He sensed it and went to her.

He just held her close, stroking her hair back from her sad face and whispered, "Shhhh, shhhh, my beautiful Liz."

Pulling her down onto the couch they curled up and held each other, listening to the music fill the room underneath the stars.

"I love you very much, and whatever you decide is best for you, will be best for us both. I now know that. At first I was angry. Hey, I've never come in contact with one of you southern types. I'm not angry anymore. I understand."

She sniffled, cleared her throat and said barely above a whisper, "I don't think that I could bear to loose you. You're my comfort, my ballast, my keel, my precious gift. But I must have time to deal with this. I don't have the anger that I need, according to Jo, but I do have perseverance." She laughed when she added that.

Liz disentangled herself, rose, looked around the studio and said, "So this is where the fabulous Lee Riley Cameron creates his magnificent art work?" She saw the piece he was working on, a clay sketch. Pictures by other artists he admired lined the rough wooden walls. There was no doubt that this was a man's room. It reeked with masculine touches. But there was a sensitive side as well. Pots of flowers at the base of the window were well taken care of. A loving, appreciative hand had seen to their needs. She had to know as much about him as she could. She'd need all the strength this man could offer her while back in Florida.

Breaking the spell, she asked, "Were you always interested in art?"

"Actually, no. It wasn't until I was at university that I discovered all this hidden talent." He laughed. It was a man's laugh, rich and filled with resonance.

"Sit beside me and I'll tell you the story of my life, my dear." He twirled his mustache.

"I hope that your rendition is a short version. I really do need to get back. We'll have to be up early. Sorry about that. I didn't mean to shatter the aura of the moment with reality, my dear."

"I was taking a required psychology class, and we were studying the brain. I had to draw a picture of said brain, and a fellow classmate saw it and commented, 'you really should take art, that's great,' and I envisioned all those nude students I'd get to draw, so signed up for art the next semester. In one day, even without the nude gals, I was hooked.

"Changed my major from advertising to art and fell in love with every phase of it. Also took classes in archaeology and ecology and fell in love with our native Americans, as they're called today. Their oneness with the earth, their history and philosophy all satisfied my innermost feelings.

"I leaned more toward the abstract and learned to work in bronze, plastic, resin and stone, but I get a great deal of satisfaction working with wood and even welded metal. As I would tell my students, I feel that combining the various materials gives you the feeling of the complete artist, the perfect master. Oh, and I also paint and sketch. Got my degree, then stayed on for my master's, and eventually taught there."

"What did your rancher father think of all this?"

"He and mom thought it was great. Mom had always done crafts and Dad's passion was working with wood. He's done some wonderful pieces. One is a duplicate of an old sea chest with brass fittings. He's promised it to Riley, and I'm jealous. But guess he'd get it eventually, anyway."

"There is more to this interview, my dear. If I could pigeonhole you as an artist, what term would I use? I mean what term would you like me to use?"

"I'm known as an ecological impressionist. No, don't laugh, really that is the term. When I'm asked to lecture, that is how I'm introduced. And besides, that is how I think of myself, that and the world's greatest lover...so come here, you delectable dish. I'm going to start with nibbling your shell-like ears, then I'll slowly kiss my way down your swan-like neck, and before you know it I'll have arrived at your cleavage, then..."

"This wasn't supposed to happen, Cam..."

"Then you shouldn't be so delightfully edible, *my dear...*"

NINETEEN

The eight-hour drive to Denver seemed much longer to Liz. All she could think of was whether Avery was going to be alive when she got home. *If he's not, then I'll feel this horrible guilt for the rest of my life, and there'll be no space for this wonderful man.* Cam tried to start a conversation but her response was halted. Finally he put in a tape and realized that it was *Ravel's Bolero* when he felt Liz take his hand and squeeze it hard.

She was smiling. "Is this to be our song, Cam?"

"Yes. I'll never hear it again that I don't think of our time together. I know you're worried almost sick, but it'll work out. I'm as sure of it as I am of my love for you."

She sighed deeply. "I'm not sure of anything right now except that I must get home before he...he..."

"Don't, honey. You've got to think on a more positive note. Let's change the subject."

"I'm all for that."

"Have I told you how I met Caroline? No, of course I haven't. Here goes. A little more of my life's story. As I told you I got a job at the university after apprenticing with Woerber Struebel in Denver. He's the famous sculptor and artist I was telling you about. When the position became available, Woerber went to bat for me. He had many friends at the university and had a lot of clout. I was scared to death, I can tell you.

"It was blowing a gale when I arrived and threatening snow. I remember that I had my head down trying to avoid the stinging rain when I heard this angry voice shout, 'Watch where you're going, you klutz!' I looked up at an unbelievably beautiful woman. She was slight, blond, very well put together in a bright blue sweater and jeans that hugged. I was smitten."

"Did she feel the same about you?"

"She said that she did later, after we got to know each other. It didn't take us long to discover that our art was extremely important to us both. That was always our connection. But as it turned out, it was our only connection aside from our sexual need. Caroline was not exactly cold, or frigid, but she always held back. I'm not sure that she was capable of giving herself totally. Some women are like that, I've read since our breakup. But at first I didn't notice, I was so in love. I don't believe that I ever really loved her because I don't think I really knew her. Is that possible? But by then Riley was on the way, and I was so excited I could hardly contain myself.

"She was not as excited. Oh, she wanted the baby, but she was away from home and pregnant, and, to make matters worse, she had morning sickness. Not a pretty sight to see when you first got up in the morning. I mean, your wife throwing up with tears streaming down her face. Made me feel so guilty. Finally, I called Mom and she spoke to Caroline. Seems that she had the same sickness when she carried me. Lasted about three months, and by then we had accustomed ourselves to it, if that's possible.

"Her folks came out to stay for the last few months before Riley arrived,and that's when I realized that I'd made a terrible mistake. She was devoted to her folks, but then so am I to mine. But her parents are very controlling and had Riley's life planned for him even before he was born. It didn't do one speck of good for me to say anything. She always sided with them.

"We managed to stay together for three more years of fighting. I could do nothing right. Absolutely every thing I said or did seemed to bother her. Her life had been disrupted by Riley. Oh, she loved him, but her life was not the same. To put it bluntly, Caroline did not take to motherhood. She wanted to be a famous and respected artist and free to hop a plane for Paris or London or New York when the notion seized her. She didn't like the responsibility."

Liz had sat quietly while Cam spoke. To herself she thought, I hope he doesn't want me to tell him about my life with Avery. I'm just not ready for that right now. Later, but not now.

"Do you need to stop? Might do us good to rest a while or at least walk a little. My butt's sore from all this sitting."

"Sure. "I'm feeling light-headed. Is the altitude higher here than at the ranches?"

"No, actually it's higher at the ranch. Almost eight thousand feet up there. Here, hon, I'll get the door. Need to fix that darned handle. The roads beat cars and trucks to death out there. But they'll be even worse next spring . Wish we had more money in the road fund."

He took her arm and helped her down. They had pulled off at a narrow gravel road intersecting route 287 leading to someone's place. A road sign said Owl Canyon, and the terrain was gorgeous. The mailbox had a sign affixed to it that read Blowing Wind Ranch. Liz thought, I'd hate to live out here away from everyone and everything. These people have to be very self sufficient to survive. No wonder there are so many suicides. Can't remember what the stats were in the "Roundup" but they were high.

They saw the dust before seeing the truck hauling it down the road.

"Someone's in a hurry. Hop in and I'll get this away from the gate. He pulled out just in time for the young lady to jump out of the truck unhook the gate and without as much as a howdy-do swing onto the hard road without bothering to close the gate. Cam called to her to ask if she needed help, but she ignored him and sped off like a bat outta hell.

"Wonder what that's all about? There's no doubt that she's in some kinda trouble."

"Should we take the time to go see?"

"Better not. I want to get you to the airport right after noon. You might have to wait a long time."

"It's not necessary for you to stay with me, you know. I mean, go on to your appointment and I'll..."

"Not on your sweet life. This'll give us a little more time to..."

"I need to think things out, Cam. I know that we'll be together. I'm sure of it, but I must think of Avery and the children. I hope you understand."

"Of course I do. I've acquired a little patience these last few years, hon. A few years back I'd not be as accommodating. Is that called aging? Well, whatever it is, I'm glad it is now part of my character."

Liz struggled to remove her suede jacket. She had not gone native but she just couldn't pass that bargain up. She'd never be able to find one for that price in Jacksonville, she had told Avery. The rich brown complemented the red glints in her dark hair and the brown in her hazel eyes, Jo had said. She felt Cam's stare. When she turned to smile he suddenly put on the brakes. Pulling off onto the road's shoulder, he reached for her. She hungrily came into his arms.

The airport was buzzing with wall-to-wall people returning home from vacation. She could tell by their golf bags and sporting equipment. I'll never get out of here tonight. Is that so bad? Oh, how I'd like one more night with my love. Avery's face appeared. Am I going to allow him to dominate my life forever? Am I?

Cam was weaving in and out of the long lines. He was mouthing something to her but the noise prevented her from hearing what he said. "I can't give up my seat," she called to him.

"You're on standby and the ticket agent said you'd probably not have any trouble getting out by nightfall. They were very accommodating, hon. Said that usually students would give up their seat for a free ride. It's done all the time." He was standing in front of her. Liz's fingers drummed on her knee. He could tell how distraught she was. Suddenly he saw a familiar face standing behind Liz at the end of a long line. Where had he seen her? Then it came to him. It was the young girl who had practically run over them, hauling it on the gravel road outside of Fort Collins . Maybe that's why she was in such a hurry. Thought she might miss her flight.

"Liz, remember the girl who almost hit us on the road to Fort Collins? You know, the young blond girl in the pickup?"

"Yes, we thought that we probably should go see what she was running from."

"Don't hafta be concerned anymore. There she is behind you. Probably just afraid that she'd miss her flight."

Liz turned around and recognized the girl. She was taller than she had thought. But then she'd only seen her for a split second when she jumped out to open the gate.

They heard her name called over the intercom, and Cam

grabbed her arm. "Think that this is it, hon. Can't say that I'm happy, but it has to be. Don't look so sad. We'll be together soon. I know it."

But there was no way that they could foresee the circumstances of their next meeting.

Leaning her head against the headrest, Liz sighed. The young man beside her asked if she had a fear of flying. "Oh, no. It's just that I've had word that my husband had a stroke and I'm concerned. I had planned to leave Wyoming in a few days, anyway, but this came out of the blue."

"I'm sorry to hear it. Do hope that he'll be all right."

"He's very healthy. Did have a slight heart attack a few years back but recovered in record time, his doctor said."

The young man could see that she was in no mood to converse, so he pulled the magazine from the pocket of the seat in front of him and began to read. Liz closed her eyes, pushed the button to recline her seat and tried to make her mind go blank. But it would not. Try as she might, Avery invaded and filled the space.

When did it go wrong? Was it on his fortieth birthday? She knew that the office was planning a surprise party for him, so she and the kids postponed their party. Maybe that was when he got the "itch" as the guys called it. SHE didn't come on the scene until a few years later. That's when the conventions and away golf tournaments became the norm. Chuck had asked his dad to attend his boy scout jamboree with him, but Avery had declined because he had already paid for and arranged to attend a golf tournament in Innisbrook outside of Tarpon Springs. She remembered how disappointed Chuck had been. It didn't seem to matter to Avery that Chuck had made eagle scout and that there was to be a big celebration. He even had his picture in the paper and a wonderful write-up.

Was that when I knew that something was wrong, terribly wrong?

Laine bounded down the long stairs. "Mom, is this all right to wear? I could wear the blue denim skirt and plaid top. What do you think? Mom, are you listening?"

"The blue denim will be fine, hon. Chuck said that it was to be casual. I'm going to wear a skirt and blouse, too, and loafers. We'll be on our feet for a long time, I'm thinking. Why can't they ever have enough chairs at these things? Oh, Laine, go to the garage and get two folding chairs for Mom and Dad. I'll not have them standing throughout the entire ceremony. And put an extra one in the back of the station wagon for me. Why should I suffer?"

"About time you got here, John. You can help me with the chairs. Where on earth have you been?" Liz asked, perturbed.

"At practice! You know that I practice every Thursday. Have been doing it for four years now. What's the big deal, anyway?"

"The big deal is that Chuck is getting his eagle badge tonight, John. That's the big deal."

"Well, if it's such a big deal why isn't Dad here? Huh?"

"That's a good question. Why indeed? He obviously had made other plans that to him were more important than to attend his son's ceremony. I was told that it had something to do with our livelihood".

Everything went downhill after that. Oh, he played the game of perfect husband and father for all to see. But their old friends knew that all was not well. Liz began taking more art courses and engulfed herself in her work. It was not the solution, but the release did help. She had garnered quite a fine reputation, and Avery was very proud of her. He made it a point to attend all of her shows up and down the East Coast: Hilton Head, Charleston, Savannah, Amelia Island and all the major Florida cities. His handshaking, smiling, oozing his practiced charm for all Liz's admirers to see were evident. They appeared to be the perfect couple, prominent lawyer and acclaimed artist.

It was all on the surface, and as Liz rested she knew that she had wasted a large part of her life. I'll not allow this to go on. No matter what it costs. I'll not allow it to continue. His selfishness will be exposed. I now know who I am and what the rest of my life is going to allow. It will not allow one Avery Bellin to destroy this chance of happiness with Cam. She tingled when she remembered their intimacy in the front seat of his truck. It's a good thing we were on a non-trafficked road. Grief! What if a state trooper had come upon them! Whew! We would have had a lot of answering to do. She began to laugh out loud, and the young man beside her asked if she was OK. "I get ditsy when I fly. Sorry."

She smiled all the way to Atlanta.

TWENTY

Gate three was crowded. Liz had no idea which one of their children would be there when she saw Terry, Chuck's wife, struggling with Ashley, who thought that she needed to help stroll little Paulie. Terry called to her and Ashley immediately forgot about her little brother and dashed toward her grandma.

"Gramma, Gramma, Paulie's got a new tooth!"

Liz put down her makeup kit and picked her up. "Would you just look at this child! I bet you've grown an inch since I've seen you."

"More like two inches, Mama Liz."

"Where's Chuck?"

"He won't leave the hospital. Been there every day and night since Avery was found." Terry was biting her lower lip. That indicated to Liz that she was distraught. She never referred to Avery as Pop or Dad—just Avery. There was no love lost between them. Terry was a common-sense girl and took no guff from anyone, not even her father-in-law. She resented his attitude toward Chuck and had every reason to. Liz was very fond of her and approved of the job she was doing with the children.

"How is he?"

Terry was hesitant. "We really don't know any more than when we talked to you last. The doctor just says that we must be patient and pray. So, that's what we're doing."

"Has he shown any sign of..."

"Nothing. We're not allowed to see him, and that's the hardest thing for Chuck to accept."

"Which hospital?"

"St. Vincent's. Ashley, don't do that. I want Paulie to get some sleep before we meet Daddy."

"I told Jo and Ben that I'd call them when I got in, but think I'll wait 'til after I see Murph. No point in calling when I have nothing to report."

"I guess not. Mama Liz, wait here at the baggage console, and I'll go for the car. Would you mind if I left Paulie with you?"

"Of course not. You and Ashley take your time. I'm sure it'll be a while before the baggage gets here."

She watched Terry go out the automatic doors and head for the parking garage. She's the best thing to have ever happened to Chuck. Now, if Avery would just make peace with him his life would be in order. That, dear Lord, is what I pray for. Give them time, please. I can handle the rest. And, Laine, where are you when he needs you? Off healing the world's ills, saving the whales or seals or polar bears or whatever. Not making enough money to even fly home to be with your father, who dotes on you.

She glanced down at Paulie. He was sound asleep. He looks just like Terry. Funny how much Ashley looks like her dad and Paulie, the spit'n' image of Terry. She saw her hanging bag and rushed to grab it, checking the tag to make sure it was hers. Setting it beside the stroller, she waited for her large suitcase. I wonder where Cam is right this minute. Is he working on his piece, or is he already on his way back to Laramie? Think I'll call Bud and Eva when I get home and leave a message for him. They're aware that there is something going on between us. I feel so free this minute that if Avery were conscious, I'd have no trouble telling him that I want a divorce. Maybe I'm numb—in shock.

She could see her bag on the other side of the console. Waiting for it to make the bend, she realized how tired she was. Think I'll go to the hospital, then head for home and take a hot bath. Fill the tub up to the rim and soak forever. Don't think I've ever been so dry.

Terry and Ashley came in waving. "I'm parked right out front. You want me to help with the luggage?"

"No, I can manage. Finally got smart and got a large bag with wheels. Don't think Paulie will know if I drape this bag over his stroller. Look at him. He's with the angels, like my mother used to say."

"He's the best baby. Ashley was easy, too, but he seldom cries. Bothered me at first, but the pediatrician said that's his nature. Here we are. Wait and I'll open the trunk. Ashley, don't bother Mama Liz. She's tired from her long trip. Mama Liz, why don't you sit in the back with Paulie and try to take a little nap. It'll be a while before we get to the hospital."

"Think I'll take you up on that, Terry. I am tired."

She climbed in beside Paulie's car seat, put her head back and gazed at the clouds rolling in. "Think we're in for some rain, Terry. We certainly could use it in Wyoming."

"We saw a documentary on TV last night about the fires in Yellowstone. Was frightening."

Liz smoothed out her tan twill skirt. She liked it with the boots. Never thought I'd enjoy wearing boots, but they are as comfortable as Jo had said. Her eyes were tired. Felt like they were filled with beach sand, like when she'd take the kids to St. Augustine and they'd stay the entire day just lazing around Anastasia Beach. Built the most awesome sand castles imaginable. I don't remember that Avery ever went there with us. Probably didn't, but I can't think about that right now. Cam said that I had to have a positive attitude, and he's right.

"Mama Liz, we're here. Think you had a little nap. I'm glad."

"I didn't get much sleep last night and certainly couldn't on the plane. We were in Atlanta before I knew it, and it was rush, rush to get the flight here."

The hospital smell hit her when she opened the heavy doors. "Chuck will be in the waiting room, I'm sure. We can't go upstairs where Avery is because of the children, but you should go on up. Dr. Murphy said that he'd be there when you got in. He's a nice man. Chuck said that you've been friends for as long as he can remember."

"Yes, Murph was on the JU basketball team with Avery. He was on a full scholarship, also, and they went to Forest High all four years. He and Helena were in our wedding. We don't see them as much as we did. Used to play bridge together about once a week when the kids were small." I sound like I'm in a vacuum. Like I've said this same thing over and over. Probably because I'm so tired.

When Liz got to the nurse's station she identified herself, and the brunette nurse paged Murph. "Mrs. Bellin take a seat in the room across the hall. Dr. Murphy is with a patient but should not be long. Oh, Mr. Bellin's condition has not changed, and that's good. A really good sign."

She thanked her and entered the pale aqua room. She looked at the large seascape and recognized the artist. *He does nice work. Didn't know he'd gone to acrylics. I still prefer his watercolors.*

Picking up *Good Housekeeping* she leisurely turned the pages, not really allowing anything to register. Glancing at the young couple sitting opposite her, she smiled. They returned the smile. They were whispering, but Liz could hear the conversation. "If she has to be in here much longer, I'm not sure her insurance will cover it. What if Betty and Hugh won't help? We'll really be in a pickle."

At least that's not one of my worries. I can be thankful for that. Poor things. They're worried sick, and all I can think of is whether he is going to be a vegetable, and if he is, then there is no way that I can ask for a divorce. I know I shouldn't be thinking that. I know it's wrong. But is it? Oh, here's Murph.

"Liz." He hugged her hard. Pushing her away he said, "He's holding his own, but there is definitely some paralysis. How much we don't know. But he's stable."

"Is there any way that you can tell…"

"Here, young lady, you sit down. I know that this came as a shock, and Chuck said that you had a helluva time getting off that mountain. You must be exhausted."

"It's good to get down to sea level, I can tell you. I love my mountain retreat, but the dry air and altitude do bother me. But it's worth it, Murph. I've needed to escape so I can paint seriously for a long time, and I think that you and Helena both know it."

"We've suspected it, but, young lady," he hesitated before continuing, "we've got to get Avery on the mend. I'll be honest with you, though, I'm not sure how far we can get with him. He is healthy, so that's in his favor, but there doesn't seem to be much fight in him. Not like the Avery of old, is it?"

"What do you mean?"

"Well, by now we usually have an indication of what's going on. But there has been no change. He's the same as when we brought him in."

"Oh, Chuck, you sit here and I'll go check your pop. This is one special son you two have, Liz. Can't force him to go home, and think Terry is getting a little put out with him. Am I right, son?"

"I'll have to admit that you are, doc. Mom, you look all done in. Why don't you let Terry drive you home so you can get some rest?"

"Murph, I'll wait 'til you check Avery and think I'll do just what Chuck mentioned. I need to call Jo and Ben soon. Know they're probably down in the little town of Bondurant waiting for my call. We're finally getting phones put in and shouldn't have this problem next year." Murph patted her back and headed for the nurse's station.

Chuck took her hand, gently stroking it. "What's really going on, Mom? "

"When did you grow the mustache? I like it, but it does make you look older. Does Terry like it?"

"You're changing the subject. Yes, she does. What's going on, Mom? Dad has been so quiet since he got back. Is something wrong between you two?"

"Things have not been going well for a long time, honey. Now is not the time to discuss it, though." She realized that the couple across from them were taking in the conversation. She smiled at Chuck, pecked him on his cheek and said they'd talk about it later. "Has John been in today?"

"He came by for a short time earlier. Couldn't stay long because they had a dinner thing to go to. Seemed to think that it was important or something."

"He's a lot like your dad, isn't he?"

"Guess he is, but maybe that's not too bad."

"Heard from Laine?"

"She called last night very late. Think she didn't realize the time difference. Don't get too upset with her, Mom. She is broke. Had to put a new transmission in her car and…"

"Always making excuses for your little sister, aren't you? I bet if some of her friends called and asked her to join them in Acapulco, she'd manage to come up with the money.

"Don't think so. She really did sound shook. I'm on to her, and you know it. Yes, she's selfish and independent, but she does love Dad, and I know she'd be here if she could."

"I hope you're right, son. I've seen her so seldom these past five years that I don't really know her anymore."

Murph opened the door and immediately took Liz's hand. He looked at Chuck and said in a low voice, "We've done everything we can for him, and now it's up to him. I'm not saying that we should give up hope, for we shouldn't, but the longer he remains this way the less his chances are. There has been a lot of damage, and even if he rallies he'll probably be incapacitated for however long he lives."

"What are you saying?"

"I'm saying that we're going to move him from ICU to the coronary care unit. We're running at capacity right now, and we just don't have the room…"

"Will that hurt his chances?"

"Chuck, we're doing everything we can. That room is needed for someone who does have a better chance than Avery. I'm sorry, but that's how it is."

Liz grabbed Chuck's arm. "Don't son. You know that Murph has to think of everyone…"

"But Dad's his good friend and…"

"Get hold of yourself. That's no way to talk to Dr. Murphy and you know it. I know that you're distraught but that's…"

"I'm sorry, Dr. Murphy. I didn't mean it like it sounded. I'm just tired, I guess."

Murph patted his shoulder and said that he understood, that he'd probably feel the same if he were in Chuck's shoes. Liz felt relieved. *At least something is happening. It's this not knowing that is killing me. Why can't I feel upset like Chuck does? Why can't I feel angry that my husband is dying a young man? Why can't I feel hurt that he's dying without telling his son that he loves him? All I feel is relief that it's almost over. I must be evil. I must be evil…*

"Thanks for the ride, Terry. I'll call you tomorrow." Liz opened the double front doors and rushed to disarm the alarm. "What on earth! They forgot to even set it! Oh, they were probably in such a dither that Adelle didn't think of it." She draped the hanging bag over the old trunk that had been her mother's. Turning to switch on the living room light she noticed that Avery's blue suede jacket was hanging on the hall rack. "What is that thing doing there?" *Oh, he took it to Wyoming, and I guess he hung it there after he came back. Not like him. He's usually so fussy about his things. Maybe he wasn't feeling well out there and that is why he wanted to come home early and didn't want me to know. I mustn't start that. Always making excuses for his behavior, like Jo says.*

She heard the phone ring in the den. Rushing for it she almost tripped over the ottoman in front of his chair. Looking around she realized that things were not in their usual place. *Has someone been in here? Are they here now? I can't panic. I can't.* Taking a deep breath, afraid to look around, she quickly picked up the phone and softly said "Hello." No answer. *I can't panic. I'll call John. No, Chuck said that he and Debbie were going out for the evening.*

"Liz, Liz, is that you?"

"Oh, Cam. I just got in. Have been to the hospital." She continued searching the room. She was relieved to see that it was just the ottoman that had been moved and the magazines that were usually stacked on the coffee table in front of Avery's leather couch were beside the chair instead of in their usual place. *Of course! Adelle hasn't been back since Avery was taken to the hospital. I'll have to call her to let her know that I'm back.*

"Whew! I was afraid that you'd not be there. You don't sound right. Are you OK?"

"I'm fine now. It's just that I feel so far away…"

He laughed. "You are, my sweet. Any news that I need to know?"

"They've moved Avery from the ICU to the CCU. He hasn't shown any signs of anything, but Murph said that he's definitely paralyzed. They don't know to what extent."

"That doesn't sound too good. I've spent most of my day at the police station."

"What on earth for?"

"Went to Woerber's after I left you, and he had the TV on, and splashed across the screen was the news about Senator Billings Brooker's son Bill being murdered. And guess where it took place."

"I have no idea, hon."

"Remember when we were on the outskirts of Fort Collins and we pulled over to walk around, and that girl came out of the road like a wild woman and…"

"Yes, and we saw her again at the airport and…"

"Seems that the ranch, Blowing Wind, you know, where we stopped at the gravel road, was where she had been. The report said that his caretakers, some Mexican couple, had found him, and he'd been shot at close range. And guess what else? The Brookers are good friends of my folks, or they used to be. Mrs. Brooker was killed in a plane crash a few years back. I barely knew their son."

"Dear Lord in the morning! Do you think that the girl did it?"

"It's not what I think. It's what they now think since I went down to the station to give them our piece of information. They've contacted American Airlines and have by now got a positive identification on her. Remember she was in the line for the St. Louis flight?"

"I didn't notice. How do they know that she did it? Maybe someone else did."

"Well, they don't know for sure, but they've got an all-points-bulletin out on her, or something like that. Liz, I'm sure you'll be called to make an identification. Don't be surprised if you get a call real soon. This is hot news out here, and the senator is very powerful."

"But what can I tell them? I only saw her twice."

"I sketched a picture of her and I'd like to fax it to you for a comparison. Do you have a fax machine at your house?"

"Yes, Avery's had one for years. The number is the same as our phone number. Are you sure that they'll get in touch with me?"

"No doubt! This is a big case, my sweet. The Brooker and Billings families are the wealthiest ranchers in the entire state, and Billings, or Bill, was to inherit the whole shebang. Seems that the two daughters were disowned by their father for marrying husbands of their choice instead of men he approved. I want you to sketch a picture of the girl to compare with my impression. Think you can do that?"

"Cam, do you think that this can wait for a while? I'm dead

tired. It's very late and…" She heard the call waiting signal and said, "Hold on, hon, Someone is trying to call. Might be the hospital. Hello. Yes, this is Elizabeth Bellin…" That's when she saw the front door close gently.

TWENTY-ONE

When Liz saw the door close she almost panicked. Trying to keep calm, she rushed to the front door and secured the lock. Leaning against it, breathing hard, whimpering, she couldn't bear to peak out the side window. What if someone was there? Why didn't Adelle set the alarm? It's not like her to not do that. I should call the police..

"This is Mrs. Avery Bellin on River Road. Someone was just in my house and…"

"Mrs. Bellin, this is Archie Vallier. You know, Chuck's friend from high school What's wrong?"

"Oh, Archie. I'm so upset! Please get here as fast as you can…"

"I'm on my way. Hang in there!"

She realized that whoever had called her would try to call again. But as she sat beside the phone waiting for it to ring nothing happened. The next thing she heard was the doorbell ringing and Archie calling to her. "You OK? Did you see anyone? Here, let me help you. You need to sit down and get your breath." Archie turned to the other officer and said, "Olan, how about getting Mrs. Bellin a glass of water, and then we'll check the place."

But before Olan left he asked Liz if she thought that anyone was still in the house. She couldn't answer. Just sat shaking her head.

"Here, Mrs. Bellin. Now you take your time and we'll get everything down on this report. You're going to be fine, just fine."

She took the glass of water from Olan and slowly unfolded the story. Archie asked her to stop before she had finished. "I don't like the sound of this. Have you checked to see if anything is missing?"

"No, I was too frightened. I need to call John, Archie. I can't stay here tonight. I just can't."

"You go ahead and do that. Olan and I'll just have a look around." He called from the bedroom and asked Liz if she had been in the room since she had returned, and when she said that she

150

hadn't, he came out to the hallway. You'd better come in now, Mrs. Bellin. Think you're right about someone being here, all right. Left a mess of your things."

Liz was astounded at the mess. All her clothes had been dumped on the floor from her dresser, but nothing from Avery's had been touched. "I wonder if they went into the safe?" She left the men, went into the large walk-in closet and moved the plastic container of purses. The safe had not been tampered with. "I don't think anything is missing. What could they have been looking for in my desk and dresser? Nothing there but bills and letters and personal things. And look, the jewelry is still in these boxes. This doesn't make sense."

"Mrs. Bellin, you'd better get hold of John and have him come on over for you. We've got a lot of work ahead of us tonight. Got to dust for prints and get this place cordoned off."

Liz knew that John and Debbie would be asleep. After all, it was well past midnight. When she picked up the receiver there was no dial tone. "It was working just a few minutes ago. Archie, the phone is dead."

He looked at her, then at Olan and said he'd check it. Sure enough, there was no dial tone. "Best check this out. Be back in a minute." He cautiously walked toward the squad car and reached for the phone. "Archie Vallier here, Peggy. We need some back up over here at River Road. Yeh, the Bellin place. You know that big house on the corner of Kingsley. Something funny going on here. And Peggy, the phone is out. Please call John Bellin over in Mandarin and tell him that his mother would like for him to come get her. She's not about to stay here the rest of the night." He felt rather than saw that someone was there. I'll just wait 'til Peggy gets someone over here before checking that phone line. He was glad to get inside.

"Olan, I called Peggy, and she's getting the print man over here. Won't be long, Mrs. Bellin. I had Peggy call John from the station. I'm sure he'll be here in jig time." He wasn't sure of a thing, but he didn't want her to know it. Never saw such as this. Entered the house and had enough know-how to turn off the house alarm. Course, maybe the maid did forget to set it. She must have been real scared when Mr. Bellin had his stroke. Could have just forgotten.

John poured Liz a cup of coffee. "Now, let's go over it all again, Mom. I know that you didn't make a whole lot of sense last night, so try again, please."

"John, I'm not on the witness stand, so don't get smart with me. I'm just about over the precipice, as my father used to say."

"I don't mean to sound harsh. It's just that I got no sleep last night. Good thing I've got a light load today. Now, you told me about the phone call from your friend, what's-his-name, and that's when you noticed the front door closing. Did you actually see it close, or did you maybe imagine that you saw it close?"

"I saw it close, John. I hadn't been frightened until then, well, not really frightened. I was tired, yes, and worried about your dad and also a little put out that Adelle left the place ...well, not a mess, but she hadn't picked the place up, nor had she set the alarm. At least, that's what I thought then."

"Well, if Adelle is telling the truth then we know that the alarm had been set. The company is sending someone out this morning, Archie said. He thinks that whoever went in the house was a professional and knew exactly what he was looking for. Maybe you surprised him before he found it. Oh, by the way, that murder case is big news even down here. Senator Brooker was well liked and very influential, so I hear. But maybe none of this has anything to do with that case."

"When are they going to get our phone fixed? And where did they cut the line?"

"Archie didn't say, but cut it they or he or she did. Oh, he's alerted the Jacksonville police station where you are in case they need to get in touch with you. The girl has turned herself in and says that she didn't kill him, but then no one expected her to admit it."

"Maybe she didn't. And even if she did, why is someone checking on me? What could I possibly know? I saw her only twice, and Cam can identify her, too. Oh, John, I need to let him know where I am. Also, call Jo and Ben's house and tell Andrea and Carlos where I am. Have you heard from Chuck this morning?"

He put his coffee cup down very gingerly and took Liz's hand.

"Mom, we just got up, or rather you just got up. Do you think anyone else in his right mind will be up this early? Huh, do you?"

About then Liz heard Jonathan's scream, "Gramma! Gramma!" He was in her arms in no time. "Did you bring me a present? Huh, did you?"

"A typical kid of the 80s. Your gramma is tired, son. Here, let me pour you some Cheerios. You want them with milk or without?"

"Widout!"

"Hey, fellow, where are those magic words?"

"Please, please and another please."

Liz hadn't laughed in several days and it felt good. *I hope it's not my last laugh today. I could use some laughter right now. I bet Cam has been trying to get in touch with me.*

The phone rang and John reached for it. "John Bellin here. Oh, hi, Chuck. We just got up. Or rather, Mom just got up. No, I haven't had a chance to get any sleep. No, you go on over to the hospital and alert Dr. Murph that Mom's here. No need calling the house. Phone's probably not fixed yet. Police everywhere."

"Tell him that Archie Vallier was there as soon as I called the police station. Such a nice young man. Always did like Archie."

"Chuck, Mom said that Archie answered her call."

"Tell him that…"

"Here, Mom, you tell him yourself. I've got to shave and get dressed. Debbie has a hair appointment this morning, and I'll drop Jon off at daycare on my way to town. You gonna be all right?"

She sighed and thought, *just like your dad, John.* "I'll have Chuck or Terry take me to the hospital. When can I go home for my car? I'll be lost without it."

"I don't want you to go near that house until the police have come up with something. I called Steve Hargrove. Now, don't give me that look! He's not just one of dad's partners but a good friend as well. He feels that we probably should get in touch with the FBI."

"What on earth for?"

"Don't know for sure if the fact that the girl left the state makes it a federal case, but won't take long to find out. Steve is a good friend of the SAC of the Jacksonville office. Mom, it'll be OK. Believe me."

"Seems to me that this is getting very involved. All I did was witness that she was there at the right time and driving like a bat outta…"

"That's the point. You also saw her in line for a flight out of the state."

"Well, son, if she says that he was alive when she left him …"

"You just said it. Why was she hauling it outta there without even seeing you guys? Huh? Don't you see? You and what's-his-face saw how upset she was, and if he had been alive when she last saw him, why was she so upset? Huh?"

"Spoken just like your father, John. And his name is Cam. You're a good lawyer, son."

"I try to be, Mom. I try to be. Now, I have to leave. Hey, Jon, you ready? Debbie?"

When Chuck picked Liz up to take her to the hospital, she still had not been able to get in touch with Cam. *I hope he's not panicking. Who should I call? Oh, I'll call Eva and Bud at the Smilin' S. He always checks in there when he returns. Or maybe I'll call Louise at the post office.*

She and Chuck caught Murph after he had finished his early morning rounds. "He's rallying somewhat, Liz, but don't get your hopes up yet. Chuck, go on to work, son. We'll call you if anything happens. Now, I mean it. This probably will be a drawn out affair."

"Chuck, I'll be fine. Debbie said that she'd swing by here on her way back from the hairdresser's. You need to get back to work. Get your mind off all this."

"Mom, if he comes to, please call me. I'd like to be here."

She kissed his cheek, hugged him hard and said, "You're the best thing that ever happened to Avery Bellin, and I believe that he now knows it. Now, I mean it. I've read that just because a person is comatose it doesn't mean that they don't know what's going on. Your dad does, honey. I know it in my heart. He knows that you're keeping vigil." A tear seeped out, and Chuck didn't try to brush it away.

Liz spent the afternoon sleeping. Debbie had insisted on her taking a sleeping pill. When she finally awakened it was late afternoon. The guest room was dark. Liz opened the sheers, and when she saw the St. Johns realized where she was. *Gracious, I'm groggy. The river looks so different from this side. Was there ever a more magnificent river? I almost wish that we'd built on this side so we could enjoy the sunsets. Everything within sight is rosy and purple. I need to paint more sunsets. I miss our cabbage palms out west and our spectacular live oak trees with the Spanish moss flowing in the gentle river breeze. I know that they have palms in other states, but when I see them they spell Florida to me. I hope Cam can learn to love Florida like I do. I'm sure that I couldn't live out west all the time.* She heard a rap on the door. When she answered it John was there. "Mom, I hope you approve of what I've done. As I said, I called Steve at Dad's office, and he went to see the SAC at the FBI. Don't remember what his name is. Anyway, Steve told him what had happened to you and what your small part in this murder was and..."

"I really don't understand, John. Do you think that I'm in some sort of danger?"

"I wanted to make sure that you're not, Mom. I also called Sloan, who is one of the best private detectives in the business, to check on a few things that I was concerned about."

"What on earth are you saying?"

"Didn't take him long to get info on the senator and his son. Was a lot of gossip about eight years ago concerning the son and his ex-wife's divorce. Just about did the senator in, according to what Sloan found out. Don't look like that. It's a public record. Just took a couple phone calls and, as they say, the rest is history.

"Seems that there was a lot of partying, boozing, other women and you name it. His ex accused him of it all. Got a big chunk of money and custody of their two children. The senator doted on them. Almost killed him. But Sloan said that Bill had kept a low profile ever since the divorce eight years ago. Mainly ran the ranch and did a lot of charitable things. Sponsored a big rodeo with proceeds going to one of the kids homes, etc. Did an about-face."

Liz was having trouble taking it all in. *I wonder why Cam hadn't mentioned any of this? But then he didn't have time on the phone. At least, I hope that's why. I need to call Jo.*

TWENTY-TWO

The yellow vacancy sign blinked in front of the Smilin' S Motel in Bondurant. Eva and Bud had just got off the phone with Liz Bellin and sat looking at each other. Bud was the first to speak. "We don't want to get into this mess, honey. A murder could get real sticky, and I imagine that the senator has important people in high places. He certainly does in Colorado and, I imagine, in Washington."

"She sounded so frightened. When is Cam returning from Laramie, do you know?"

"Riley dropped by yesterday while you were doing the sheets, and even he didn't know. Did say that Robert had told them to keep their mouths shut about Cam and Liz being witnesses. Nobody's business according to Robert. I'm thinking that he knows more than he's letting on. He and Sarah have been friends with the Brookers for years. Went to university with them, I think."

Eva put down her knitting, rolled the loose yarn around the skein and put it back in the bag.

"I wish that Jo and Ben hadn't decided to leave early. Oh, I know what you're going to say, that she's their best friend, but honey, she needs to rely on her own judgement. Reminds me of your sister Audrey and her best friend over in Rock Springs. Now, she got herself in a real mess trying to help what's her name."

"You're right on that one. Thought that ex-husband of hers was going to get real nasty when he found out that Audrey had given her advice. Don't think that she'll ever get over him threatening to kill her. Beecher said that the man was serious."

"How many years did he get? Bet he's about ready to get out. Know that Audrey is probably ready to move from there."

"Is that a truck I heard? Might be Cam. Sure hope so."

Jamie Stroebel stuck his head inside the front door. "You guys seen Manny?"

"Well, no we haven't. Anything wrong?"

"Maybe yes and maybe no. Miss Irma thinks he's been poking his nose around Charlie's Mountain and she's laying for him with that shotgun she's got. He's not long for this world if she aims. Ever see that old woman shoot a gun?"

"Nope, and I don't want to either."

"She gave me some pointers the other day. Never saw the likes of her. Been downright peculiar ever since the Daultons left. You'd have thought that they were getting even with her for something the way she's carrying on. Told Doc about it and he said people like Miss Irma get that way when they've had a bad shock. You know like her daughter getting killed and then Charlie dying and…"

"Hell, Jamie, that happens to folks all the time and they don't get peculiar."

"Not according to Doc. Said as how folks who are real creative like Miss Irma react different. Well, if you see Manny, better tell him that he'd best not be going up to Charlie's Mountain. Think he was just waiting for the Daultons to leave before poking around. He's in for a peck of trouble."

"Well, none of us know what trouble is. You read the *Jackson Hole News* this morning? Now that's trouble. Fellow over in the Wolf Creek area of Yellowstone said that the whole month of August had been the scariest time in his life. Said that when they first built their cabin grizzlies gnawed at his front door and snowstorms have left him and his family cut off from the outside world for days at a time. But he ain't ever seen the likes of those fires just one ridge away from him. Managed to save his place using some kinda makeshift sprinkler system.

"Now, if Miss Irma Barksdale had that to worry about, then I'd feel sorry for her, but a crazy Manny roaming around don't do all her worrying justice. Course those fires ain't that far away, so maybe she'll have a legitimate reason for her stewing."

"Don't know why Jo Daulton has taken such an interest in her, do you Jamie?"

"Yessum, I do. She's got a good heart and loves the out of doors just like Miss Irma. She's just about the nicest lady I ever met. Her husband is nice too."

"I ain't saying that they aren't nice. What I'm trying to say is why all this interest in Irma? Is it because she's famous? Or is it because of something else?"

"What you trying to say, Miss Eva? I'm not following your thinking."

"I'm just perplexed about all that attention she's giving Irma; that's all, Jamie. I ain't implying anything is really wrong with it, but a body does wonder."

"Well, reckon you're the only one who's wondering. Everyone else I know thinks that it's real nice for Mrs. Daulton to try to help the old soul get over her hurt. That's what I'm thinking."

"Don't be getting on Eva now, Jamie. She's just voicing her opinion, that's all."

"That's right, honey. You know how we Westerners are, Jamie. Just gotta state our opinion." Eva and Bud laughed, but Jamie did not. He tipped his hat and left.

Ben and Jo had decided to leave after Liz had called them and left a message at the Triangle F Restaurant and pool hall. She knew that Ben filled his truck with gas there every Friday and that Monta was very reliable about getting messages to them. When Ben read the note he knew that they had to leave. There was no way that Jo would be able to stay with Liz in that condition.

"I wish we could fly back, hon, but then what would we do with Maggie?"

"We could ask Irma to look after her. No, that's not such a hot idea. We were returning next week anyway. So we leave a little early. I've done almost everything I wanted to do this year. Glad we got the holding tank in though. From the looks of things in Yellowstone we might need it before we return next year."

Jo was biting her lower lip. "What'll I tell Irma? I mean I've finally broken through. Could you believe it when she came down the day Liz left and asked me if I wanted to walk? I almost dropped right on the spot."

"It was a surprise. But I can't believe that she didn't seem to want to talk. Didn't say more than a few words, you said, and most of those were directed at Maggie."

"She just seemed to want someone with her. I didn't feel like talking either. Think she knew how much I missed Liz. We did go by Liz's cabin, and she said Liz had made a good choice for her studio. That's about all."

"Why don't you tell her the truth? Liz needs someone with her right now, and it's not just because of Avery's condition. She probably doesn't know about her and Cam being important witnesses in the Brooker case. If she knew that she'd understand how important it is for you to get back to Jacksonville."

Jo left her rocker and bent down to kiss the top of Ben's head. "You're a smart man, Ben Daulton. She might even know Billings Brooker. Robert Cameron and his wife are good friends of his, Doc said. Said that Sarah Cameron is taking Bill's death real hard. Seems that he was about Cam's age; however, he and Cam barely knew each other."

"Honey, think I'll leave a lot of my clothes out here this year. Most of them are too western for Florida. That'll save time. Will you have Billy close up the house? I mean drain the pipes and all that?"

"He's already been contacted. Stopped by on the way back from Triangle F yesterday and told him that it looked like we'd be leaving early."

Jo went to the mud room and started to open the closet door when she saw Irma sitting on the porch on the park bench against the wall. Opening the front door cautiously Jo started to ask why she was there when Irma interrupted."

"Leaving early I've been told. Wanted to tell Maggie goodbye." She was sullen, and Jo was concerned about how to answer her.

"Yes, I was going to tell you about it before we left. I'm real concerned about Liz. Not about her husband's condition but about a new development…"

"Gotta have something to do with that Cam…"

"Not exactly. On their way to the airport in Denver it seems they were witnesses to a murder suspect…"

"That's the Brooker case I heard about."

So she does listen to the radio. "Yes, they saw a young woman rushing out of the Blowing Wind Ranch and again at the airport, and Cam reported it. His folks are good friends of the Senator and

159

his late wife."

"Knew that. Charlie mounted a lot of Billing's African kills. Got to know the stuffed shirt a little. Did like his wife though. She could have done better."

"Anyway, Irma, Liz has had a scare about all this. Seems that someone's been snooping in her house, going through her things, and she thinks that it has something to do with the fact that she's going to be called to testify about...what's her name?"

"Robin Davenport of the St. Louis Davenports, the paper said. Seems that she was sweet on Bill."

"I feel so far away from her out here. If we had a phone it'd not be so bad. I can hardly wait 'til next year. Ben said they've already begun laying the lines on Rim Road."

"Don't care! Next thing you know they'll let in all the riff raff like they did in Jackson. Won't be the West anymore." She reached down and rubbed Maggie's neck and left without saying goodbye. Hopped on her four wheeler and spewed gravel all the way up the mountain.

"Irma," Jo called, but she didn't stop. "You forgot to close your gate, and I bet that Manny will..." I mustn't think that. Jo went over to the gate and secured the new padlock. Tears were streaming down her face. I thought that this would be a true haven. Have more excitement here than in Jacksonville.

TWENTY-THREE

It took Ben and Jo four hard days of traveling to get to Jacksonville. They felt that they had to stop often to let Maggie out to run. She wasn't used to a confined area even in Jacksonville. Carlos loved to run her around the neighborhood, and she was out often in Wyoming. Jo had been so quiet that Ben was concerned about her.

They had stopped at a rest area off of US 75 just north of the Florida line and Jo had bought a newspaper. Ben heard her gasp. "What's wrong?"

"Robin Davenport has confessed that the murder of Billings (Bill) Brooker was an accident. Look, right here on the front page of the *Times Union*. She said that they had been having an argument, that he had been drinking all morning and that—listen to this—'He was threatening to kill Joe Burgess, his horse trainer, and when I tried to keep him from leaving the room we struggled and the gun went off.' It goes on to say that Senator Brooker is not buying that account, that his son had been on the wagon for years, and the entire story was a fabrication to save her skin."

"Liz and Cam will have to testify anyway, honey. They're the only witnesses to what her condition was when they saw her driving like a bat…"

"She was upset! Why wouldn't she be? There's no way they can tell if it was an accident. How would you feel if it were Ruthann? Would you believe her or some big shot senator?"

"Hey! Slow down! I'm not saying that she killed him purposely."

"Then what are you saying?"

"They'll be able to tell from the autopsy about his being drunk, and I'm not saying anything but that Cam and Liz will have to testify for the prosecution. Don't know how much weight it'll carry since Cam's family is friends with the Brookers. That's up to the defendants. I'm not a lawyer and don't know all the ins and outs of a case like this, but you can bet that it'll be a sticky one."

Jo pursed her lips and said, "I just don't want Liz to be hurt. She's been through enough and finally has met someone who appreciates her and…"

"Honey, it'll all work out. I don't think that they'll go into her personal life. At least I hope they won't."

Andrea and Carlos greeted them at the front door. Maggie wiggled all over, constrained by Carlos telling her to stay down. He had trained her well but she couldn't control herself. "Take her out for a run, Carlos. She's really missed you." Jo said.

"Missy, you had a call from John Bellin to tell you that his mother is staying at his house. He left his number. He said he'd like you to call him as soon as you got in."

"Go on in, hon. I'll start unloading, and Carlos can help me after Maggie has her run. Andrea, have we had any rain? The hibiscus looks droopy."

"They've rationed the water, Mister Daulton. We do the best we can, but it hasn't rained a drop for over two weeks. The TV said that we'll be put on an every-other-day schedule and can't water for more than twenty minutes at a time. Carlos is real worried. You can see how brown the lawn has gotten."

"Yes, I noticed that when we drove up. But it's nothing like we're experiencing in Wyoming. Has the office called me?"

"No sir, but Mister Chet has. Said for you to call him at the office when you get in."

"He'll just want to chat. I'll get settled and let Jo get her calling done. Have the kids called? Jo has stewed for the entire four days about being out of touch with them."

"Miss Ruthann called last night. She was surprised that you hadn't arrived. And Mister Robbie called and let Casey talk to Carlos. Guess what she asked him?"

"That one probably asked him to make sure that the pool was cleaned so she could go swimming."

"That's exactly what she did say. Carlos got a laugh out of that one." She continued laughing as she went to the foyer to open the hall closet for Ben to store the binoculars and maps. "Saw a lot of antelope out of Pinedale and a couple coyotes on the way to Laramie but not much else, I'm afraid. They're really hurting with this drought."

"Debbie, this is Jo Daulton. Yes, we just got in. Ben got an extra week off so we could stay in Wyoming a little longer, but you know how I feel about Liz. Yes, we love it out there, but it's good to be home.

"Is Liz there?

Pause...

"I thought she might be. Any news on Avery?"

Pause...

"Well, a little progress is better than none. How are the kids? I bet Jonathan has really grown since we saw him last. How old is Amanda now? Can't believe how fast they grow up, can you? I'll call John at his office, if that's all right. He had left a message to have me call him."

Pause...

"Yes, I'll not be a stranger. I'll tell Ben what you said. Bye for now."

Jo called to Ben, "Debbie says to say hi. Liz is at the hospital, and she also said that Avery has made some progress. I'm going to call John at his office, and then I'd like a tall drink out beside the pool. How does that sound to you?"

"That's a winner. Andrea said that she made a crab salad and there was leftover baked chicken if you're real hungry."

"I'll have the salad, but first want to get this call over with. I'm not looking forward to it."

"What'd you say, hon? Crab or chicken?"

One of the things I like about Wyoming is that the house is so much smaller and I don't have to yell to be heard. "I said crab and put in your hearing aid. I'll declare I'll be worn out by nightfall if I have to yell any more. Did you hear that, Ben?"

Ben went to the great room and was grinning. "You know what Andrea said?"

"No, I don't but I bet I can guess."

"She said that it's like old times around here and she likes it. She missed us. Oh, the Sinclairs down the street had their house broken into. Took all Mae's jewelry except what was in the safe. You'd better put yours up, hon. Don't want your mother's stuff taken."

Jo sighed. "Don't know what this world's coming to. Hurry with that drink."

"John Bellin, please. This is Jo Daulton returning his call." She waited forever, it seemed. "Aunt Jo. When did you get in?"

"Just got here, and Andrea said that you wanted me to call. Talked to Debbie and she said that Avery had made some progress. Well, some is better than none, John."

"Don't know how much you know about that Brooker murder, Aunt Jo, but Mom is real worried about having to testify. Is there anything that you can tell me?"

"Heavens no. The only thing I know is what Liz said the one and only time we talked."

"I was hoping that you could enlighten me. She seems to be holding something back."

"Your mother has a personal life, John. Now, I realize that our children don't ever consider that, but it's true, nevertheless. I'm sure that she's not keeping anything from you that is pertinent to the case. What she told you is all she wants you to know for now. It should not be a shock to you to know that she and Avery have not been on the best of terms for a very long time. Or do you kids wear blinders?"

Pause…

"Yes, I know I'm out of sorts and tired, but you should all take your heads out of the sand, as the saying goes. Your mother is my best friend, and her feelings are very important to me. If she wants you and Chuck and Laine to understand her problems, I'm sure that she can now talk about them. Yes, I'm a little put out."

"What's that all about, hon?" Ben called from the den.

"I've had about all I can stand dealing with children whose instincts are nil. I bet Chuck knows that something's wrong with his parents' relationship. But John? Not a clue. He's just like Avery."

"Let's sit down, sip these tall ones and change the subject."

"You're on, Sir Ben. Boy, are you ever!" They went to the patio arm in arm.

Manny could smell the acrid smoke filtering down from the Yellowstone fires. "If'n I set this whole place afire no one would even know. Burn the ugly old woman up!" He sat in the front of his pickup, grinning, and popped another beer out of the cooler. Hope I see that Jamie come around Rim. Think I'll have a little fun with him. Smart ass kid. Thinks he can steal my job away from me and get by with it. He ain't ever seen the day that he can do my job. He scratched his privates and thought, 'bout time you got to go to Pinedale for some fixin, huh? Bet if I got all dressed up and went for a visit with Daphne's gals you'd be perking up. But need some money. Son-of-a-bitch! Took my job and I ain't even got enough money to visit Daphne's. Son-of-a-bitch!

He saw a cloud of dust approaching. Bet that's Jamie. I just bet. But when the truck rounded Elk he could see that it was the water conditioner man from Jackson. "I'll just wait a little longer. Ain't got no place to go and no money to spend if I had. But I'll get you, Jamie Stroebel!" he yelled.

Betty and Jack Sheffield had almost finished packing for their return to Florida. They'd have Jerry and Gordon come in and winterize their place after they left. Draining all the pipes, pouring anti-freeze down the drains and covering all the high windows with heavy canvas took almost an entire day. Betty had not known to do that their first year out but found out on their return that the winter sun was lethal. Her favorite painting in the living room had been bleached almost white, and the candles likewise. Irma had told her, "You gotta know how to live out here, Betty. This isn't your gentle Florida, tropical sun. This sun bounces off the snow and will almost blind a person." She learned her lesson and paid dearly for it. That painting was a Dockham and was valued at over a thousand dollars. She did save the frame and gave it to the church for its August bazaar. It brought in fifty dollars for the church.

"I want to take this up to the outhouse and leave it for Irma, Jack. Now, don't say that she'll probably throw it out. I don't care if she does. I just want her to know that we're leaving and we're thinking of her."

"What is it?"

"These are our old bridge scores that I'd kept for all these years. You know, we kept a running score of all our games and how she and Charlie got such a kick out of 'em. Think she'll get a chuckle out of the comments he'd jot down when they'd win a rubber or..."

"Betty, just because Jo got through to her, don't you start. I mean it! She's got a fragile mind. We don't have a right to tamper with it. Jo should have just left well enough alone."

"I almost never disagree with you, but on this one I do. She truly seems to have changed. Jo says that she is just lonely. It's not going to hurt."

Betty put the small box on the back of her four wheeler and rode down the long hill to Elk. When she got there she saw the dust rise from an approaching vehicle. "Who can that be? Doesn't look like Jerry." She stopped to let the truck pass. The young man waved and stopped. It was Riley. What on earth is he doing out here? He should be back east at school.

"Hi, Mrs. Sheffield. Just took some wood to the Daulton's basement. Dad had some extra left from that mountain man he's working on. Mr. Daulton likes working with his hands and asked dad for any extra burl he had. "

"Why aren't you back in school, Riley?"

"My school doesn't start 'til next week. We're always later than public schools. I was hoping for an early snowfall, but doesn't look like we're gonna get one. Wanted to go skiing with Dad."

"I imagine that your dad has more on his mind than snow and mountain men, Riley. Heard when he and Liz are going to be called to testify?"

"He said probably not until next month or so. They haven't even selected the jury yet. He thinks that it'll be a long drawn affair. You see that Manny hanging around? Dad and I saw him up in the pines on Rim. He tried to scrunch down in his truck, but we knew it was him. He could be dangerous, Dad says. You and the doc should watch out."

"Doc's never trusted him. I'll tell him."

When Betty stopped the four wheeler, she could tell that someone was amongst the trees. She didn't know how she knew, but she did. "Irma, I'm leaving these old bridge scores from when you and Charlie and Doc and I used to play. Thought you would get a kick out of them. We're leaving tomorrow. If you need us, have Jamie get in touch with us. Now, I mean it. We love you and miss our time together. I hope you have a good winter." She opened the outhouse door and before she turned the wooden latch, Irma appeared.

"I'll take that, Betty. No need to sneak around my place."

"I'm not sneaking around. And since you're here, you better be on the lookout for Manny. Riley Cameron said that he and Cam saw him up on Rim Road and he tried to hide in that old truck of his. He's not to be trusted, Irma. I worry about you up on that mountain all by yourself."

"What makes you think that I'm all by myself? Ain't you heard? I've got myself a house full of whores up there working for me, making me rich. I'm giving that Daphne some competition."

She actually cackled, she told Jack later. "And Jack, she pulled a rifle out from behind that old skirt she was wearing and held it up above her head and shot it right toward the sky and yelled, 'That oughta get Manny off my mountain, Betty. He might be dumb but he ain't quite crazy yet. He knows I'm layin' for him.' Then she said, 'He ain't nothing but a cur dog, anyhow.'"

TWENTY-FOUR

Life in Jacksonville resumed its tedious pace. The only excitement came when the Daultons heard from Bondurant. Billy and Fern Parker would write once in a while or call, and Jo and Ben did get the *Community Club Newsletter.* That kept them up on the Hoback's news. Billy said that Manny had caused such a commotion one night in Pinedale that he'd ended up in the clinker again. Never did find out who paid his bail, but he suspected that Irma had. She had told Jamie that without Manny sneaking around the mountain she'd almost been bored, something that she had never believed in.

Liz had moved back into her house. They still did not know who was responsible for the alarm and phone's being disconnected, but since Robin Davenport had confessed that the murder was an accident and she was in custody of her family while awaiting the trial, nothing else had happened to Liz or Cam. His place in the Hoback Ranches had been ransacked while he had been in Denver and Laramie, but nothing had happened since Robin's confession. They all surmised that the Davenport family had hired someone either to frighten the two witnesses or to try to get some dirt in order to intimidate them, and when that didn't work the contract was cancelled.

"Jo, I'm going to the hospital. Chuck and John will be there to help me get Avery's insurance papers filled out and make the final arrangements. I have never seen as much paperwork in my life. How do older people manage? No wonder there are those shysters out there ready to con the poor old souls. We're lucky to have our boys around to help. I'll call you later."

Avery had recovered enough to be transferred to a nursing home with care around the clock. Liz had managed to get him in the one in Orange Park so she wouldn't have to drive the heavily trafficked road into Jacksonville. He recognized the family and made guttural sounds but had not recovered the use of his left side. Liz could not believe how old he looked. But Chuck didn't or couldn't see it. "Boy, he's really coming along, isn't he, Mom? I can see improvement every day." She answered in the affirmative but did not agree. All she really wanted was to be in Wyoming with Cam.

After Jo and Ben had returned to Jacksonville and Jo had the little talk with John, Liz had felt free to speak to the boys about her feelings about Cam. It hadn't been as hard as she had thought it would be. It was in the hospital. Murph had been to see them with the prognosis, and it was not good. He could live for years in that condition, but a chance for recovery, even partial, was remote. They were all so quiet. They just listened. Finally, Liz spoke. "Boys, it's time we had a talk. I'll buy the coffee." They had gone downstairs to the coffee shop, and Liz began. She felt confident, assured. She didn't feel it necessary to tell them of their father's infidelity, but she indicated it. She also said that she should have ended the marriage long before then, but because she had always felt that marriage was forever, she hadn't. But she had been wrong.

"There are times when you have to take a stand, be brave and know that you, too, are important. My self-confidence had been shattered. I had no one to turn to except Jo. I couldn't go to our minister because he was Avery's minister, too, and Avery was on the vestry. I had become an Episcopalian because your dad decided that that was the church that he felt was best for us. In other words, I was a sheep just tagging along. What Avery said, I did. As you both know, I had been brought up Methodist and had always been uncomfortable in the Episcopal Church. But I played the good little wife, whatever that is."

John sat with his head bowed. Chuck sipped his coffee and finally said, "I knew that things weren't right, Mom. I don't mean that I ever heard you fight or anything like that, but there seemed to be a lot of tension..."

"I never noticed any tension!" John interrupted. "I always thought that you and Dad had a wonderful marriage. I even said that to Debbie, I don't know how many times. You deceived us, Mom." He said it barely above a whisper.

Chuck lowered his voice when he responded, "That's not quite right, John. It was Dad who deceived, not Mom. She's been carrying this burden for a long time. I think you need to apologize, big brother."

"Don't! I'll not have this. We are still a family and need to stick together. That's what I've been here for, for our togetherness. That's so important to me, John.

"I've met someone who is a wonderful person, and he loves me for who I am. He appreciates my work and my predicament. He understands that people change. And sometimes the change hurts those we love. He is divorced and has a seventeen-year-old-son. He married late and is a sculptor. Yes, John, he's the man who drove me to the Denver airport. He is respected as a sculptor, a son, a father and is very important to me. I love him very much, but..."

"That's enough!" John shouted. There were only two other people in the coffee shop besides the clean-up girl, but they all stared.

Chuck got up and said softly and slowly, "That's about enough, John. We're in a public place, and if that doesn't bother you, it does me. Now, calm down. This is your mother you're yelling at."

John rose and was obviously shaken. Liz then realized what a toll Avery's illness had taken on him. He had difficulty expressing it. Unlike Chuck, John kept his feelings inside. *I wonder if Avery has been doing this for all these years? I can't think this. I must finish what I started.*

"Please sit down. Please. This is very important to me. I want you to know that as long as your father is alive I'll not divorce him. Cam understands my predicament and agrees that for my sake we'll wait to...we'll wait to build our marriage. That is what we both want, boys. You'll like him and I hope that you learn to respect him. He is an honest man, a man who does not judge others..."

"Is he a man who covets another man's wife? Is he?" John almost shouted.

That was more than Chuck could take. The couple across from them had left so Chuck felt that now was the time. "All right, big brother, we're not going to embarrass our mother with a fist fight, though I would enjoy it immensely. It is time, Mr. Lawyer, to have a real man to man talk. Our mother has…"

"That's enough! I'll not have this! Your father is in no condition to be of any help, but if he were he'd not like this either. I shall remain in Orange Park for as long as your father needs me, but then I'll join Cam in Wyoming. And for your information, if I decide to visit him from time to time, I'll do so. He is very important to me, and I intend to make darned sure that he is not neglected like I have been for fifteen years. That is all I'm going to say on the subject, and you two can go to the parking lot to resume your…your…"

Liz turned, said goodbye and left.

It was the spring of '89 when Liz and Cam were finally called to testify in the Brooker and Davenport case. They had not seen each other since Denver but had called and written often. She was thinner, and Cam could tell that the strain had taken its toll. He met her at the Denver airport, and without even speaking they were in each other's arms. When the photographers spotted them they broke apart and patted each other's backs in a friendly gesture. All they were allowed to say was, "No comment." They were relieved about that. The photographers and reporters followed them closely to Cam's truck, but he managed to lose them before arriving at Woerber's.

There was not much conversation while Cam executed the back roads and side roads. When he had to stop for a traffic light, he just took her hand and held it tightly, squeezing it often. But the smiles were broad. Finally, Liz spoke. "This is going to be difficult for us. Anyone who sees us will certainly know that there is more than a friendship between us. We'll have to be careful."

"Your boys know about us, but did you tell Laine?"

"I haven't, but she plans to come home for two weeks this summer, and I'll tell her then. But I think she knows or has known for a long time that her dad and I haven't gotten along. I think it's called woman's intuition or something like that." She laughed when she said it.

"Maybe it's called awareness. A lot of men are tuned in, too. Remember, Liz, that I instinctively knew that you did not love Avery. It didn't take an atom bomb falling on me to see it."

"Now, Cam, I hope it wasn't that obvious. When I first saw you I was miffed by Avery's behavior with one cute twenty-year-old stewardess. It had nothing to do with love. I was just disgusted, that's all."

"You might be right, hon, but when I saw you later—and I'm not referring to the nude scene—it was obvious to me that you were looking."

"Cam, that's just not true. You ask Jo. You're the first and only man I've even looked at since I met Avery! And I mean met him—not fell in love with him. You see my sweet, I had those same feelings for him that I felt for you. That's why I'm having a difficult time handling this. I need to be sure that this is not just infatuation."

"Just how difficult is it? Should I be worried?"

She grabbed his arm. "You indeed should not. Its just that if I felt that way about him and my feelings changed, maybe they'll change for you, in time, that is."

"I'll not do to you what he did, Liz. You can go to the bank with that one. Even when Caroline and I were having our problems I didn't have an affair with anyone. Oh, I could have. Those darlings at the university were ripe, and they let me know it. And it wasn't for a good grade, either."

"I just bet they couldn't keep their hands off you. You are a handsome devil, sir."

They arrived at Woerber's home, and Liz was immediately taken with it. It was part log but mostly glass, contemporary. "This could be a Frank Lloyd Wright! Look at how he's worked the landscape right into the foyer. I'm anxious to meet him."

It didn't take Woerber long to make his appearance. Liz was not prepared for it. Cam had not mentioned that he was a dwarf, a Toulouse Lautrec type. But when he looked up at her, his eyes said so much. There was so much wonder in them and warmth. She could understand why Cam had not even thought to mention his condition to her. When you saw his beauty of spirit you saw nothing else.

He took her by the elbow and spoke in a heavy accent. "As long as I haff been in dis country you'd tink dat I vould learn to speak American, huh? If you do not understand me, just ask me to repeat vat I say. My students learned dat early. Huh, my friend?"

Cam nodded with a broad smile. "But what a teacher! If you had even the smallest amount of talent, Woerber found it and made you work. And I mean work."

"Dat's vat you vere der for, huh?"

"Woerber, you'll probably have as much trouble with my southern accent as I have with your German one."

"Oh, my pretty one, yours I like. I tink you should be Cam's next model..."

"Hey, that's not what I had in mind. I want her for my wife. Then, perhaps, my model. But first things first. We've got to get you settled in. I talked Woerber into letting you sleep in the studio. I want you to have the experience of waking in the morning to the sunrise over the mountains. It's unbelievable. Maybe I can talk her into allowing me to be with her, what do you think?'

Woerber laughed along with them. "If I veren't so ugly, I'd beat you to it, Cam."

"Your beauty is within, Woerber. I wish more people had the beauty of spirit. The world would be better for it, wouldn't it, Liz?"

"You know how I feel about that. We need more of that going around."

TWENTY-FIVE

The futon bed in Woerber's studio was smaller than a regular double bed, but Liz and Cam didn't mind. She awakened. Smiling, she remembered the previous evening and night. Should I awaken him? No, I'll be quiet as a mouse and die a little as I remember. We were meant to be together. Dear Lord, I do so hope that this is not wrong in your eyes. You know how unhappy I have been and how hard I've tried to be a good wife to Avery. If you can find it in your heart to forgive me…

Woerber was a glorious cook. That's the only way to describe his dinner. GLORIOUS! They had sat out among the pine, fir and spruce trees in the heavily treed, rocky back yard on his stone patio that literally was one with the terrain. It was cool but not unbearable, and there was still plenty of snow on the mountains to add to the ambience. She had packed heavy sweaters, and Cam asked her if she'd like for him to get one of them, and she said yes. "And, Liz, Woerber wants to know if the lady from the South wants a mint julep?" Liz laughed and Cam said, "He is serious, Liz."

"Tell him that the lady from the South would enjoy a cold German beer, if the gentleman from Germany happens to have one?"

"He'll love that. He has a great sense of humor. I'm glad you two have hit it off. He's my best friend, you know."

"I gathered that there was a great bond between you, but if he has gone to a lot of trouble to get the fixings for a julep, then I'd love one. Anything would taste like ambrosia in this setting." She snuggled up in the heavy wooden chair. The cushions felt soft underneath her legs, and while she waited for Cam she began fantasizing about the night with her love. Her reverie was broken when she heard him return.

Putting the tray of drinks down on the table beside her he took her hand and said, "He has fixed a shank of lamb—I hope you like lamb—and those little red potatoes, browned and roasted. Then there's fresh asparagus with an unbelievable lemon and herb sauce, his home grown herbs, I might add, and a fresh salad right out of his garden. Actually it's a greenhouse and..."

"Please, no more, my sweet. I've lost weight and I don't want to regain it in just one sitting." They laughed, then Cam grinned, reached down and stroked her breasts. "You've not lost too much. Methinks you're just right. And Woerber would be as disappointed as I if you do not allow me to share your bed tonight. He told me so. He can see how much we need to be together, my Liz."

She rose, held him tight and whispered, "I've dreamed of this first meeting, Cam, but I hadn't pictured such a beautiful setting. More like a hay field..."

"That, too, can be arranged. Just happen to know one not far from here if you'd rather go..."

"I was teasing. Right here will be perfect. Would it be rude to dine then excuse ourselves?"

"He'd encourage it, I'm sure."

But there was no rushing after dinner. Woerber took Liz on a tour of his home, and she was surprised that there were so few of his sculptures around. When she questioned him, he shrugged his heavy shoulders and said, "I do dem for udders and I paint for myself. I'm not good at abstract yet, but I work on it. Your Cam is de master of dose." Liz challenged Woerber to a game of cribbage, and Cam relaxed in the tan leather chair, well worn from years of use, and listened to the soft music and their bantering. Is this happiness false? Will it end tomorrow when we are called to testify? The attorney representing the Brookers thought that a simple questioning was all that was called for, but in a case this hot and with the hotshot lawyer the Davenports had hired from L.A. he couldn't be sure. He just hoped that they wouldn't get into his and Liz's personal life. They had not been assured that it wouldn't happen. "He'll try to discredit you anyway that he can," Chester had told them.

He was apparently dozing when he heard Liz comment, "Well, Professor, that's one skunk for me and you've got me down by two games. Heaven's, I hadn't realized how late it was. If the trial ends

175

early tomorrow, I'll challenge you to a rematch. Are you game? I haven't played cribbage in years. Avery and I used to play, but that was a long time..."

"About time that you allowed me to have some time with my lady love, Woerber. Who'd you fly all this way to see, anyway?" Liz gave him her Cheshire-cat grin and kissed Woeber's bulging forehead.

She soon joined Cam in the oversized chair, snuggled in and said teasingly, "Dear friend, I believe that he's jealous. Good!"

"Good, is it!" He began to tickle her unmercifully. "Stop that this minute, Cam! Woerber, make him stop! He knows I can't handle this..."

"Shhhh! You two go to your room and let an old man finish his chores. Now, I mean it. Go—go! The dishes won't wash demselves. Now, go—go!"

"Liz, the bathroom is free," Cam called. "Your towels are the cream ones with seashells. Woerber went out and bought them especially for you. Said that he didn't want you to miss your Florida beaches."

She peeked around the corner of the heavy pine door that joined the bath and dressing area and asked if he was decent?

"I sincerely hope not, my sweet."

"You're getting frisky with me, Lee Riley Cameron. I thought that you western men were slow and thorough..."

"Don't you believe it! Can be, yes, but when the occasion warrants, we can outdistance any thoroughbred you've ever known. Your cowboy awaits, my little filly." He twirled his mustache and went into his villain stance. Liz left laughing. She called over her shoulder, "Your little filly will not be long, pardner."

She was glowing. "I'm blushing. Can you believe it? Actually blushing." She continued brushing her medium length hair and after brushing her teeth, put on the carefully selected short satin brocade gown. The peach color made her even more rosy. Hope it's the altitude and not high blood pressure. Now wouldn't that be a hoot! Witness dies of heart attack while in her lover's arms. What is it that the comedians say, "What a way to go!"

Liz could tell that Cam had stripped and had pulled just a sheet over him. He turned her side of the sheet back for her to climb in. "Oh, wait! I forgot to hit the tape button." She laughed when she heard Ravel's Bolero playing. "Now, where were we?"

Liz had chosen a plain medium brown wool suit and a soft rose and taupe print blouse for the trial. She had pulled her rich brown hair back from her face in a chignon. Chester Robbins, Brooker's lawyer, had asked her to dress in a feminine style, not austere and not too frilly. The cowl neckline of the blouse softened her look, and she added understated, simple gold jewelry. Cam was in a western cut suit of dove gray. He looked so handsome. I bet there's not a woman in here who wouldn't give her right arm to be where I was last night, Liz thought. I can't let my feelings show, though. Why am I not frightened? I should be worried. Our testimony might ruin a young woman's life. But, it might also see that justice is done. I can't think about the outcome, like Jo said. Just do what you're there for and let the lawyers do their jobs. I'm the one who should have thought that. After all, I'm the one with a lawyer husband and son.

When Liz was called, and after she had been sworn in, things moved slowly. Robin Davenport sat, emotionless, dressed in a powder blue suit. Her long blond hair was pulled back with a large pearl barrette, and she wore little makeup. She was so young looking, Liz thought, but the papers said that she was thirty. The lawyer was Hollywood through and through—shock of white hair, deeply tanned by the California sun, bright blue twinkling eyes, dead behind his practiced stare.

Why am I finding this amusing? I feel like a third person witnessing this scenario or watching TV or a movie. I don't feel that I am even here. Am I still on a high from last night? God! Who wouldn't be! Whew! I'm probably just exhausted.

"Oh, I'm sorry, I didn't understand the question. I am very tired from my long trip, and the altitude does affect me." She exaggerated her southern accent.

"The question was a very simple one, Mrs.—it is Mrs., isn't it?"

Oh, oh, here we go. Chester said that he was pretty sure that their lawyer wouldn't get personal. I think he was wrong.

"Yes, I'm married. Have been for a very long time." She smiled sweetly. *Two can play this game. I think the old Liz has returned. I wish Jo were here. Oh, how she'd love it. After all, I wasn't selected to play the lead in our high school play for nothing, Mr. Hotshot lawyer.*

"The question was, "Why were you on that road at that time? And why..."

"I'll be happy to answer the first question; then you may ask me another. Doesn't that seem fairer to you?"

The spectators laughed. *Think that threw the smart-ass, as John would have called him, but he's gearing up to bombard me, and I'll just become more southern by the minute. They don't know how to handle that.*

"As I recall the first question was this—why was I on that road at that time? The answer is that it's the road that goes to Denver from Laramie, where we had just been. We were on our way to the airport. Do you want me to go on?"

He just shook his head and softly said, "Continue, please, Mrs. Bellin." He paced briskly back and forth.

"Thank you. See, isn't this easier?" More laughter from the room. She didn't dare look at Cam. *It would have started her giggling for sure.* "I had just got word that my husband had suffered a stroke in Florida, where we live, and I was very upset. I was way out in the Hoback Ranches, where we had just bought a cabin. That's in Wyoming, the Hoback Ranches, I mean..."

"The deed says that it was YOU who bought the cabin, Mrs. Bellin," he said loudly, pointing his finger at her.

"Why, yes, Avery, my husband, thought that I should invest the money my dear mother had left me in some property. You see, we were told that the property value was excellent..."

"Mrs. Bellin, would you do me the favor of deleting some of the detail..."

"But, that's just not how Southerners explain things," she laughed. "My Yankee friends say that it takes a Southerner a whole paragraph to say what they can say in just one little old sentence."

"Please, Mrs. Bellin. Let's get to the point. My patience is wearing thin."

"Oh, I'm sorry. But it was you who said that the cabin was in my name, and I felt that I had to explain why it was in my name. Shouldn't I have explained it?"

"No, it was not necessary to go into such detail. Just answer the questions yes or no. Thank you."

She shrugged her shoulders and pursed her lips and gave the audience her disappointed expression. They were with her, she could tell. Oh, how I'm loving this.

But she wasn't prepared for the next question. "Mrs. Bellin, are you and Mr. Cameron lovers? Yes or no."

Caught off guard, she jumped up and said in such a soft voice. "What a thing to ask me!" Sitting down, she regained her composure. "Well, I never."

Chester Robbins shouted, "What is this? What can this possibly have to do with witnessing Miss Davenport on that road at that time driving like a race car driver! You're out of..."

"You're both out of line. Mr. Brewster, retract the question and stick to the correct line of questioning. Mr. Robbins, take your seat and no more outbursts." Judge Edmond Pope had almost had his fill.

Liz looked Brewster right in his too blue eyes and waited for the next question, but he could see that she had won over the gallery and probably the jury as well, so he said, "No more questions, your honor."

"Mr. Robbins, have you any questions for the witness. And make it quick. They might be slow as molasses in the South, but out here we like to get to the bottom of things. Do you understand, Mrs. Bellin?"

She looked at him sweetly and replied, "I like that, your honor. I'll behave. Honest." The entire courtroom howled.

Chester straightened his tie, got up and approached the chair. "Now, Mrs. Bellin, in your own words tell us why you were at the road when Miss Davenport appeared, and, as judge Pope ordered, make it short."

"I'll try. As I tried to say before, I had word that my husband had suffered a stroke and was trying to get a plane back home to be with him. But you know, it's just about impossible to get one out of Jackson. So Mr. Cameron—he's my neighbor, you know—was going to Denver to take one of his pieces to be cast—he's a sculptor, you know—and he offered to take me to the airport so I could be on stand-by. That's the whole thing in a nutshell."

"Tell the jury about seeing Miss Davenport. Please, just like it happened."

"Well, Mr. Cameron said that his butt—oh, I'm sorry—his bottom was sore from sitting so long, and he'd like to stop and walk around a while. I thought that it was a good idea because my butt...oops! Sorry. I was sore too, so we stopped at this road. I noticed the name on the mailbox that said Blowing Wind Ranch, and I thought to myself that I was glad I didn't live that far out and that it probably got terribly lonely. About then we saw all this dust coming down the road, and Cam, I mean Mr. Cameron, said that he'd better move the truck 'cause someone was in a terrible hurry. So, he did. About then the truck came to a screeching halt, and this young girl hopped out, opened the gate and tore outta there without even a howdy do. I asked Mr. Cameron if maybe we should go see why she was so scared, and…"

"I object! "

"Objection sustained. Mrs. Bellin, please refrain from…"

"But your honor, she was scared to death, you could tell."

"Mr. Robbins, would you please instruct your witness that it is not necessary to embellish…"

"Yes, your honor.." He approached the chair and whispered, "Keep it up. You've got old Brewster messing his pants."

"Oh, thank you. I'll behave. I just thought that you wanted me to tell just what I saw as honestly as I…"

"Oh, come on, judge! Let her tell it like she wants!" someone yelled from the gallery.

"That does it. Recess! Right now! Mr. Brewster and Mr. Rollins, I want to see you in my chambers. This will not do!"

"Oh, Jo, you would have been so proud of me. I don't think I've ever had such a hilarious time. I had old blue-eye Brewster messing his pants, Chester said."

"What did Cam say? I mean how did he do?"

"He almost one-upped me. Went into his best western cowboy, good-old-boy routine. Oh, Jo, I'm so happy. I wish it could last forever, but I know it can't." Jo didn't say a word.

Ben asked, "Why didn't you tell her, Jo? Avery might not last the night."

"I couldn't, honey. I've not heard her this happy in so long. I just couldn't."

"Come here. Of course you couldn't. Let her enjoy her time with Cam. When Avery's time comes and she gets word of it, she'll no doubt have one helluva guilt trip. Chuck said that Murph thinks it's just a matter of time. There's no hope now."

TWENTY-SIX

"Miss Irma, you shouldn't be making fun of Manny. He's not smart, but he does have feelings. We grew up together, and I used to like him, but since he's been hitting the bottle he's changed. Even Doc says he's dangerous."

"They're the best kind, Jamie. Not any fun stalking a docile animal. Manny's nothing but an animal. You see how he drools all the time? Well, that's the sign that he's like any other animal, just pacing up and down in his cage. Now, Manny's built his own cage. I'll grant you that, but a cage it is, anyway. Hey, hand me that old tarp. That'll be a good cover."

"Miss Irma, he'll be able to see you because of the snow. That tarp is just going to look like…"

"Jamie, with all the dead trees around here you think Manny'll be able to see us? We'll blend in with all the dead wood. That little bit of snow that's left isn't gonna make us stand out. You can bet on that. Why Charlie was the best hunter this place has ever seen, and he taught me how to build a blind. How'd you think we got all those trophies, anyway?"

"I haven't seen any trophies."

"Well, go to Faler's in Pinedale, and you'll see the walls covered with them. Must have given them twenty-five or thirty when Charlie died. Got three beautiful pronghorns. Just about the most beautiful elk you'll ever see he got up at Water Dog Lake."

Irma had talked Jamie into laying an ambush for Manny. He'd continued sneaking up into The Ranches every chance he got. How he thought that she couldn't see his old truck in the dead of winter she couldn't understand. Hell, she could see for miles from her mountain and certainly could hear. Every vehicle, including snowmobiles, could be heard and seen from her perch.

"You hear anything, Jamie?"

"No ma'am." He listened carefully. He saw Irma pull her old red wool cap back from her ear and put her head down to the ground. "He's coming! Yep, that dumb-ass is on his way. Right into our trap."

Jamie shook his head. "Miss Irma, I don't want to show any disrespect, but this isn't right. What you gonna do? Shoot him?"

She had a wild look about her. "You good goddamned right, I'm gonna shoot him. He's on my property, and I shoot trespassers. It's my right! It's my duty!"

Jamie got down beside her on the tarp, and trying as hard as he could, didn't hear a thing. But Irma seemed to know just which way the vehicle was coming from. "It's a truck. Can't you tell, Jamie? Listen!" She resumed her position on the ground. "Yep! It's a truck!"

"How can you tell? Just sounds like any other vehicle to me."

"That's cause you've allowed your senses to go dead just like any other flatlander I've known. When you're a mountain person you've gotta have your senses keen. How'd you think the mountain men lived out here? Huh?"

"Can't say as I've ever given it any thought."

"Said like a true goddamned flatlander, Jamie. God, how you people managed to survive out here I'll never know. Must've been that God you're always talking about. You know, the one who's gonna save you, and you'll float up to heaven, and everything will be glorious. Bullshit, Jamie! Bullshit!"

"Miss Irma, you'd better not be talking 'bout God like that. He doesn't take kindly to that kind of talk." He was ashamed of her, she could tell.

"Oh, Jamie, that's just the ravings of a disgruntled old woman." Irma knew instinctively when she had overstepped her bounds. Jamie's company had come to mean as much as Jo's had.

"You're just lonely. Mrs. Daulton has done you a lot of good. She is a true friend to you. Why, Eva Young said just that the other day, said that she is always taking up for you when anyone says anything bad, I mean, when they talk..."

"I know full well what you mean, Jamie. But I don't need any goddamned Easterner taking up for me. I don't need her to take up for me."

"It's all right. She's coming back early this year. Billy and Fern heard from her today, and she and Mr. Daulton are flying out to open up the house, and he's going to stay for a little while and then fly back to Florida and come back out to join her with Maggie."

"When did you hear that?"

"Just this morning at the post office."

"Oh, hell! Its just that damned Cam! Thought for sure that it'd be Manny." She could see Cam's truck turn onto Mountain View. "Already lost interest in killing him, anyway. When'd you say that the Daultons are coming out?"

"Eva said in about two weeks. Since her husband died, Mrs. Bellin wants to come out with her daughter, and Mrs. Daulton wants to be with them for a while. Seems that she's real upset 'cause she was at that trial when he died and she wasn't with him."

"Humph! Upset my eye! She could hardly wait for the fool to die so she could screw around with that Cam, that's what! Probably just guilty 'cause she was getting herself a good f…"

"Don't talk that way, Miss Irma. She's Mrs. Daulton's best friend, you know."

Jamie could tell that Irma had other things on her mind. He'd learned to read her moods and knew when to shut up and leave her to her memories. "Better be going on home. Told mama I'd help her with the moving of all that hay. Don't know why she's in need of another barn, anyway. Things haven't been that good around here the past few years, what with the drought and all. But when things get slow, as papa used to say, mama's just got to build herself something. She dearly loves to have all those outbuildings surrounding the place." He chuckled when he said it.

Irma looked up at his handsome face and said, "You're a good son, Jamie Stroebel, a good son. I had a good little girl once upon a time. Did you know that, Jamie? Her name was Patty. Named her for Charlie's sister Pat. Now, that was one smart little girl. But your God took her from me, Jamie, and I'll never forgive him. He first sent her to me as a surprise, then he….I'll never forgive him. He took my Patty."

He reached down and patted her gently. Even with all those layers of clothing he could feel her bony back. "It'll be all right, Miss Irma. You'll be with her one of these days."

She looked up at him, and instead of tears she had a diabolic expression on her contorted face, and began to yell at the top of her lungs, "I've outsmarted that goddamned God of yours, Jamie Stroebel! Ha, Ha, Ha! I'm already with her! Ha! That God of yours ain't so goddamned smart after all!"

When the tears finally came, Jamie Stroebel was there for her. He patted her back and, rocking her back and forth, said, "Shhhh, Miss Irma. It'll be all right. It'll be all right. It takes a lot of time for some of us to heal. I remember when Elsie moved up to Alaska with her folks, I truly thought I'd die. I don't know when I've had such a pain."

Irma sniffled, wiped her runny nose on the back of her tattered glove and pushed Jamie from her. "You mean that little Eddinfield gal? The one not bigger than a minute and freckles every place they could stick?"

"Yes ma'am. Elsie and I were going to get married when we got out of school. But then her papa got that real good job on the pipeline, and off they went. Oh, we wrote every week at first but…"

"You mean to tell me that you've been harboring a longing for her ever since she left, Jamie? Hell, that's gotta be at least twenty years now."

"The truth is, I haven't found anyone who is as sweet and gentle. I have to have a girl who's gentle, Miss Irma. Oh, I've had them come on to me the few times I've been at the Elkhorn with Bruce, but they're just too fast for me."

"Jamie are you telling me that you've never poked a girl? I mean except that Elsie?"

"Miss Irma, you're out of line. I loved Elsie and wanted her to be my bride. I'd never have—well, you know—had her before we were wed. That wouldn't have been right."

"Well now, I've heard it all. Thought you young men said howdy do and hopped right on the fillies. If the news is right most the time, you don't even wait to get introduced before you're groping each other. Guess those national pollsters haven't been to Bondurant, Wyoming. They'd surely have to change their statistics. Why, Bondurant, Wyoming would be a laughing stock for those sophisticated New Yorkers and Washingtonians for sure."

Jamie had a far away look. "I'd surely like to find a girl. But she'd have to be able to live at Big Bear, 'cause Mama needs me. Since Jake and Hiram moved to Idaho, we're down to just the two of us boys and the girls' husbands. It takes a lot of hands to run the Bear."

"Hey, Jamie, got an idea. Maybe that daughter of Liz Bellin would suit you. Jo said that she was with Greenpeace, so she must like animals and has to be sensitive if she's gonna save the world."

"You're making fun of me, I know. She's one of those well educated girls and would like a faster pace, maybe like she could find in Jackson. You know, with all those bright lights and loud music. I like the peace of the Bear and a good book and to hear the coyotes call to each other at night. I like to sleep out in the open and look at the stars and dream and…"

"Well, son, I'm afraid that you've got a lonely life ahead of you. That God of yours doesn't make that kind of girl anymore. You'll just hafta move up to Charlie's Mountain and keep an old woman company, Jamie. I'm thinking that you don't have any red blood rushing through your veins. But I can tell you that my Charlie surely did. Did you know my Charlie?"

"Yes, Ma'am, I knew Charlie. He was as strong a man as I ever saw. I remember once when he came up to see my papa for something. He helped him move a tree trunk from the road, but before papa could get hold of it, Charlie had the thing off the road by several feet. I'll never forget that."

She sighed. "He was strong in more ways than that, Jamie. He was strong inside…" She thumped her chest and sighed again. "Hey, we'd better get a move on before we get frostbite." She hopped up and turning to look up at Jamie said, "Not changing the subject, but how about taking some of this jam off my hands? Know Eileen always liked my wild strawberry jam. Used to buy me out at the church bazaar, she did."

"I'm sure she'd like some. Bet you've got about a hundred jars of it in your basement."

Irma turned on him, "You been poking around in my basement, Jamie Stroebel?" She was now screaming at him. "Have you?"

He was taken aback. "Calm down, Miss Irma. I don't poke into anyone's business unless they invite me. It was you who said that's where you keep your jam."

She heaved a big sigh. "You better not start that poking like Manny was prone to. You'd better not, or you'll end up on the receiving end of this!" She raised her rifle high over her head.

TWENTY-SEVEN

"Laine, Laura Swanson wants you to call her. Think she wants you to go to a movie or at least to get out of the house. Hey, why don't you go to the Club for lunch? Just put it on our tab. Wouldn't that be fun?"

"Sure, Mom, I'll call. Did you get her number?"

"She's in the book, honey, living at home, and they're still on Pine Avenue, I believe. Don't think that Royce and Betty have moved. Getting so congested down there that the last time I saw Betty she said they were thinking of it."

"Is she still at Burdines?"

"Last I heard she was an assistant buyer, I think. I believe for the children's department. Her folks re-did the guest house for her. You know, facing the river. Simmone Grayson said that it was darling. Laura has always had wonderful taste. Haven't heard that she's serious with anyone but know she dates." Liz was in the bedroom emptying Avery's dresser drawers, a job she hated. Jo had volunteered to help, but she just couldn't allow her to. "Saw her with Hugh Branch at a Friday night happy hour before we went to Wyoming. Looks the same. Still skinny as a rail. Laine, why don't you plan to play tennis one day this week? I bet she could get a day off. And if she can't, then Rachael Borders might be available. Kirk has a great job, and I don't think she works. Seems that every time I play tennis or go to the club she's there."

"OK. I'll take the portable out on the pier and get some sun while I talk to Laura."

Liz watched her walk down the brick walk that led to the river. She hates all this. She'd rather be out on a boat spotting whales or out in the woods searching for some critter. If she still had Marshall she'd have something to hold onto. When that horse died I truly believe something died in my little girl. I remember saying that to Avery, and he said that I was reading things into her rela-

188

tionship with that horse. I'd forgotten how quiet she was. Almost like she's not here. I'm so glad she's going to the ranch with me. She said that she'd missed riding in Seattle. Maybe I can call Billy Parker and have him call Jerry or Gordon to see if they can rent a horse for her. I'm not sure I'll be able to see much of Cam while she's there, but he understands. Actually he has been almost too understanding. Almost wish he'd kick up a fuss. Guess that mountain man has turned into a mountain of a job.

"Laura, this is Laine. Mom said that you called."

"I'm so glad you returned my call. I know how upset you are. About your dad, I mean. And, why wouldn't you be?"

"It wasn't the shock that it could have been. I tried to prepare for it, but it's something you can't prepare for. Guess you just have to go through it and let time do the healing. At least that's what everyone says."

"Well, it's still hard. Hey, there's a neat movie playing at the mall. Would you like to go?"

"You know what I'd really like to do? I haven't had dinner at the club in a long time. Mom said I could put it on her tab. I'd like to go to the River House and sit on one of the swings on the porch overlooking the river and toss down a few cold ones and chat. You know like we used to when I'd come back from college."

"You know, I'd like that. Saw Simmone at the Friday night bash, and she suggested the same thing. We used to have such fun just hanging out, didn't we?"

"Sure did. I have lots of friends in Seattle, and that's just about all we do. Seldom go to a movie or watch TV. Most of them are with Greenpeace, so we have lots in common and are always broke. That's the only thing I don't like about it. Never seem to have enough money to do anything. Wouldn't have been able to get home if John hadn't sent me the money. And the jerk had the nerve to say that if I had a decent job he'd not have had to bail me out. Naturally I'll pay him back."

"That was unkind of him. I always liked John. Think maybe he's changed."

"Not really. He's just more vocal. He's really taking Dad's death hard. Can't talk about it like Chuck and I can. Chuck and I have always been able to talk though."

"You want me to pick you up or are you going to walk?"

"Think I'll bike. Heavens, haven't used that thing since a year ago Christmas. I hadn't realized that it's been that long since I've been home. Things surely have changed around here. Doesn't look a bit like the little sleepy Orange Park we grew up in, does it?"

"You can say that again. They're talking about adding on to the mall. Again! But in some ways it's nice. Just about anything a person could want is right here. I get to go to Atlanta and New York at least twice a year, so that breaks it for me. You serious with anyone?"

"Not really. I go out quite often with one of the guys, but there's not really any fire in it. He's a good friend. I'd like to have a meaningful relationship, but guess I'll have to get out of Greenpeace to find someone. How about you?"

"Same here. Oh, I date. The folks say that I'm married to Burdines, but they couldn't be more wrong. I really think that if I had an offer to leave here I'd hop at it. It's a great job, but I'm getting a little bored with it."

"Laura, Mom is calling. I'll meet you at the River House about 5:00 p m. OK?"

"Sure. Don't dress. I'm going to wear jeans. Never seem to be able to just hang out. Bye."

"Hi, Sweetie, did you get hold of Laura?"

"Yeh, we're going to meet at the River House for a drink then go to the club for dinner, if that's all right?"

"Jo called. That's why I called to you, but I see you have plans. She invited us over for dinner. We want to make plans for the trip out west. But I'd rather you be with your friends."

"It'll be fun. Didn't get to even see Laura when I was here last. Think she was in the mountains skiing with her folks or something."

"They have a place in North Carolina, I believe. Royce has done really well in real estate. I'm happy for Betty. Bless her heart. She was one of the children in our first grade who had no shoes. I'm not kidding. They were so poor that they could not afford shoes. She is so appreciative of her life with Royce, and he seems to dote on her. Laura is a lucky young woman to have them for parents.".

"Mom, were you able to get reservations? You never did say."

"I'm sorry, honey. Yes, Mildred called back, and you're flying Delta to Atlanta, change for Seattle; then on your return trip to Wyoming you'll fly to Salt Lake, then take a puddle jumper to Jackson. Jo called Billy and he'll open up our houses, and we'll drive out with Maggie. Later Ben will follow with Robbie and family. It's not as complicated as it sounds, honest. Tell Laura that you'll have only a few more days to hang out. Maybe you two can hit St. Augustine for a short while. I'll spring for a hotel, if you'd like."

"I'd love that. Remember Anastasia? Oh, how I loved that beach. I thought that Australia and New Zealand would have beaches that could compare, but, none did. Here I've traveled all over the place and haven't found a thing that could compare with what was right in my own back yard. Isn't that funny?"

"If I'd told you that, Laine, you wouldn't have believed me, now would you?"

"I'm sure you're right, Mom."

"Is this like old times, or what!" Laine called to Laura.

"You look great! Like the short hair. Its really you! Is that the latest Greenpeace style?"

"No, not really. Its just that when you're out half the time and there's no hot water, you're afraid of getting lice and all those glamorous things. Besides, I like it. Tried the long hair with the braid down the back, you know, real New York model type..."

"Sure, Laine. You were always feminine but not fussy like Donna Chapell. God! What a trip! Guess what happened to her? You haven't heard have you?"

"No, haven't heard a word."

"Graduated from Bryn Mawr with honors, naturally, went to Washington to work for some hotshot senator and proceeded to get herself pregnant. Refused to have an abortion and threatened to sue the son-of-a-bitch, and he ended up divorcing his wife, or she divorced him, and our own prom queen is hooked with a jerk, I'm told, and a son and..."

"I'm sorry to hear that. I always felt sorry for Donna. She

seemed so lonely."

"Am I hearing you right? Sorry for her? She would have nailed your hide to a wall if you had stood in her way."

"That's what I mean. She was missing something , some ingredient. Hey, let's not get started on that. Isn't this a great setting!"

"I never tire of looking out over the river. Bet it's two miles wide here. Wasn't this building the old golf clubhouse, and they moved it from its original place? You know, the one that the Palmolive Soap man, a Mr. Johnson, built? Think the big house was his private residence before they turned it into the club, and he had his own private golf course. I'm sure that Caleb said that it was built in the twenties."

"I didn't really appreciate it until we went to Italy. You know when Ms. Mock, our French teacher, took the six of us girls to France and Italy? It was after we graduated from high school. Where were you, anyway?"

"Oh, that was the summer that we went to Canada, and the family had been planning it forever. I'd forgotten all about your trip."

"Well, when we got back from Italy and I saw all this marble and wrought iron that the man had brought from over there, then I appreciated the club more. Some of the mantles are priceless, I've been told. There's something not just old world about it, but it's comfortable and not stuffy like some of the clubs."

"Anyway, I love the River House. So rustic, and I love what they've done with it. Kept it the same with the old bar and pool table. Don't you just love the pictures above the bar of the semi-nude ladies lounging with just a hint of gauze draped discretely over them." Laine laughed.

"Remember our graduation night? We all came here, and the porch swings were filled and swinging full-tilt,and the rockers the same? Was it Dave Whitson who got so smashed that he ended up skinny dipping in the river? What a jerk!"

"Did you know that he's an aide to some big wig in D.C.?"

"It figures. Sometimes when I can't sleep, I dream of this place. No, I really do. I dream of Anastasia Beach and my beautiful horse Marshall and this. I've seen magnificent trees in many parts of the world, but none can compare with that live oak in front of the

Club Continental. I even had Mother take a picture of it so I could show it to my mates, but it didn't do it justice. The redwoods in California are really awesome, but they don't look like trees. Our live oaks look like trees ought to. I never tire of looking at them. The one in our front yard beside the river is magnificent, but I've never seen anything like the one here. Must be a block wide."

"Want another beer? Think I'll call Hugh to see if he wants to join us. Do you mind?"

"Oh, no. See if he has a friend."

"Are you serious?"

"Why not?"

"OK. Oops! Do you have a quarter? Don't worry. I'll get change inside at the bar. Hey Tim. Laine, there's Tim Fennell. Remember him from high school? Varsity basketball. Right?"

"Yeh, right. Hi, Tim. How's it going?"

"I'm going to call Hugh to see if he wants to join us. You wanta sit here? Laine and I are celebrating old times, then we're going to have dinner at the club."

"I swear, if it isn't Laine Bellin. Grief! Haven't seen you since we graduated. Heard you joined Greenpeace."

"Sure did, Tim. You went to Florida State, didn't you?"

"Yeh, and you went to Gainesville. Still got your horse? Seems to me that's the reason you didn't go to Smith."

Laine laughed. "Now, how'd you remember that? But, you're right. Dad couldn't talk me into giving up Marshall. He dangled all sorts of fabulous gifts in front of me if I'd go to Smith, but none worked. I was in love with my Marshall. Unfortunately he died when I was a senior. Still miss him."

Tim draped his lean body over the wooden captain's chair and faced Laine. "Heard about your dad, Laine. I was sorry to hear it. My dad thought a lot of him. They played for JU together, you know."

"No, I didn't know that. Always more to our folks than we think, huh?"

"Yep, you're right on that one. They're getting up there. Hey, I can't stay for dinner with you two, but maybe I can take a rain check. I'd like to see you while you're here. I mean that, Laine. God, you look good!"

"Well, thank you, sir. We're leaving in a few days. Sorry. Mom's talking of putting the house on the market and buying a condo or small cottage in St. Augustine. Too much house now that Dad's gone."

"Smart thing to do, I guess. As I recall it's a mansion. Always liked the setting. Just about the prettiest part of the river to me."

"She bought a cabin up in the mountains in Wyoming. Just loves it there. I plan to go there after I return to Seattle to turn in my resignation."

"How long have you been with Greenpeace?"

"Five years. Want to go back to school and get the courses I need for vet school. Couldn't handle it back when I was younger, but I'm ready now. At least I think I'm ready. Either that or animal husbandry. Both fields interest me. Probably be in school for the rest of my life." She laughed her low laugh.

"I always loved your laugh, Laine. Very different. Did you know that?"

"That's what Chuck says. You remember Chuck, don't you?"

"Sure. Eat at his Sonny's often. He looks great and has the cutest kids. Wife isn't bad either."

"Love that gal. She's so right for him. He's the lucky one, Tim. Leads his own life and is so strong within. The world could use more Chuck Bellins."

Laura motioned to Laine. "Excuse me, Tim. I'll see what Laura wants. Be right back."

"What's up?"

"Hugh said that he can call Jack Downs. Remember him? Gorgeous and well healed."

"Sorry, Laura. I've had a change of heart. Can we have dinner together or maybe with just Hugh? I'm not as up to this as I thought. I'm really sorry."

"Hey, don't sweat it! No problem. Hugh and I are real good friends, and he'll understand. What's Tim doing? Is he busy?"

"Yeh. He has other plans but did ask me out while I'm here. Can't though. I'll be leaving in a few days."

"Hugh asked if your cabin is near Jackson, and I said that I thought it was. Am I right?"

"Yes, according to Mom it's about forty or so miles southeast.

She said the trip out to Bondurant through the Hoback Canyon with the Hoback River running beside the highway has got to be the most gorgeous scenery you can imagine. Even see mountain sheep up on the hillside sometimes. I'm getting anxious to get there."

"Liz, you've got to tell her about Cam. You'll be seeing him in a few days, and then it'll be too late. She's going to be able to see..."

"Jo, I know it, but the opportunity just hasn't come up. I've tried to broach it but..."

"There are no buts about it, honey. It's not fair to Laine. I'm surprised that John hasn't told her, or maybe Chuck, since they're so close."

"I don't think they have though. Think I'd know it if she had that on her mind. She's so quiet, Jo. She worries me. Hang on a minute. Think I hear her."

"Wrong. It was the local paperboy collecting. Cutest little redhead you ever saw."

"She was always quiet, Liz. This is nothing new. You used to say the only ones Laine ever had a conversation with were Chuck and her horse Marshall. Remember?"

"But I thought that the last time she was home she was more talkative. I guess that this visit has to be different, though. She's not as devastated as I thought she'd be. I'm surprised. She's grown to be a very introspective young lady. Deep like my father was. Do you remember how Dad was? We used to call him the great philosopher, remember?"

"I surely do. What's she going to do with the money Avery left her? Has she said?"

"Yes, she has. Seems that she's been thinking of going back to college and going into animal husbandry or perhaps even trying to get in a vet school. I mentioned the University of Wyoming and was surprised when she didn't pooh pooh that idea. After all, I'll be a resident, and it'll cost less. Maybe Cam has some pull in that department. I'd love to see her go for it. She's never had a lot of drive, but once she makes up her mind there's no dissuading her. Avery found that out."

"Is that a call coming in on your line? Never can figure these things out."

"Yes, and I'll call you later tonight. Bye. This is the Bellin residence. Oh, Cam. I was hoping you'd call. You sound funny. Is anything wrong?

Pause…

"Oh, no! I'm so sorry, hon. Do you want me to come out earlier? Are you sure? I'll come if you'd like. What about your trip to Riley's graduation? Will you be able to make it?"

Pause…

"Did you say that you are the executor of his estate?"

Pause…

"That's quite a responsibility. But I'm glad that you'll be going east to visit Riley. That's more important."

"Jo, Liz. It was Cam. His good friend Woerber Stuebing died this morning of an apparent heart attack. He's really shaken, I can tell. He was his closest friend. I need to be with him. What am I going to do?"

"Wait a minute, Liz. A news flash just came on the TV. I take it that you haven't heard the news. Robin Davenport got off scot-free. The jury ruled Bill Brooker's death an accident. Apparently the caretakers corroborated her story about his wild behavior when he was hitting the bottle, and the autopsy confirmed a large amount of alcohol. And the jury bought it. Maybe she's telling the truth. I hope so. Liz, did Cam ask you to come out? Did he?"

"Actually he said that it wasn't necessary, that he'd be all right. But he sounded so far away, so far away from me. I don't like that, and who knows, his plans to go to Riley's graduation might change."

"Give him some space, honey. He's used to being alone and figuring out things on his own. He just might need to be by himself. You know, like Laine. There are people who need to be alone, Liz." She thought of Irma. I must write her tonight. I haven't written her in over a week. Hope she's behaving. I know that she's laying for that Manny. Jamie told Eva that she has her rifle on ready and enjoying every minute of the hunt. He's worried about her.

TWENTY-EIGHT

"Mom, do you want me to help you with Dad's things? I don't mind, honest."

Liz had just finished taking a box of Avery's clothing to the garage when Laine called to her. "I thought I could get everything finished by this afternoon, but I was wrong. I'd forgotten how many clothes your dad had. Since he seldom changed sizes he rarely threw anything out or gave any away. Your help would be wonderful, if you're sure you want to."

"No problem. It's a little sad, but I've been gone from home for so long now that's it not like it would be if I still lived here. I mean that I've gotten used to not being with him, if you know what I mean."

Liz walked around the twin bed, hugged Laine to her and said, "I know full well what you mean, honey."

"Tell you what I want you to do. Go to the kitchen and get a big Husky bag out of the pantry, and that'll give us a place to put his belts, shoes and bulky things. The Goodwill should be here in about an hour. They said pick-up was between 2:00 p.m. and 4:00 p.m. That doesn't give us much time, does it?" She laughed nervously when she said it. I think now is the time to tell her about Cam. I've got to do it. I just hope her reaction isn't like John's was. I don't think I could handle that right now. I can't get over Woerber dying. I wish I were with Cam. Oh, how I wish …

"Oh, there's the phone, again. Laine, please get that for me. If it isn't important tell them that I'm not taking calls right now."

"OK. Hello."

Pause…"

Yes, this is the Bellin residence."

Pause…

"I'm Laine, his daughter. Who did you say is calling?"

Pause…"

"Just a minute, please. Mom, someone says that she would like

197

to speak to you and that it's personal. Do you want to take it?"

Liz thought it might be Cam, but when Laine said that it was "she" the curiosity set in. Who would be calling me at a time like this and say that it's personal. Hmmm.

"I'll take it in the kitchen, honey. You finish up packing the things I put on the bed, and we'll be almost finished. Thanks."

She was apprehensive. Why do I have this foreboding. My Lord, my heart's racing. "Hello, this is Liz Bellin."

Pause...

"Who did you say this is? A friend of my husband's? I guess you aren't aware that my husband died over a week ago."

Pause...

"I don't understand what you're saying. What does this have to do with me?"

Pause...

"Listen! If you know what's good for you, and you obviously don't, you will get lost! You're not shaking me down, and if you call again, I'll bury your overactive ass! Are you hearing me?" Liz was visibly shaking she was so angry. And Jo thought I couldn't get angry. Well, the new Liz certainly can.

She hadn't realized that she had been yelling, but when Laine rushed into the kitchen calling, "Mom, are you all right?" she heaved and answered, "I'm fine. Can you imagine the vultures! They don't wait 'til the body's cold before they start hounding you for...oh, honey, some people have no tact. I guess they can't help it, but it does annoy me. Yes, I'm fine now. Let's finish what we started. Come on. Then we'll go on the patio and have a nice, cool lemonade. Maybe throw some gin in it, huh?"

"Didn't know that you were a drinker."

"I usually have a cocktail before dinner, and when we go out I'll have wine with the meal. Does that constitute a DRINKER to you?"

"No, not really. But it is a little early, that's all."

"I guess I'm not aware of the time right now. Hey, how about you finishing up for me? I forgot I told John that I'd call him about some of the business we still have to go over. OK?"

"No problem. You do what you have to to. Won't take me long."

All the way to the den, where Liz closed the double doors, she said, "BITCH! BITCH! I'll not have it! I simply will not! So she was his last cutie. Well, little cutie, if you want to smear his name in dirt go right ahead. I protected the son-of-a-bitch while he was alive, and I don't care what they do to him now. I hope you're listening, Avery! I felt horrible that I wasn't here when you died. I really was torn, but mister, I'm sure as hell over it. I can't believe I'm even saying these things to myself.

"Hi, Robin, is John available? Oh, this is his mom. Yes, I'll hold. Thank you."

Well, this time he'll find out just what kind of man his wonderful father was. I hate to put that pin in your balloon, dear little boy, but I've carried the burden too darned long. "Hi, son. Had a call from, uhh, from one of your father's girlfriends. Seems that she is in need of money, and I told her in no uncertain terms that she was not going to shake us down. Now, I know that you might think otherwise, but John, there will be no blackmail money paid to keep your father's name squeaky clean. He's gone, and I'll not be a part of any such scheme, and neither will you or any other member of my family. I just want you to know where I stand, and I intend to call his office and tell Spencer the same."

Pause...

"I was very firm with her. She did not give her name. I don't want to know her name, but John, I mean it when I say there will be no money paid out to keep your father's immaculate reputation intact. I'm at a point in my life when I don't care about his reputation, and neither should you.

"He is not, and I repeat, not going to reach out of the grave to hurt us. He did too much damage while he was alive. There will be no more said about this, but if she contacts you, and I'm sure she will, you are to be just as firm. I mean this!"

Pause...

"Listen, if I have to, I'll alert Debbie about this. She has your future and the kids' future to think about, and some bimbo shouldn't be given the upper hand. Put your personal feelings aside, John. This is business, pure and simple. I have to go. Laine and I are packing up your father's belongings, and I can't get them out of this house fast enough. Bye."

Now is the time to tell her about Cam, and I'll not have a problem in the world with it. Glory be! I'm rid of him at last. You're dead and gone, Avery, and I hope that I'll never have to think of you again. It seems that I've spent most of my life lying for you and about you, and now I'm free to think of Elizabeth Laine. About time!

John sat still. He was numb. He couldn't comprehend what his mother had just said to him. I don't understand. I don't understand. How can you live with a man, love and admire him and not even know him. I thought I knew Dad. I thought he was just about the greatest man alive. My God! I've spent thirty-two years loving a man who was a cheat, an adulterer, and God knows what all. I need to call Spencer at dad's office. I wonder if he knew what was going on? Am I the only one in town who didn't know? Chuck seemed to know that there was something wrong with their marriage, and I didn't even have an inkling. Am I that dumb? Am I that insensitive? He sat and continued to sit until the phone rang.

"Yes, Robin, who is it?"

"Your beautiful wife, John. Does that mean that we'll not be able to have our, you know, our usual...?"

"Get off the line, Robin. I mean it! Right now! This is none of your business ..."

"Hi, honey, what's up?"

"Just got a call from some woman, and she said the strangest things about Daddy Bellin. I don't understand what she means, honey. But I got her number for you to call. I hope it was all right. I didn't really understand what it was all about, but I think that she was a client of his and didn't realize that he had died. At least I think that's ..."

It's started! What am I going to do? His head quickly found his hands and he began to sob. I'm as guilty as he...

Jamie called to his mom. "Going to Miss Irma's, and don't let Bruiser follow. That darned dog is going to get killed on the highway yet. Mom, did you hear me?"

"All right, honey, I'll keep him in the house until you're out of sight."

"Not that that will do the trick. Love that dog, but he just won't mind." Jamie was whistling. Eileen smiled when she heard him. Haven't heard Jamie whistle like that for a very long time. Probably since that Elsie moved to Alaska. Grief! That has to have been darned near twenty years ago. That's music to my ears, son. Pure music. "Get off that couch, Bruiser! Darned dog is loved almost to death and just won't mind a body."

Eileen got the mop bucket from the back porch and stood looking at the Sleeping Indian, or what folks said looked like a sleeping Indian, a silhouette of part of the Gros Ventre Range. In the other direction folks said there was an eagle perched on the side of the mountain, but she figured that it was just some ever-greens that made that shape. Is this Laine Bellin going to be the one for my boy? I'm worried that he'll get hurt. She's a pretty thing and very sensitive like Jamie. But is she right for him? Where are you when I need you, Harve? Why'd God decide to take you so soon and leave me with all the burdens of the Bear? She sighed, went into the kitchen, called to Bruiser and told him to stay on the porch. But the minute he landed on the step, he was off running down the lane. Darned dog! Clucking at him, she shook her head in resignation.

Jamie floored the old Chevy truck. God, it felt good to have someone to think about, and he surely thought about Laine. He'd never forget when he first saw her. As Bruce would have said, she sure filled out a pair of jeans to perfection. And he liked them tall and lanky with long legs, not that her shape meant all that much to him, because it didn't. What he liked about her was that easy way her low laugher just seemed to tumble out and how her soft brown eyes sparkled when she laughed. Reminded him of his first calf, Bunny. Oh, how he loved that little heifer.

Pulling into the Elkhorn for gas he realized that he'd forgotten Miss Irma's gas can. Darn! I'm not going to go back for it now. That'll give me another excuse to go up to Charlie's Mountain. Maybe I'll see her riding. She sure mounts a horse nice. I wonder if she even knows I exist. Probably not. After all, she's educated and been out in the world, and what have I ever done, or where have I ever gone? Haven't been farther than Denver and sure haven't done anything but work the Bear. What'd she ever want with me?

"Bart, you suppose I could put this gas on Miss Irma's tab? Do you want me to get her written OK?"

"Don't need to. She used to do it for that Manny. You seen that critter around lately? I'm getting worried. When he ain't around snarling at me, then I worry. That means he's hatching up something. You can bet on it!"

"Not seen him and don't want to either. Sure as heck don't want to see him up in the Ranches. Miss Irma is laying for him with that rifle, and I'm afraid that she's gonna cause a fire, things are so dry. That's all we need up there."

"That Manny was up at Dead Shot working on one of Earle's tractors and drunk as a skunk. Had trouble holding onto the tools, and Wilson said that he was carrying on about Miss Irma something awful. Said that we were all such dumb asses. Jamie, you see anything peculiar going on up there?"

"No I haven't and neither has he. Just forget his crazy talk, Bart."

"Changing the subject, I heard that that little heifer of Mrs. Bellin's is a knockout, Jamie. Or haven't you noticed?"

Jamie knew that the boys at the Elkhorn were talking about him being cow-eyed about Laine, but as usual he took it all in stride. He smiled and answered, "She's that, all right, Bart. And she's as nice as they come, too. Have you seen her sit a horse? If you haven't, then you've missed a truly beautiful sight."

Bart knew that Eileen was concerned about Jamie's getting hurt "She's an Easterner, Jamie, and you rightly know they're different. Best you set your cap for one of your own kind. You know, like Tiffany Oberhelman. Now, that's a cute little trick."

"Tiffany is all right, but she doesn't have what I want or need. I'll keep looking, at least for a while. I know Mama thinks that I'll not find a wife, that when she's gone there'll be no one to tend the Bear. But I'm patient. That's one of my charms, Bart. One of my charms, like Miss Irma says."

"One of your charms might be patience but doubt that it'll last past your fortieth year, Jamie, so you'd better get a move on, I'm thinking." He laughed when he said it, but Jamie thought to himself,

I've already got a plan, Bart. That Laine fits right in with it.

The main highway was heavy with traffic. Wonder where all these folks are going, Jamie thought. Don't usually see this many folks except in July when they haul it to the Rendezvous in Pinedale. Maybe they're going to Yellowstone or the Teton National Forest. I'd like to take Laine up there. She'd really enjoy seeing the view from Signal Mountain. Think I'll ask her. But he knew he wouldn't. He'd barely spoken two sentences to her.

He shifted into four-wheel drive when he approached the hill up to Charlie's Mountain. Slowing down, looking all around in hopes of seeing Laine or Liz or even Jo, he threw on his brakes in time to miss a doe, fat with a baby, that bounded in front of him. "Watch it!" he yelled. He hadn't seen the horse galloping around Mountain View until he sat, shaking. "Darned thing. Just about got yourself and your fawn killed." He revved up the engine and when he looked into his rearview mirror saw Laine on Lucky Charm, the horse she had rented for the summer.

What should I do? Should I stick my head out and call to her? Should I wait for her to catch up with me? God, please be my companion, he muttered. I don't want to make a bad impression. Please, God, be my companion. That was a saying that he'd said since he was just a youngster. Learned it from his grandpa when they worked the range together.

Laine pulled rein on Lucky Charm. "Whoa, boy, think that's that handsome Marlboro Man." She had told Liz when she first saw Jamie that he could have posed for the ad. She loved the twinkle in his bright blue eyes and had asked Gordon and Jerry a dozen or more questions about Jamie. They had teased her and said that he was no match for an eastern gal, that he was just a laid back cowpoke whose mom owned about the largest ranch in the basin. But she pumped them anyway.

She pulled up beside the truck. Jamie stuck his head out and finally said, "Miss Laine, have you seen that Manny hanging around here? Cause if you have, I'd better get word to Miss Irma."

She knew that he was just making conversation. She loved the deep resonance of his voice. Had such a soothing sound to it.

"Jamie, please just call me Laine, and no, I haven't seen Manny. Should I alert Irma if I do? I mean would she shoot me if I decided to trespass?"

"Oh, please don't do that, Laine! I mean, she doesn't like for anyone to go up there except me. Once Mrs. Daulton decided to climb up, and Miss Irma sure kicked up a fuss. Mrs. Daulton won't be doing that again, I assure you."

"Guess I don't understand your Miss Irma, but I love her work. She's a true artist with her camera. What's she like in person? I mean, is she a happy person, or is she a grump? Some people get cantankerous when they get older."

Jamie began to laugh, then cough. "Did I say something funny?"

"No, ma'am, it's just that Miss Irma is just Miss Irma. She's a true maverick from the git-go. You can't ever tell what she's going to do or say. Maybe that's why I like her. She is as honest as the day is long, she is. You'll just have to meet her. I'll try to arrange a meeting for you, but don't hold your breath." She's not so hard to talk to after all, he thought.

"Do you really think you can?" By now she had slipped off Lucky Charm and was leaning on the window ledge. Jamie could smell her freshly shampooed hair. It was shiny, just like he had brushed it himself. As pretty as any hair he'd ever seen. The sun bounced off it, and her long slender hands held the rein with such firmness. She began stroking Lucky Charm's sleek neck. Jamie realized that he wanted them to stroke him like that. Dear Lord, be my companion. Miss Irma, I sure do have red blood rushing through my veins. I just hope I'm not letting on to her. Sure hope I'm not blushing. That'd be awful.

"Jamie, did you hear me?"

"I guess my mind was wandering, Laine." Oh, how he loved the sound of her name. When she laughed her low, husky laugh, he thought he'd die right there on Elk.

"I said, why don't you stop by our cabin on your way back and we'll have a glass of lemonade or iced tea, and we can get acquainted. I haven't met any of the young people out here, and frankly, I get lonesome for them. Am I being too forward? I don't mean to but guess I'm like Miss Irma in that I'm very direct and don't know how to make small talk."

"I'd like that, Laine. That would be real nice. I get lonesome, too. I don't do much but work and read and visit Miss Irma."

Laine thought, I'd certainly like to change that. I don't think I'd ever tire of just looking at you. And I love your easy manner. Why can't more men be like Jamie? I mean, why do they think that we enjoy being hit on? He is so beautiful. He reminds me of my Marshall, that same easy gait and strength of character. Don't think that he'd like to be compared to my horse, though, but he's probably the only man I'll ever meet who'd not take offense if I did. I think that I've finally found Mister Right, as Mom would call him, like her Cam.

Even before Laine got off of Lucky Charm, she was calling to Liz. "There, there, old boy. I'll put you in the corral and prepare for my guest. Yippee! Hey, Mom!" She opened the front door and looked around and realized that Liz was not there. Don't think she went to Cam's. He's so busy with the Mountain Man that he'd not have time for her or anyone else, he said.

She bustled around and found the tin of powdered lemonade, a large pitcher and long spoon and measuring cup. "I know that he's probably not fussy, but I'd like this to be perfect."

It seemed like only a few minutes before she heard the truck bumping down the lane. We need to get that darned thing fixed before it tears up someone's auto. I'll have to speak to Mom.

She ran to the front door and called, "You wanta sit on the deck, Jamie? It's not too cool, and the view is spectacular. Oh, I know it's probably not like the view from the Bear, but to us it's great. Florida is mostly flat. We do have high sand dunes and rolling land down the center of the state, but nothing like here."

Why am I so nervous? He's just a fellow, and I'd think nothing of this if he were one of the Peace guys. Guess I want him to like me as much as I like him.

"I worked on that deck when the Simpsons built it, so I know about your view. Our view at the Bear isn't that much more spectacular, Laine. It's just different, that's all."

"I'll get the lemonade. Just be a jiffy. Go ahead and put your boots on the rail if you want. We all do it. We like the easy living of the Ranches."

Jamie did as she suggested. He drew up the log deck chair, rested his long legs up on the rail and thought, why am I so calm? You'd think that I'd be tongue-tied, but she's so easy to be around. No airs like I thought eastern girls would have. She's as easy to talk to as Elsie was.

"Here, I'll set this down on the table. Taste it and tell me if it's too tart or sweet. I can add sugar or water or whatever."

He took the glass from her but could not force his eyes off hers. Without even tasting it he said, "It's perfect, but then I knew that it would be."

Laine began to giggle, then he began to laugh at what he had said, and when Liz came trudging up the hill from the spring she saw them. She got a lump in her throat, and when they saw her she was grinning—not smiling, but grinning. I think my Laine has caught herself a cowboy, too. Hey, maybe we can have a double wedding. "Hi, you two! Guess what I just saw? A bull moose with a rack like I've never seen before. Keep looking at the spring, and he should emerge from the willows any minute." Not that they'd care whether he did or didn't. Gracious, I can feel those vibes all the way down here.

TWENTY-NINE

"Maggie, you get up here, young lady! If I see you go up to Irma's again, I'll swat you a good one. Jamie said that she was feeling poorly, as my mama would have said. Don't think I've used that expression in a long time, Liz. Did your mother ever say that?"

"Guess all Southerners say that. Must be one of our southernisms, like Laine calls them. Did she give you a printout of the southernisms she got off the Internet? Some of them are priceless. I thought Cam was going to laugh himself silly when I showed them to him."

"Why am I so antsy when Ben isn't here? I'll be so glad when he drives out. Robbie and the girls said they've charted their course. Robbie has charted it, of course. The girls are too young to know what's out this way, although Julie did say that Rachel wanted to see the bison at Yellowstone, and Casey said she wanted to pet some antelope. Oh, I can hardly wait. But Liz, I'm frightened. It's so blasted dry. What'll happen if we do have some of those afternoon thunderstorms with the dry lightning I've been reading about? Would we have time to get out of the Ranches? That's what frightens me."

"Cam and Jamie were talking about that last night. Jamie was telling us of the terrible time they had up Jack Creek a few years back. Took all the firemen from both counties, Teton and Sublette, to put it out. That was one of the dry-lightning fires you're talking about, and it was not in the tall timber, either."

"Not to change the subject, but is Laine really interested in Jamie? I mean…"

"I know what you mean, Jo. And the answer is yes. Crazy as that might seem to some people, it's not crazy to me. Laine has always walked her own rope. If you remember, she would not be a part of the coming-out parties and the cotillion in Orange Park that Avery wanted her to participate in, nor would she consider going to

Smith in Massachusetts. She informed him in no uncertain terms that she was not going to leave Marshall. And he caved in. He knew her strength. And I know her strength. She is not only in love with Jamie, she appreciates him. He's a beautiful human being, and she knows it. He's a deep thinker like Laine, and although he has not much formal education, I was surprised how well read he is. Says he is an avid reader and reads everything from the *National Geographic* to almost every new book our little library gets in. Laine was impressed. I'm not worried about a future arrangement with those two. And Jamie would settle for nothing less than marriage, she told me."

"I didn't realize that it had gone that far. I mean they're really serious. I've never seen her looking more beautiful. She just seems to glow. I wonder if that's what is bothering Irma? She didn't get poorly until Jamie started seeing Laine. She's peculiar, and I know it, but this is a new wrinkle."

Jo tossed a stick for Maggie to fetch. "I love this time of evening when it's cool and the flies aren't everywhere. Now, aren't you glad that I insisted on driving out with you? That gave us a chance to really talk and Laine the opportunity to go to Seattle to close her apartment and pack and..."

"It gave me and Cam some time to be together before she returned. I thank you for that, my friend. These last few weeks have been heaven, even with Laine here. Did she tell you that she's looking at a place in Pinedale? Well, there's a darling little house right in the downtown area with a white picket fence and English garden. I'm not kidding. Even has hollyhocks and a vegetable garden. She's enthralled with it, and of course Jamie thinks it's great. He's encouraged her, as I knew he would."

"But what about her schooling? I thought she was going to try to get into veterinary school."

"She is, but she'll have to use the satellite system with the University of Wyoming or something like that. Don't ask. I don't understand any of it, but she and Jamie do. He's taken some courses that he thought were fun, Spanish and, I believe, forestry. Anyway, they're working it all out, they say."

"Is that the phone? Listen. No, guess I'm hearing things. Next year I'm going to get a cordless, or maybe Ben's already bought one. He hinted that he might have a surprise for me, and I just bet that's what it is. It's hard to remember when we didn't have phones, isn't it? Betty and Jack said that they just might sell their ATV's because they almost never use them now that we have phones. I think Ben wants to buy them so the kids can ride when they come out, but I'm hoping that he'll rent a couple ponies instead. Think the little ones will enjoy them a lot more."

"I'd better be getting back. Think I've given Laine and Jamie enough alone time. She's been great about allowing Cam and me time. It was hard to confess to her about us, but I think she must have been told something by Chuck before she left for Seattle, or why wasn't she shocked? I told you how she hugged me and said, 'Mom, I want you to have a great life, and if he is what you want, then I'm all for it.' Imagine!"

"Like you said, Laine is a very deep child, Liz. Jamie is a lucky young man, and I think he knows it, and so does Eileen. Fern said the other day at Guild that Eileen had told her how much she likes Laine and that she is thrilled for Jamie. Thought he'd be a bachelor."

"Not a chance. Laine said the first time she saw him that her heart told her he was the one. But Jo, that's how I felt about Avery and Cam too. People do change, don't they?"

"Hey, you want another cup of tea? Tastes so good on a cool evening, doesn't it? And do I detect a little doubt creeping into your and Cam's relationship, young lady?"

"Think I'll go on home. I'm getting cool, and, Jo, I do not doubt my feelings for Cam or his for me, but I'm just not ready to make a commitment. Does that make sense?"

"It makes perfect sense. Is he pressuring you?"

Liz thought, then slowly said, "He is, in a way, but he knows that I've been widowed such a short time, and things still aren't settled. I mean there is still a lot of paper work to be done on the estate and..."

What she didn't tell Jo, and probably never would, was that she had received a call from one of Avery's conquests. Why she hadn't told her she didn't know. She had always shared all her problems with her, but she somehow wanted to handle this one by herself. Maybe I'm trying to prove that I can, that I can be tough and that

I can get angry when I need to. At least I think that's what is going on in this muddled head.

"Jo, I'm not going to go to the Fyr SyWrens meeting tomorrow. Would you tell Fern that I'll help her with the art show and rummage sale if she wants. Think I need a day to myself. Laine is going to Pinedale to put a month's rent on the little house, and I'll have time to paint, and I need to finish that table I've been putting off doing for ever, it seems."

Jo raised her eyebrow. "Is that all?"

"That's all. I seem to need some time alone. I told Cam that last night, and he got this funny expression, and I had to assure him that women need time to do their hair and nails and get their wardrobe together and in my case to paint. You know, just like he needs time to work on his Mountain Man and his other sculptures.

"No, I guess I don't understand, Liz. Have I done or said anything to cause you to…"

"Oh, for heaven's sake! Between you and Cam I don't have any breathing room!" She looked down at Jo and said, "You are my best friend, but…I need to be by myself right now to work some things out. I need to do it alone and to think on my own like everyone has been telling me to do for years. Especially you, Jo. I think I'm strong enough now to do that. A month ago I wouldn't have been, but today I think I can. I hope you understand."

She turned to leave, and Jo called to her. "Liz, I believe you've finally come to terms with who you are and realize that your needs can actually come first—for once. I'm proud of you. Come here and let me hug you."

They were in each other's arms when the phone rang.

Jo rushed inside and grabbed the phone off the pass-through. "Hello, this is Jo Daulton. What did you say? What! Who is it? What's wrong with you!"

Liz rushed into the house. "What's wrong, Jo?"

"Someone threatened me. It was a man, and I've no doubt that it was that Manny. He apparently had a handkerchief over the receiver, so he wasn't very clear, but threaten me he did."

"Well, what did he say? "

"He said that we foreigners had caused enough trouble and

that...that we'll be sorry, that he was going to fry our asses. And...he said that old woman...oh, Liz..."

"Cam, Liz here. Jo has just had a very disturbing phone call, and we think that it was Manny who called."

Pause...

"But he threatened her. He said that we foreigners had caused a lot of trouble, and he mentioned that old woman, meaning Irma, I'm sure, and that he was going to fry our asses and, oh, I don't remember what all."

"Liz, I think he's gone too far this time. I'm going to call Joey Shiffar and tell him what's going on. He needs to go talk to Manny's mom and also Eileen Stroebel. She'll straighten him out. After all, they live on the Bear, and I'm sure Reba will get tough with him."

"But what about us in the meantime? Jo is beside herself with fear. I asked her to come over here, but she's afraid of getting me involved, I think."

"Riley got in yesterday from his trip to Europe. I'll call Dad and ask if Riley can come over to stay with Jo until Ben gets back. Do you think she'll go for that?"

"That might be the solution in more ways than one. That'll give you two some time together and I'm sure Jo will welcome his company. You're brilliant, my love. Don't laugh! I mean it. I never would have thought of that."

"Call her and tell her what I proposed and ask her to spend tonight with you. At least that will give me time to get Riley over here."

"Cam, I'll do better than that. I'll drive up for her when Laine gets back from Pinedale. Maybe she'll have supper with us. You wanta come too? It won't be fancy, but if I know you, you'll just open a can of tuna..."

"How'd you know? Had planned to add crackers and cheese to it. As much as I'd like to dine with you, my love, I am so far behind. Someone I know keeps me from finishing my work. Can't imagine who it is, can you?"

"Certainly can't. They must be very selfish. Bye for now."

"Bring your big coat, Jo. My cabin isn't as comfy as your house, you know. And better take an extra blanket. Laine and I do fine with what we have, but you might need another one. I'll be there as soon as she returns from the post office. And don't you dare mention any of this to Ben. Knowing him, he'll hop the next plane out here. I'll be so glad when they get Laine's car fixed. It's almost impossible to get along with just one."

"Don't understand why I can't drive down there, Liz."

"Cam suggested it, and I think he's right. We don't want Manny to know that you're here. If your car is at the house, then he will think that you're there. And it's just until Riley gets here."

"Has Cam spoken to him about his trip to Europe, or has he had time?"

"Riley called when he got back, and they had a short visit, I think. He said that he had a much better time than he anticipated. He loves his grandparents, but they're getting up in age and tire easily, I guess, whereas Robert and Sarah are filled with energy. But he did see a lot and was pleased that they gave him such a nice graduation present. They've not accepted the fact that he's taking a year off before deciding where to attend college, though. Cam's pretty sure that it'll be the University. At least he hopes that it will. I've no doubt about it."

"Liz, I hear Maggie barking. I'll see you a little later."

Jo went to the front door cautiously. Looking out the side window she saw nothing, but when she opened the door a crack she smelled an unmistakable odor. She slammed the door hard and locked it. She went to the sliding glass door leading to the deck and saw a shadow, then saw Manny trying the door to the den. Thank goodness she had locked it the night before and had not unlocked it. Rushing to the sliding door she quickly locked it and hid beside the door leading to the basement. Oh, my God! Did I lock the door leading to the garage! And the garage door. Did I lower it? She couldn't think. Her mind was racing so hard that she hadn't heard the commotion out front. Maggie was still barking.

The next thing she heard was a gunshot. It was unmistakable. She rushed to the front door and saw someone running toward the backyard. Another shot and she began to panic. What's happening! Where are you Ben? Where are you? Sliding down the wall whimpering, she sat on the floor in front of the front door.

It seemed like forever, and when the heavy pounding began on the front door she came to her senses. She was afraid to look out the window. Then she heard her name being called. She didn't recognize the voice but knew it wasn't Manny's.

"Yes, who is it?"

"Jo, it's me, Doc. Are you all right?"

She unlocked the door and literally fell into his arms. "Think that Irma might have winged him, but if she didn't, he's too scared to be coming back any time soon. Cam had just talked to me about the phone call, and I'd decided to ride down to check on you when I saw Irma round the bend with her rifle raised up high. I thought she'd flipped until I saw Manny round the corner of your house."

"But, I don't understand! What has he got against me? I've never done anything to him."

"Think he holds you responsible for everything that's gone bad in his life. You know, losing his position with Irma and you befriending Jamie and...who knows? He's tetched, as we say in the South."

"Where's Irma? I need to thank her. How'd she know that he was down here, anyway?"

"Just like she knows almost everything else that's going on around here. She has that extra sense, that instinct. She's a remarkable lady, Jo."

"I'm well aware of that. If she winged Manny, shouldn't we be looking for him? He might be bleeding to death. I wouldn't want that."

They heard Irma come up on the porch. "Thought you'd like to know that Manny won't be back for a while, Mrs. Daulton. I didn't hit him, although I could have. Just wanted to scare him bad enough to keep him away from you until your husband gets here. But the next time he causes trouble on my mountain, I'll not miss. And, Jack, you'd better get word to him that I mean business this time. Use that phone of yours to alert the basin and everybody else in The Ranches. Irma Barksdale has had her fill of one Manny

Markos." She raised her rifle high above her head, stomped off the porch and almost ran down the driveway.

Doc stood looking at her, shaking his head in amazement. He turned to Jo and said, "She means it. Jo, she won't allow him to hurt or frighten you again. Irma takes care of her own. She always has. When Patty was buried, she and Charlie wouldn't allow anyone to attend the burial. When Charlie died, the same. She said that they were her concern and no one else's. And now you're her concern, like it or not."

The siren wailed into the night. The little town of Bondurant awakened with a start, and all the men of eligible age hopped out of bed and headed for the volunteer fire department. There were over twenty of them. Jamie Stroebel was among them, as were his brother and brothers-in-law. Sleep had been hard to come by for Jamie. He couldn't relax enough to allow it to invade his mind. Laine Bellin occupied his every thought. Tossing and turning, throwing off the blanket then pulling it back over his long, muscled body he wrestled with it. When the siren pierced the star studded night he was on ready. His nerves were on edge anyway, he told Bruce.

"Got a case of the hots, little brother?" Bruce asked Jamie, teasing him.

"I guess that's what you might call it. I just know that I can't seem to relax. She's with me every minute of every day. Its great, but also I can't seem to do anything right. Both my feet are left and my hands that have always done my bidding don't seem to know what to do with themselves." He laughed when he confessed to Bruce his dilemma.

"We'd better get another jacket. This might be a very long night. I didn't hear any thunder, did you?"

"Come to think of it, I didn't. But maybe the fire is over in Pinedale or Daniel. Could even be up at Hoback Junction."

"Lets just hope that it isn't up at your little filly's place…"

"Hey! I hadn't even given that a thought! Get a rush on, Bruce! Hand me my boots." They rushed toward their bunkhouse door. He and Bruce preferred their own place, and Eileen understood.

After all, they were in their late thirties and should have had a wife to share a house with them, she rationalized. She had built smaller houses for the three daughters on the place, and Jamie laughingly referred to it as the Stroebel commune. Told his mother that she had started her own town, but she just called it the Big Bear.

"What time is it, Bruce? Left my watch on the dresser."

"All of two o'clock, little brother. This better not be a false alarm!" They passed by the cemetery and sped across the Jack Creek bridge. "Hope it's not as bad as the Dell Creek fire last year. Didn't think we'd ever get that one out. We sure owe a debt to the Forest Service guys. God, they were something else. Sure learned a lot that night."

"Every one of us needs to take that class again. Let's see if J.D. will approve it. Maybe we can have another turkey shoot to raise the money. Let's mention that to him next meeting."

"Good idea. Gawd almighty! Who is that hauling it down the road? It's that crazy Manny, and he's gotta be drunk! Hey, Manny," Bruce shouted out the window, but Manny just kept on weaving down the highway. "We've gotta do something about him! When we get back to the Bear I'm gonna have a little talk with Miss Reba and Mama. If we can't lock him up permanently, then he's gonna hafta have his beer taken away from him. He's a menace, little brother."

THIRTY

Bruce Stroebel was livid. "It was that goddamned Manny Markos, J.D.! Something's gotta be done. I've already told Jamie that we're going to speak to Miss Reba and Mama about him. I don't give a damn if they lock him up for good."

"Now, Bruce, you don't know for sure that he set off the alarm. Could have been another nut. Now, I'll allow as how it probably was Manny, but we gotta have proof. I'll call Joey and talk to him."

"You do that! And while you're about it, you just might tell him that some of us are gonna take things into our own hands if they don't set that bastard straight. I've had it!"

Bailey Held piped up. "Getting us up at two o'clock ain't funny, J.D. What if it had been haying time? I guarantee you this minute I'd not be waiting on any Joey Shiffar to tend to him. Me and Elway and Lavon already decided that if he causes us any more pain, we're going to put him out of his misery."

"Just what the hell you talking about, Bailey? What're you gonna do? Lynch him? Is that what you're talking about? This ain't the Old West, boys. You been seeing too much Gun Smoke. We do have the law around now. You boys go on home and get some rest. I said that I'll tend to it."

"Come on, Bruce. If Mama is up we'll talk to her tonight. Manny is probably already home if he didn't run off the road, that is." Jamie took Bruce by the arm, and they headed for their truck. Bruce continued to grumble all the way home.

Cam drove over to Liz's as soon as Doc called him. When he got out of the truck he could see Maggie looking out of the front window and knew that Doc had driven Jo over and that he'd not have to go for her. Opening the front door, he knew immediately that someone would have to stay there that night. The air was charged, nerves shot, and all because no one had had the nerve to

216

take care of one Manny Markos. Even Irma had decided to give him another chance. Why? Why, when she knew full well that she, or someone else, would need to put an end to his terrorizing the ranches?

"Your knight has arrived, damsels. Fear not, the Duke of Cameron is here." No laughter did he receive, but Liz did rush over to hug him. It was obvious that they were upset, and even with Maggie barking happily, wiggling and jumping up for her welcome rub the tension persisted.

"I brought my bed roll and plan to stay the night. Where can I stash it, Liz?"

"Oh, Cam, can you? I mean, we're so relieved. Doc had mentioned staying here, but then Betty would be alone. He asked us to come up there, but Jo was afraid that Ben might call and knew that if he couldn't get her at her house that he'd call here. So, my sweet, we were in a dilemma."

"Get out the supper and a decks of cards. You do play bridge, don't you, Laine?"

"I'm not very good, but yes, I do play. I used to in college, but that was some time ago. But you know what, think I'd like to learn. Eileen asked me the other day if I played. Seems that the ladies in Bondurant are bridge and cribbage players. She also said that if I am going to be a part of their band of winter women I'd better learn, just to keep the winter blues away. I wanted to say that I didn't think that I'd get blue with Jamie around but had the good sense to keep my mouth shut."

They all laughed. Cam thought, you were able to do what I couldn't, Laine, get Liz's and Jo's minds off Manny. But they are smart enough to know that Manny will try again. He's got it in for Jo, just like he does for Irma and Jamie.

When the truck light's beam hit the main house at Big Bear, Bruce and Jamie could tell that their mama was already up. The kitchen light was shining out the side window, and they could see her sitting at the kitchen table. "Bet she has the coffee on, little brother. I just bet."

"You don't have to sneak up on the stoop, boys. I heard the

others come home even before you got to Jack Creek bridge. What kept you? Afraid that I wasn't awake?"

"We stayed behind to have a few words with J.D. about Manny. Did the others tell you what happened?"

"Nope, they must have gone home and fallen in bed immediately. Was the fire out by the time you got there?"

"No, there was no fire to put out, Mama. We think that Manny set off the alarm. Jamie and I saw him weaving all over the road, driving like a bat outta hell before we got to the station. Something's gotta be done about him, Mama. You'd best speak to Miss Reba and soon. The boys are really getting riled up about him."

"I don't doubt it. They have every right to. I'll speak to her as soon as it's light. There is no reason to delay, but, boys, I'd like to do it alone. Reba and I speak the same language, we understand each other and I believe she'd appreciate it if I handle it. You do understand, don't you?"

"Of course we do," Jamie answered. "I think that's the right thing to do, but you'll have to be really firm with her. Miss Irma has just about had it with him. I honestly think that if she hadn't been poorly of late that she would've taken care of Manny. I mean it. She's laying for him her every waking minute. Said the other day that if he sets foot on Charlie's Mountain, that's the only cause she'll need, that he'd be trespassing on her property, and she's posted it all over creation." Jamie reached down and kissed Eileen's cheek, then continued. "I don't agree with her. He needs help, Mama. He needs psychiactric help. We should do what is right and look into it."

"We should have done that years ago, Jamie. If anything happens to Manny, or if he causes anyone else to come to harm, we can lay the blame right here on Big Bear. Reba didn't have the financial means to help him. We should have."

Bruce shook his head, took off his hat, scratched his head and said in a low voice, "Think I'd better have a cup of that coffee, Mama. We need to discuss this. Now, I don't mean that we shouldn't have looked into his problem, but what are our taxes supposed to be paying for? Huh? They raise our taxes every year and Pinedale gets it all. They're even trying to close our little library so they can build a gigantic one in Pinedale. We don't get a damned thing. We should take Manny to Pinedale to the county doctor for an evaluation and let the county take care of him. But first we'd have to dip him in Lysol to get the stench off him, or they wouldn't even let him in the place."

Eileen ignored Bruce and said, "I'll suggest to Reba that we plan to call the county health department first thing tomorrow to get her reaction. I think she'll go along with us. What else can she do?"

Bruce finished his coffee, and he and Jamie told Eileen that they were going to try to get a little shut-eye before daybreak. On the way back to their bunkhouse Bruce started laughing. "What's so funny?" Jamie asked. "Didn't want to say anything to Mama, but one of the boys at the Elkhorn told a bunch of us about Manny trying to get into Daphne's the other night, and she chased him out, kicking and screaming about how he'd be frying in hell before he ever poked one of her girls. That there wasn't enough soap on this earth to clean him up enough to ever let him in there again."

"What did Manny do?"

"He yelled some cuss words at her, saying that he had the money and that his money was as good as any of those other whore pokers' in there, and Daphne high-tailed it back inside and came out with her shot gun. They said that he began running for his truck, but Daphne's big fat ass was right after him, and she began shooting toward the sky, and that got Judge Black out of there. He was running while trying to pull up his pants with his boots tied around his neck bouncing up and down, and he didn't know if he should hang onto his hat or his boots. Bailey said that he wished he'd had a camera—just about the funniest thing he'd ever seen."

"I doubt that the judge's wife would've thought it was very funny. Come to think of it I bet Bailey's wouldn't have either."

"I swear, Jamie, don't you have a mean bone in your body? You do beat all, you do."

"Oh, I have lots of mean bones, Bruce. I just hide them better than you do, that's all." He slapped Bruce on his back, and the two of them tumbled into bed with their boots still on. About then Jamie started laughing. "What's so damned funny?"

"I wish I could have seen the judge. Did he remember his

toupee? We sure do have some characters in this place, don't we? I was telling Laine about some of them just last night. She sure got a kick out of it."

"That's what's keeping me here, little brother. I gotta have something to laugh about. The rear end of a cow just won't do it. Yep, gotta have humor to keep the engine going."

"When I told Laine what Miss Irma told me Charlie said about the county commissioners, she really howled. It seems that when Charlie was a commissioner he was so frustrated with them that he told Miss Irma that 'all their brains would fit in a gnat's navel,' and when I told Miss Irma that I didn't know that gnats had navels she really got the giggles. She said that he went one better with 'all their brains would fit in a gnat's navel and there would still be room for lint.' Remember when Mama would check our bellybuttons when we were little to check for fuzz or lint? Miss Irma is really funny. Laine wants to meet her, but I'm not sure it's such a good idea. She's like Manny in that she's unpredictable."

Jamie pulled the blanket over him, curled up on his side and it wasn't long before both were sound asleep.

Eileen pushed her coffee cup away from her and rose. "Now's the time. I've gotta do it. Harve, I thank you for your advice. Even if you were here, I'd have to be the one to tell her. Now, I appreciate my time with you, but honey, I'm on my own with this one. You've helped me run the Bear all these years. Don't think I'd have been able to make it without you and the good Lord's letting us visit, but I'll be fine with His assistance, of course."

She had accepted Harve's death, but since the Lord had decided to take him before she was ready to let go, she did call on him from time to time for help. She didn't think that was too much to ask of the Lord. She believed in the Almighty and the hereafter, but she sure as heck didn't believe in being set adrift. A woman alone wasn't much good out in this part of the country, and she understood that is why He had given her sons. She was grateful that at least two had remained with her.

She got her hat off the hat rack beside the kitchen door and went out onto the worn, wooden stoop. She knew that Reba was an early riser and that Manny was probably still asleep. There was no activity. Not even the grandchildren were awake, because school was out and they didn't have to get up so early. Eileen loved the peace of the Bear. That was one of the things she had fallen in love with. She'd asked the Lord for a mate for Jamie, and He'd come through again. That pretty Laine was more than she had hoped for, and she was grateful. *She'll love the Bear just the way I do, and Jamie will come into his own with her beside him. They'll have the strength to carry on.* She'd told Harve that very thing last night. She was glad that he agreed.

The cold air filled her lungs as she walked down to Reba's. *Well, it's going to be a glorious day. I hope that Reba doesn't buck me off.* She started to knock but before she did the door opened. Reba walked out onto the stoop and said, "Shhhh! I don't want to awaken Manny. Not that I think he'd stir. Eileen, I think I know why you're here. I'm beside myself with worry. He's drunk all the time and doesn't seem to know what he's doing." When she began to cry, Eileen knew just how upset she really was. Reba was a strong woman.

Dear Lord, did you have to hand me this one? Well, I guess you did. Oh, my.

She hugged Reba to her, patted her on her firm back and made soothing noises. Finally, Reba shuddered, and wiping her eyes and running nose on her apron, calmed down.

"I spoke to the boys this morning. Manny apparently set off the fire alarm at the station and has twenty or more men angry at him for doing it. Plus, he's been causing lots of trouble up at Miss Irma's. He's threatened her and Jamie and even Mrs. Daulton. We need to get help for him, and Bruce suggested that we contact the county office to see what we can do at that level. We have no choice, and neither does he, Reba. And if he gives us any more trouble, we'll have to have him committed. I don't want that to happen. I'm sure that you don't want that either."

"You are the most wonderful person I've ever known, Eileen Stroebel. You never asked any questions about Manny's father, and I'm grateful that you didn't. I'm going to tell you something that I've never told a living soul—not a living soul." She drew in a deep breath and continued slowly. "My own father, my very own father, is Manny's father. My mother died when I was but ten years old, and there were just the two of us up at Shoal Creek in Idaho…"

"Reba, you don't have to tell me this, dear…"

"Yes, I do. I have to. I want you to understand why I am not against us doing what we can for Manny. As I said, we lived way out from everyone. My father made his own shine and when he was drunk he'd…he'd…"

"That's enough! I know what he did. Now, what are we going to do about Manny?"

The sky was a dark grey with even darker grey clouds hovering over the Wyoming Range. Jo had left Liz and Laine at their cabin and had walked home, Maggie running ahead of her. "I hope that we have a downpour without any lightning. Boy, do we need it." Maggie chased the chiselers without any success, their straight tails erect as they scurried toward the safety of their hole. It was a game Maggie loved, and Jo had never seen a sign that she had actually caught one. It was the chase that she liked.

To herself she thought that Cam was right in that Manny had enough sense, as mixed up as he was, to make himself scarce on Charlie's Mountain. I'll not alert Ben before they leave, she had decided. There is no need to alarm him or Robbie. Maybe Irma and Doc taught Manny a lesson, and he will know we aren't going to put up with his shenanigans.

Maggie began to bark, and Jo, looking all around, became frightened. When she saw Doc on his four wheeler she relaxed and hailed him. "Going back to my cabin in the sky, Jack. Cam thinks that it's safe and that Manny won't dare show his face around here for a long time. What do you think?"

"You can never tell what they'll do, Jo. Sorry about that. When I first warned Irma and Charlie about him, they laughed at me. But I think that by now Irma knows that I was right. His mind is disturbed, and kindness and any other salve we can administer won't heal it. The do-gooders don't seem to understand that, but it's true. I worked in a mental hospital in Gainesville, Florida, at the University and we found that the Mannys were unpredictable and cunning. So, my sweet, don't count on anything. Just be on the alert, and we will, too. Ben should be here within the week, correct?"

"Yes, he and Robbie plan to leave next Saturday, but they want to take a week to get out here. There is so much that he wants to show the grandchildren. I'm tempted to call him and ask him to cut it short. What do you think?"

"I think that if he knew about Manny, he'd fly out and let your son drive out later. That's what I think."

She sighed. "You're right about that. Ben is very protective."

Joey Shiffar paced back and forth. He'd had a rough night at Stockman's Bar subduing some drunks, and he was in a foul mood. "J.D., you don't know that it was Manny! You just suspect it was. So what do ya want me to do, huh? You want me to take out a warrant for his arrest? We'd all look like a bunch of dumb-ass fools if he was home sleeping like a baby, that's what!" He was almost in J.D.'s face.

"Now did I say that you had to arrest him? Did I? I just want you to warn him about the boys getting their balls in an uproar. That's all. They're laying for him and a big ol' scratchy rope is what they have in mind. Now, Joey, I ain't kidding. They've had their fill, and so have I! And you don't hafta yell at me! I'm only doing my duty and I expect you to do yours, Deputy Shiffar!"

Reba had not told Eileen that she had become afraid of Manny when he was drinking. His actions took her back to her youth and how her father had acted. *He's becoming just like Pop. I'll not mention what Eileen said to me and will just let the boys handle him. That's the best I can do for him.* She decided to not go back inside even though she was cold. Opening the heavy door she reached inside and pulled her sweater off the hook. She thought she heard Manny snoring, but she was wrong. He had awakened and needed to relieve himself, and when he climbed down the narrow stairs from the loft he had overheard Eileen and Reba talking outside. He made up his mind right at that moment. Now was the time. He'd been planning it for a long time. Wiping the saliva from his mouth he went outside to the privy. He had his heavy jacket with him and his gun was already in the truck.

Reba heard the truck start up, but before she got around the house to ask where he was going, he was racing down the gravel road. Should I alert the boys? What should I do? Did he overhear us? Dear Lord, haven't you already given me more than I can bear? Haven't you? She sat down on the stoop and began to cry. But she should have alerted the boys...

THIRTY-ONE

Earth, parched by the wind and sun, stung Manny's sweaty face as the wind picked up. His head was bowed. His jacket sleeve managed to find the dripping saliva on his chin, wiping it, only to have to repeat the nervous habit again. He could see Irma's house through the Douglas firs. "When that ugly old witch sticks her head out, I'm gonna remove it from her shoulders!" he yelled loudly. He was tired from too little sleep and hung over. Lordy, he wanted a drink. Even water would taste good, but all the ponds in the area were but dust bowls. *I should've brought some water.* He shook his head trying to focus better. Having to walk from Rim Road through the back woods had been rough, because the underbrush was so thick, but *that'll help burn that old witch down to her bones. She'll be but ashes when I'm through with her.*

The most difficult part of his plan had been where to hide his truck, but he had figured that out last week and had gathered enough brush to camouflage it. The time couldn't have been better. Most of the ladies in the area would be at the Fyr SyWren's meeting in the little log church/community building in town, if you could call Bondurant a town. Often the husbands would go with them and hang out at the fire station adjacent to the church. Then they'd join the ladies for refreshments afterwards. Manny figured that he'd be able to cut through Irma's back woods undetected with so few people around. He'd crawl up on her back porch and sneak in the back door when she went down to the outhouse to deliver her packages to Jamie for pick-up.

They think they're so goddamned smart. What'll they say when I show them that crazy old freak's pictures? Huh? What'll they say then?

Liz heard Jo honk the horn and told Cam that she'd be right back. "I really should go with her but have had so little time to myself. Did you see what I did to the landscape? Think that tint of umber was what the mountains needed. I'm coming, Jo," she called.

"Need anything at the Triangle F? I'm out of milk. Maggie drinks more milk here. Don't say it! I know that she's not supposed to have it, but she loves it so."

"Could use some bread. See if Monta has whole wheat. Laine doesn't like the sourdough. Oh, if she stops off at the meeting on her way back from Jackson with her car, tell her that Jamie called and said that he'd pick her up after he goes to Irma's. Eileen had some extra chores for him, and he's running late. But she might come on home to avoid the storm. Did you put Maggie in the basement? She'll go nuts when it starts thundering."

"I didn't know what else to do with her. If I leave her out she'll high tail it up to Irma's, and you know it. I hate to leave her with the weather like this."

"Cam will be leaving soon. Do you want me to have him go get her and bring her here? Won't be a bother, honest."

"Oh, Liz, would you? It is so upsetting for her when she's alone and it's thundering. Give me a hug. Gotta go."

"Is that new? Like the pleated slacks. Are they washable? I've decided to buy only washables from now on. Dry cleaning is so expensive out here."

Cam came out onto the porch and called to Jo. "You'd better hurry, Jo. We might get a downpour. Goodness knows we need one, but I hate it when there is lightning accompanying it."

Liz turned around and asked Cam, "Would you be a dear and go to Jo's to get Maggie? I'll keep her here, and Jo can pick her up when she gets back from town. Do you want anything from the Triangle F?"

"First, yes, I'll go to Jo's and fetch Maggie. And, I do not need anything from town, thank you very much. Oh, Jo. Riley called and said that he'll be here before dark. Dad wanted him to go into Pinedale with him to get some supplies, and I think they'll stop by St. Andrew's to see Fr. Bret. Riley has decided to join the church. How about that? Seems that he got interested in religion while in Europe." He pecked Liz's cheek and hugged her. Jo got a lump in her throat. My friend, I'm so happy for you. Even if you two decide to not marry, I'm happy that you have such a wonderfully warm relationship. Oh, I miss my Ben…

All the way to town Jo reflected on their decision to build in the ranches. It was a good decision. Look at all the interesting friends we've made since being here. I wouldn't want to make it a permanent residence but I would like to stay out for at least six months after Ben retires. Maybe Liz has the right idea. Buy a smaller place in the Jacksonville area with little upkeep and split our time between the two.

Manny heard Jo's rented car leave and tried to see who it was but could not because of the growth. But he knew that it was not Jamie because he always drove his truck. He knew engine noises.

He sat back down trying to get comfortable. When the thunder began he cursed it. God he was miserable. There wasn't any place that he could find to curl up and doze. That's really what he wanted to do. That Jamie wouldn't be out here for a long while yet, he figured. And I bet he's poking that damn foreigner, when I'm not even allowed to service one of Daphne's whores. That burns the shit outta me. But you'll be paid back for stealing my job, you son-of-a-bitch! Again he moved brush trying to make a pallet. Finally giving up, he began to doze.

Irma opened the front door and peered out. Shielding her eyes with her bony hand, she pierced the darkened sky. No Jamie nor Jo did she see. She had hoped that Maggie would come running up the gravel road but realized that Jo probably had stuck her in the basement. It's Fyr SyWrens day at the church, and she was sure that Jo had gone. Probably went down with Betty and Liz. Why am I not better today? It's not like me to be poorly for this long. You don't suppose that their Lord is preparing a place for me? She laughed and decided that if He was, it had to be down deep and not in His lofty sky floating around with His pretty angels with their flowing golden locks. How can anyone with any brains believe in that hogwash? Well, Sir, I'm here if you want me. I'm tired enough to quit fighting you. She sat down hard. Suddenly she was so tired that even walking back into the house seemed too much.

The wind picked up and Irma realized that the storm was not going to blow over. "This one means business," she said loudly.

A clap of thunder resounded from mountain top to mountain top. *I wish Maggie were here. I know she's afraid down there.* With a sudden and unexpected burst of energy she hopped up, held onto the porch banister and rounded the house. "I'll be down, Maggie. She shouldn't leave you all by yourself." Climbing onto her four wheeler, she revved it up and hung toward the side of the road trying to avoid the spattering of rain that had begun. "Good, we're finally going to get some! Make it a good one, Mr. Man up there."

Manny stirred. "What the hell! Is that crazy old woman trying to get away from me?" Grabbing his rifle he worked his way down the hill to Irma's. It was slow going. "Dumb ass old woman left it just for me. Ha! Now, I'll show 'em! I'll show all of 'em!"

He was uneasy when he opened the back door. He had to practically turn sideways there was so much stuff cluttering the mudroom. *Doesn't that old fool ever throw anything away?* But Manny knew just what he wanted and where she kept it. He had peeked at her often enough. *She thinks she's so damned smart.* He purposely avoided the bedroom, not even glancing at it as he went into the living room. *God! Junk everywhere you look. Has she moved it? Better not have.* Suddenly he heard the four wheeler coming up the road. Panicking, he didn't know whether to go out the front door or the back. Crouching behind the couch he listened. No noise. *Where are you, old woman? Where are you? Manny's here. It's my turn now. Your friend Manny's here, old woman...*

Cam kissed Liz thoroughly. "Yum, I like that, but, my sweet, you'd better rush or you won't make it home before the storm hits," she murmured.

"I wish I could stay. No, don't look at me like that. I mean it. Have you ever made love during a Wyoming storm? No, the lady says coyly. Well, my dear one, then you've not been properly loved, and this seems like the perfect time to rectify your lack of education."

A loud clap of thunder roared and one frightened Maggie found her way onto the couch and into Liz's arms. "See what you've done, Cam! You've waited too long, and even Maggie knows it. Poor baby. Maggie, poor baby," she said stroking Maggie's smooth coat. Maggie was panting heavily.

Cam began to laugh and took Maggie from Liz. "Here, old girl, come to Cam and I'll get you some towels. She'll start to pant now. My old Poker used to do that. That dog hated storms as much as you, Maggie. I still miss that dog. One of these days I'll tell you about Poker, who was the pride of the University campus."

Liz went to the large living room window, that overlooked the deck, with a panoramic view of the Wyoming Range. The lightning zigzagged across the sky, but only a few raindrops did the sky relinquish. "I'm afraid we're really in for it, Liz," he said, softly nuzzling her neck.

"What makes you say that?"

"This parched land does not need lightning. It needs rain. I'd not be a bit surprised if we get a call soon from the fire station. One good thing is that there are a lot of men already down there."

"Are you really frightened?"

"Frightened, no, but concerned, yes. So many people up here built among the trees, not paying any attention to what they've been told. Jo and Ben had the right idea. Billy was wise to caution them."

Another loud clap. "That sounded more like gunfire! There! Did you hear that?"

"I couldn't tell. Sounded like thunder to me."

Liz was becoming very alarmed. "Do you suppose that Irma is shooting at something?"

"More like someone, honey. She's really been out of it lately, Jamie said. He's worried about her."

"I wish Laine had made it back. I don't like for her to be out on a day like this. What time is it? Heavens, I can't believe that it's only 4:30. It's so dark. Feels more like 6:00. Oops! There go the lights."

Cam went to the kitchen pass-through and picked up the phone receiver. Nothing! Should I tell Liz? God, without the phones how will the firemen alert anyone?

"Is that a motor? Cam, is that Laine?" She dashed around the couch and headed for the front door, but when she opened it she saw no one. Turning toward Cam she asked, "Did you hear a motor? Am I going crazy?"

"No, you're not crazy. I did hear something." He went out on the porch and peered around the house toward the corral but saw no one or any vehicle. This is getting spooky, he thought, but I can't let Liz know that I'm concerned. About then a bolt shot out of the sky and he scampered back inside glad to be under cover. It started then. Hail bounced off the metal roof, and again he was sure that he heard a motor of some kind, but he couldn't tell how close because of the noise from the wind in the high timber.

Then Maggie started barking...

Jo sat about midway on one of the church pews. The sunlight shone through the stained glass window of St. Hubert the Hunter above the log altar. I love this church and its history. It's difficult for me to conceive of the hazardous job it was to build it. I'm so glad that Eileen wrote down the history for me to send the children. Even Julie found it interesting. Imagine snaking these huge logs out of the forest and getting them across icy streams and bringing them all the way down here! And even the bishop helped! I can't imagine that happening anywhere else in the world. This is truly a unique part of your world, Lord. I don't think that I could have been a pioneer out here. Guess I'm just a Florida gal.

Eileen had finished the minutes from the last meeting, and Fern was giving the treasurer's report. The sun suddenly disappeared, and Hazel got up and turned on the overhead lights. "Going to have a humdinger of a storm, I'm afraid, ladies," she said.

Swede put his head inside the heavy log door and said, "Excuse me, ladies, but we're in for a doozey. You might be smart to get a ride back home, 'cause it looks like we men might be needed down here. This is fire time, I'm afraid."

"Eileen, I for one think we should adjourn," Fern said. Martha piped up, "I'm on my way back home. Anyone want a ride?"

"Jack and Tom can ride together, Eileen. If you'll give us a lift home maybe Jamie can take them home after things calm down here."

"Good idea. Jo, if Laine comes back from town before the men are called out, she'd better be alerted about the Hoback. I wouldn't want her to be up there during a lightning storm. That underbrush is hazardous. Jamie was talking about it just the other night. Come

230

to think of it, you and Betty would be wise to come on home with me. We'll call Liz from my place."

"I really appreciate the offer, Eileen, but Liz is up there alone. I don't like the idea of leaving her. Oh, I know that Cam is close by, but he might be called down to help. I need to get home. Besides, Maggie is with her, and Irma is all alone, too."

"I know how fond you are of Irma, Jo, but that old turkey will outlast all of us. She's seasoned, so to speak."

"Thanks, but Betty and I'll go on back. I know that Doc will want her home. He'd have come down with us but wanted to finish that woodcarving for the church sale. I'm sure we'll be all right." But she wasn't sure at all, and Eileen Stroebel knew it. She's a spunky one, she thought. Jamie surely likes those folks up there. I just hope that You don't decide to test them, Lord. Harve, are you there? What should I do? Should I send our Jamie up there to help out? Send me a sign, Harve. My mind is muddled today what with that fool Manny running off like that. Harve, send me a sign.

About then a clap of thunder sent her feet moving for her car. "That's all I needed to know, Harve. I'll get Jamie."

Jack Sheffield went to the basement to start the generator. "I wish the girls were back," he said aloud. I'll need to alert the fire department about the lights and phones. I'm glad that I have my cell phone. Always seem to need a backup out here.

"J.D. this is Doc Sheffield up on the Hoback. Our phones and electricity are out so you might get a truck headed our way. The hail has started and the lightening is fierce. Almost no rain accompanying it, though."

Pause"

"No, I haven't seen Manny. Why? What's up?"

Pause...

"I wouldn't put anything past him. You're right on that one. He's gone over the edge, I'm afraid. But you know Irma. She thinks she can take care of herself and needs no one."

Pause...

"When did he say that? Was it recently?"

Pause...

"I'll put the glasses up that way but doubt that I will be able to see anything. Usually I can spot his truck but haven't lately."

Pause...

"Signing off. I'll try to get in touch with you, but don't count on it."

Jack sat down on the straight chair beside the phone in the basement. "Son-of-a-bitch! I told Irma to be on the alert, but would she listen? Hell no!"

He went wearily upstairs and pulled the binoculars off the wall peg beside the kitchen door. "Why wouldn't she listen to me?" Jack walked to the floor-to-ceiling window in the living room that faced Charlie's Mountain and focused the glasses. Just as I thought. Not a damn thing but trees. He turned toward Rim Road, where he usually saw Manny's truck, and he could have sworn that he picked up a glimpse of blue among the trees. Trying to focus better he swore. "Can't seem to make these goddamned things work!" He was totally frustrated when all of a sudden the truck appeared. "My God! He tried to hide it, but the high wind blew the brush away! He's up to something! I feel it in my bones!"

When the hail began to pelt the large window, Jack made his decision. I know his type. He'll not be out in this. Not Manny. He'll find a safe, dry place to hide, and that place will be either Jo's or Irma's barn or garage. He didn't hesitate. Picking out the rifle that he'd used when he hunted with Charlie and Irma, he checked it, took the box of cartridges out of the gun rack's drawer and loaded the rifle. He hadn't touched that gun in over five years. Methodically he went about the business of preparing for the kill. The hail had stopped and a light rain followed, but the lightning hadn't let up. It continued to dominate the sky with its high-powered designs.

Jack decided to drive to Liz's to see if Cam was still there. His truck was. But before going in he decided on another course and sped off toward Elk. "I'll not draw you in on this, Cam. This is my fight. I should have had him committed long ago. I'm sorry, Charlie. I shouldn't have listened to Irma. She just needed someone around so she wouldn't get so lonely. Somehow she thought she could control Manny. I should have seen the symptoms.

"Sorry, Charlie..."

Irma turned off the four wheeler's motor and with her hands shading her face from the rain and hail managed to reach the front porch. She grabbed the old rug from the log chair and wiped off her boots. Then she sniffed. She sniffed again and aloud said, "Glory Be, I've got him!" She was breathing heavily. The ride down to Jo's only to find out that Maggie was not there had taken its toll, but she was grinning. God, this is exciting! She was salivating. "You sure as hell ain't an elk, Manny Markos, and you sure as hell ain't a beautiful buck or an antelope. You're just a mangy old dog that's hurting and has hydrophobia."

She lifted her gun from beside the front door and, kicking it in, went in shooting.

Jack Sheffield had reached Irma's gate. He had thought he'd have to climb over, but she had been in such a hurry that she had not bothered to lock it. "Good!" Then he heard the gun shots and even before he could get his truck in gear there was a roar from behind, then a screech of tires and he saw Jamie swerve past him hauling it up Charlie's Mountain like a bat outta hell.

It struck! There had been warning enough, goodness knows. But when the lightening hit the cabin, Jack was to say later, it sent sparks flying like the biggest fourth of July fireworks you'd ever want to see. The entire sky was lit up. He braked and by the time he got to Irma's, Jamie had already returned to the porch. He was cuddling her slight, lifeless, bloody body and crying...sobbing. Jamie kept on walking, cradling Irma, not noticing the rain pelting them. When Maggie passed him barking loudly he barely noticed. He managed to say to Jack, "Don't go in there. You don't want to see." But Jack did want to see. He wanted to see what Irma had been hiding all those years. He had to see. He knew that he'd never have peace of mind if he didn't know the secret of Charlie's Mountain. He owed it to Charlie.

The flames were higher now. "God, what a mess!" he exclaimed aloud. Holding his handkerchief over his face he breathed shallowly and tried to avoid the piles of magazines and newspapers that appeared to be everywhere. He saw Manny, or what was left of Manny. He was sprawled out on the floor behind the couch holding a photograph album. He had no face left. Jack pried the album from his grubby hand. The flames had moved to the living area, and Jack decided that he'd better get out while he had a chance. The bedroom door was open, and when he peered in and realized what he was seeing, when he accepted the horror he was seeing, he let out a gasp. "God almighty!" He didn't seem to see or hear Maggie, who was on the bed hovering over Patty, protecting her and barking loudly. The horrible sight of Patty blocked everything else from his disbelieving mind.

A sooty-faced Jack Sheffield, struggling for breath, in a trance, stumbled down the steps and fumbled with the handle of his truck's door. He sat, his hands shaking as he opened the album that Manny had held. It smelled of smoke. There was Patty, mummified, all dressed up like she had just gone to a ball. On the next page she was dressed in her riding outfit. And on each page Irma had made her an outfit and dressed her in it for her photo session. Her tea-stained skin was taut on her skull and was grotesque to Jack. It sickened him. The bitterness began in the back of his throat and soon found its way out. He vomited until there was nothing left. Wiping his mouth and nose he rested his weary head on the back of the front seat and sobbed. "My friends! My friends! Why didn't you ask for help? Why?" But, he knew, oh, how he knew. Patty was beautiful to Irma and Charlie. It didn't matter to them that she was dead. She was their Patty and she had to be with them, always.

The fire truck roared up Elk with its lights flashing. Jo and Betty, Liz and Cam and every one in the Hoback Ranches were there to help. Jo had told J.D. that they could use the water out of their holding tank if they needed it. And did they ever—their's and every available holding tank on Elk. They radioed the fire stations in Daniel, Pinedale and the Hoback Junction plus the Forest Service to send a helicopter. They were able to supply buckets of water from the two remaining ponds of water. There were fifty firefighters working until the early morning hours trying to contain the fire on Charlie's Mountain. Later, the weary, soot-covered men and women gladly went to the Sheffields', where every woman on the Hoback had gathered to serve them sandwiches, lemonade and coffee. Jack managed to find some Jack Daniels to sooth their weary bones.

J.D. said, "Funny, that Irma's place was the only one hit. The way that lightening was bouncing around, I didn't think we'd have a house left up here."

Jack Sheffield and Jamie Stroebel looked at each other. They knew otherwise. It was not funny at all. It was as it should have been.

Jo began calling Maggie, and it was then that Jamie remembered seeing her run up the road to Charlie's Mountain. He later told Eileen that, being part shepherd, she needed to be near Patty. Irma had understood that. Eileen was the only one Jamie ever told about the secret on Charlie's Mountain. He never even told Laine. Jack Sheffield knew that he had to show the album to Jo, but he never told another person, and Jo could not tell even Ben. The evidence was consumed by fire, and no one was the wiser. But Jo and Jack would be haunted by Irma's and Charlie's deep love for Patty and their inability to relinquish her.

Eva and Bud Young decided on their own to phone Ben to tell him about the fire and Irma and Manny. He got the next available flight out of Jacksonville, canceling their family's trip. He had to get to Jo.

Charlie's Mountain smoldered for days, but by the time Ben had packed Jo and the things they were taking back to Florida only the acrid odor remained. Billy Parker said that he would winterize their house if they decided to not return that summer, but Liz and Laine remained in the Ranches.

It didn't take Jamie long to propose to Laine, and a Christmas wedding in the little log church, St. Hubert The Hunter, was planned. They wanted to be married at the annual Christmas party that the Fyr SyWrens and Ladie's Guild held every Christmas with Santa and Mrs. Santa present along with all the children and grandchildren in the area. Laine wanted to be surrounded by her new family. When Cam proposed a double wedding, Liz demurred. "This is Laine's and Jamie's special day, my sweet. Let's look at next summer after Jo has regained her sanity and things are back to normal—if things are ever normal again. I'm not sure that is possible.

"Casey, don't jump on your Granny like that," Jo lamented. "I was trying to write in my journal."

"Granny, don't you wanta see me dive? I've been practicing ever since you've been in Wyoming. Are you still upset about your friend Miss Irma?"

"You remind me a lot of Irma, little one. You've got her spunk and her daring. Oh, I wish you had met her and she you. She had a little girl like you once. But she died."

"What of? Was it an earache?"

"No, my sweet, she was killed in a car accident."

"Come on, Granny, come watch me dive! You can think of your friend later. Come on. Maybe her little girl just pretended to die."

Ben knocked softly on the bedroom door. "Are you all right? Do you want me to get you anything?""

"I want you to hold me. Hold me close, Ben."

"That's an order I've always enjoyed. I mean it. Are you all right?"

"I am now. I'll try to do what Ruthann suggested, take one day at a time and think of only the good times."

"That was wise advice."

"I want to tell you something that I've kept to myself."

"I hope that it doesn't hurt too much."

"I hope so, too. Do you remember when Liz was called back here because of Avery's stroke?"

"Yes, I remember it well."

"And Irma showed up on our front porch the next morning and asked if I wanted to take a walk? And how surprised I was but went with her anyway. When I got back you asked what we had talked about, and I said that actually we said nothing, that she talked to Maggie and commented on Liz purchasing the cabin. Well, what I didn't tell you was that—was that I have never felt more like I was joined to another person than I was to her that day. It was as though we were one. It was a very strange feeling that I have never experienced with anyone else, not even you."

"Is there a reason that you didn't want to tell me about it?"

"I was afraid that it might hurt you. After all, you are my

husband, and you and I are supposed to be one."

"Was it a spiritual feeling like you read so much about these days?"

"I don't know. In reflection I believe that we tapped into another realm of being. I seemed to be removed from my body and was looking down on us. And I felt that we were thinking the same thoughts and feeling the same feelings and, oh, I don't know. I've thought about it so much lately. But I do know that it hasn't sustained me. It's just got me more confused about what happened."

"Jo, Irma walked her own path after Patty and Charlie died, not needing anyone, not wanting anyone. Then you came into her life. You tried to bring her back to reality, but, honey, I think she was too far gone. Maybe she let you witness her loneliness to warn you about your own future. Maybe it was her way of telling you to not follow her path, to accept that we all need someone, each other."

"Do you really think that's what she was conveying? Oh, how I would like to believe that! I hear Casey calling me. Coming, honey. Granny's coming."

Jo grabbed the towel off the rack and reached up to kiss Ben's cheek. "You've helped me more than you could possibly know. I've been so alone. Thanks hon. Coming, Casey! And, Ben," she held him away from her, sighed deeply and said, "I truly need you. You're my life, my love."

Ben swatted her on her bottom and replied, "Why, Miss Jo, I do believe you've put another nail in your coffin with that big sigh. And I love you, too. Now, go watch your granddaughter." He watched her walk with renewed bounce. He, too, sighed. *Now, maybe we can get back to normal. But I guess I'll always wonder what you're keeping from me, Jo. What mystery did you uncover on Charlie's Mountain?*

Whatever it was, I know that your undying loyalty to Irma will always exclude me. That I know.

Ben's deep, steady breathing invaded the quiet. Jo had not been to sleep and knew that she would not until she disposed of the album. She hadn't known what to do with it when Jack Sheffield had given it to her, but she knew that no one should see it—they simply could not see it!

She decided to wait 'til Ben was asleep, clear off the dining room table and pretend to be cutting out Rachel's and Casey's Christmas dresses. It was a tradition she had begun when the girls were tiny. In case he awakened and inquired, she'd say that she had not been able to sleep and thought that she'd get a jump on making the dresses. Her plan was to cut the pictures in tiny pieces, place them in a paper sack and dispose of them later.

She had thought of burning the pictures in the grill, but fires had been prohibited because of the drought, and Ben would certainly become suspicious because she never touched the grill. It was too hot to use the fireplace, so the logical solution was to cut up the evidence and dispose of it in the compactor.

I'll be so glad to have this behind me. I'm grateful to you, Irma, for teaching me such a wonderful lesson. We take things for granted. At least, I do, and, I imagine, everyone else does, too. I'll never fall into that trap again. I know that the pictures were grotesque, but when I made myself look at them the second time, I saw your and Charlie's love. I've never experienced love like that. If you have taught me anything, it is that we are so very shallow, living only on the surface. If life is worth living we have to love to the fullest. I'll never be the same and I'm grateful, Irma, dear friend…

"Jo, its Liz. Jamie and Laine just called. Guess what?"

"Give me a minute and I'll try."

"Oh, I'm so excited that I can't wait. Irma left the entire estate to Jamie. Can you believe it! Well, all except a few hundred thousand that she left to the University. There's a condition, of course—you know Irma. He can use Charlie's Mountain only as an animal preserve. He's allowed to build one building; sleeping area, kitchen, restrooms and a large room for workshops, lectures, etc. And he's required to provide city children the opportunity to view nature firsthand on the trails or whatever he deems educational or informative in the summer months and during holidays. Laine is so excited she can hardly stand it. She's already making plans to begin a children's class in horse grooming and I don't know what all. Oh, it's to be called the Patty Barksdale Animal Preserve."

"What? I'm sorry. There's so much static." Jo began to laugh and added, "That's probably Irma throwing a clinker in the phone line. She loved her work but hated the fuss even before Patty was killed. I think that's wonderful, Liz. Really I do."

"And oh, her lawyer gave Jamie a copy of the will and what Irma wrote to him personally. It sounds just like her. Here, I'll read it to you. 'Jamie, you're the kind of person my Patty would have become if your God had allowed it. You love the land as she did. You love the creatures as she did. You appreciate space and quiet and the beauty of the Hoback, and I know in my heart, if I have one, that you will protect it 'til your death. I would have been proud to call you son. I love you, Miss Irma.' Jo, she wrote it on the back of a Cheerios box. Jamie said that that made it all the more special because Miss Irma loved her Cheerios. They had a beautiful relationship, just as you two did. Wasn't that precious, Jo?"

"Liz, I hope Irma isn't listening. She'd hate to be called precious. But, yes, that was beautiful…just like she was…"

THE END

Amaro Books

Are you unable to find *"Walking With Irma"*
in your bookstores?

Mail to:
AMARO BOOKS
9765-C S.W. 92nd Court
Ocala, Florida 34481
E-Mail: amarobooks@aol.com

Please send check or money order (no cash or C.O.D.s)

Enclosed is $ _____ for books indicated.

Book Title: _____

Number of Books: _____

Name: _____

Address: _____

City: _____

State: _____ Zip: _____

Please enclose $14.95 per book plus $2.00 for postage and handling
of first book and $1.00 for each additional book. Florida residents
add 6% sales tax. Please allow 2-4 weeks for delivery.